Radio Nowhere

Lee Beard

"Is there anyone alive out there?"

Cover by: Deranged Doctor Design

ISBN: 978-0-692-87613-8

10 9 8 7 6 5 4 3 2

http://lee-beard.com/

Dedication

To the Kid; thanks for being my kick-butt motivator and late-night deadline enforcer.

To Mom; thank you for dutifully prescribing snack breaks and being my eternal cheerleader through it all.

To Dad; thanks for letting me bounce ideas off you until your ears fell off, and for pushing me to keep going when I wanted to burn everything and call it quits.

To my collective family and friends; I appreciate your love and support more than I can say.
To George R. Stewart, Stephen King, and Terry Nation, whose visions of the apocalypse haunted my childhood and inspired this novel: thank you.

Contents

Chapter One

Newark, NJ
Wednesday, Week One

The man swung his camera bag lightly over his shoulder and yawned broadly, bumping his way through the crowded airport. He'd been running on very little sleep since the photoshoot for National Geographic had ended; the week-long excursion to one of the most remote communities in Zambia allowed his four-person team to document some of the most intimate facets of life in the tiny village. He'd even gotten to witness a burial ritual when one of the members passed away suddenly toward the end of their visit. The fact that the villager died while in the prime of life with hardly any prior symptoms didn't even register as the man moved through the crowds, dooming everyone he breathed on.

"Luggage can be picked up at stations 13 and 14. Have a safe journey, and thank you for flying Air International. Welcome home."

Three connecting flights later, he was finally back in New Jersey and what he assumed were the effects of sleep deprivation were beginning to wear on him. If he could just make it home, he could recoup the lost sleep and then some. After picking up his luggage, the man made his way to the airport's parking garage where he loaded up his Jeep, paid the parking stub, and began the two-hour drive home. About an hour into the trek, he began to seriously regret the decision to not stay at a nearby hotel. He turned on the radio to try and fight the exhaustion, settling back in his seat as a Creedence Clearwater Revival song crooned.

Suddenly, the Jeep swerved off the interstate and slammed into a lamppost. The three cars that were on the road pulled over immediately, the passengers running to the totaled Jeep. The man opened his eyes for just a second to see a blurry figure at his window before losing consciousness.

Chapter Two

Watertown, NY
Saturday, Week Two

Only two of the four lights on this row of mobile homes worked, giving the shadows and shapes an eerie glow in the hours before the sun rose. Zach adjusted the backpack on his shoulder as he made his way down the narrow roadway, avoiding the puddles left by last night's storm. Suddenly, headlights illuminated his shadow in front of him, and he quickly spun around just in time to jump back and off the asphalt as a silver pickup barreled past him. His string of curses was returned by a middle finger out the driver's window; with that, the near-daily ritual was complete. Zach gritted his teeth, green eyes narrowing, and made a mental note to "accidentally" drop nails on that guy's driveway later. It was only a matter of time before the truck's owner wrecked or mowed down somebody important, and Zach would be there with popcorn to watch the fallout.

"Heya, Bub!" An elderly man with a short white beard stuck his head out of a nearby white tin trailer and grinned at Zach.

"Hey, Oleson." Zach waved, anger dissipating. Oleson had lived in the same trailer longer than Zach had been alive, greeting him the same way every morning.

"Pretty strange weather we're having, isn't it?" Oleson adjusted his round glasses slightly, glancing to the dark sky.

"Sure enough." Zach stopped walking to talk to him.

"The weather man says there's talk that there might be sunshine next week, but I learnt way back that you can't trust a man in a suit, 'specially –" Oleson stopped, a coughing fit cutting off the last of his sentence. "Beg your pardon, Bub. I guess these old lungs is finally starting to go on me," he shook his head and cackled. "Oh, by the way," Oleson snapped his fingers in remembrance, "I found a new antenna for my radio! We can talk to them Canucks again!"

"Oh, yeah?"

A retired engineer, Oleson had been collecting parts for his Ham Radio station in the front of his trailer for years, drafting anything from bits of tin foil to discarded speakers to join his radio army. It wasn't unusual for Oleson to ride his "Olesmobile" – a custom-made three-wheeled bicycle with a large basket attached to the back – out the chain-link fence early one morning and return at midnight with a wagonload of metal bits.

The old man grinned again. "Got to rewire things, but it'll do! Make sense?"

"Makes total sense," Zach smiled.

"Good! I like makin' sense. Should have it fixed when you get back!"

"I can't wait to see it," Zach said truthfully, "Here's hoping it'll be a short work day, though they're really trying to get to most out of us before school's back in."

"Good!" The old man nodded happily, his head bobbing like a bird. "Tell that foreman that Oleson says to let you slip out early today and see what happens."

Zach chuckled. "Will do. See you later, Oleson. You take care of that cough, okay?"

"Will do, Bub!" Oleson turned and shuffled back into his trailer. Zach continued to the fence and began the slow walk to work.

***

Isherwood, PA
Saturday, Week Two

Millie lightly thudded down the hallway, drawn in by the smell of bacon wafting from the kitchen. She padded across the dining room floor in her fuzzy bunny slippers and *thump!* stubbed her big toe on the kitchen doorjamb for the thirtieth time since her family had moved in at the start of the summer.

"Gah!" Millie's face contorted as she clutched her foot.

"Millie?" Nana called, "Is that you?" Millie hobbled the rest of the way into the kitchen and forced a smile onto her face. Nana chuckled from behind the stove. "Ai, you have got to be more wary of that doorjamb. It's a sneaky little thing!" Millie put her foot down and wiggled her toes to make sure they were still working. Nana skillfully slid the bacon from the pan directly onto the awaiting plate. Millie scanned the kitchen table. Bacon, eggs, and French toast were nicely arranged on blue china, which were centered beside a full glass of orange juice on the frilly placemats in front of three of the chairs that surrounded the table.

"What's the special occasion?" Millie nicked a piece of bacon from one of the plates.

"It's your father's birthday, remember?" Steam hissed angrily as Nana washed out the hot pan.

Oh, shoot. Millie swallowed hard.

"You didn't *forget*, did you Amelia?" Nana's face was stern as she dried the pan with a dishtowel, but her dark eyes danced with amusement.

"Who, me?" Millie pouted innocently and dodged the dishtowel Nana flicked at her. "Why would I do such a *terrible* thing?"

"I assume it was not on purpose, but you must be more careful of such things," Nana waggled a plump finger at Millie, suppressing a smile.

Millie smiled at her great-aunt's odd manner of speaking, a direct result of living next to a bookstore that specialized in out-of-print books when she was growing up.

"I thought it would be a kind gesture to send your father off to the clinic with a good breakfast," Nana continued, "He needs to keep up his strength if he's going to be fixing broken people all day! Now, help your dear Nana. Get two brooms and the dustpan out of the storage room. If we hurry, we can clean the floor before breakfast!"

Millie studied Nana fondly as they swept. Her short black hair had silver streaks woven throughout. "I got this one," Nana told her years earlier, pointing out a gray strip, "When you stood on the back of the couch and decided to fly; and this one came when you tried to cheer up that scary bald man in the park!"

Nana dumped the dustpan into the trash, tapping it against the side to loosen any stubborn particles. "All done!" She turned back to Millie and caught her staring. "What is it?"

"I was just thinking." Millie leaned her broom against the wall. "It's going to be really different around here when you leave."

"No, no." Nana placed her broom and dustpan next to the other broom before taking Millie's face in her hands. "It will be just like this, only I won't be here." Millie laughed and Nana patted her face gently. "It will only be for two months. Just enough time to visit and get reacquainted with old friends. California is not a world away."

Millie raised a hand to cover Nana's, closing her dark eyes. "I'm just going to miss you."

"I know you will, beloved," Nana said softly. "And I'll miss you both as well. But you'll see me again." The old woman pulled the younger into a hug. They stayed like that until they heard a familiar whistling from the hallway. "Now," Nana pulled back, "Be happy! It's time to celebrate!"

"Something smells amaz-"-*Thump!*-"Gah!" The two turned toward the door as Dr. Tim Macaraeg's grimacing face appeared in the doorway. "We've got to do something about that doorway."

"Like daughter, like father!" Nana chortled.

"Maybe we should hang a sign in the entryway," he drew a box in the air, "'Caution: This doorjamb is malicious and will take your toes off.'" Millie grinned as he limped over.

"Or perhaps you should have listened to me as a child and learned to pick your feet up when you walk," Nana tsk-tsked, a gleam in her eye. "Happy birthday, Timothy," she stood on tiptoe to receive a hug.

"Thanks Auntie," Tim smiled, turning to Millie. "Morning, Mil!"

"Happy birthday, Father Dear," Millie said, kissing his cheek. She looked at Nana before leaning in to whisper loudly. "Regardless of what she tells you, I did NOT forget."

Tim glanced at Nana, made an "ok" with his fingers, and gave an overdramatic wink before turning back to Millie. "Of course you didn't. I'd have to disown you for such an unforgivable sin!"

Millie laughed and Nana clucked her tongue. She grabbed their wrists and pulled them toward the kitchen table. "Enough of your tomfoolery. The food is getting cold!"

***

Treaten, TX
Saturday, Week Two

"Mike, stop it. Get off me!" Gina pushed the boy away and sat up. She scooted back over in the passenger's seat of the old pickup and turned off the radio, cutting Elvis off mid-croon. The parking lot was deserted, the only light coming from a lone lamppost in the middle of the asphalt.

"What's the matter, Baby?" Mike gave her a quick look-over.

"Don't 'baby' me. I want to go home." Gina tugged her t-shirt back into place and leaned against the door.

"Works for me."

"No, I mean I want you to drop me off."

"Aw, c'mon, Babe." Mike tried to slide an arm around her. "I'll make it worth your while."

She pulled away from his arm. "I said no. Not tonight. Please, take me home now."

"In a bit. There's no rush," he said, leaning in to kiss her neck.

"Back off!" Gina shoved him away.

"Damnit, Gina!" he banged his fists on the wheel exasperatedly. "One minute you're all over me and the next you're Miss Prude. Can you just make up your fool mind already?" They sat in silence for a moment before Mike slid his hand to above her knee, just below the hem of her cutoff jean skirt. "Do you love me or not?"

Gina's mouth opened to form a response, but nothing came out. Mike suddenly moved his hand higher and she grabbed his wrist.

"'Love' isn't a free pass," she snapped, pushing his hand off her leg. She threw open the car door and jumped out, slamming it angrily behind her. She folded her arms and headed toward the deserted parking lot's edge.

"Gina! Where do you think you're going? Come back here!" Mike yelled out the open passenger door's window. "Fine, who needs you! We are through, hear me? Through!"

"Good riddance!" Gina yelled over her shoulder as the truck squealed off into the night. She straightened her skirt and attempted to wipe the remainder of free-sample lipstick from around her mouth with the back of her hand. Her well-worn, brown boots crunched angrily on the sand that blended the parking lot's edge with the ten-acre field next to it. The Piggly Wiggly store's owner tried to keep the lot clean, but the arid West Texas wind wouldn't hear of it. Gina brushed her short ginger hair back with the headband that sat askew on her head, frowning as her bangs fell defiantly back into her eyes.

As the patches of sand gave way to dry grass, she became suddenly aware of the dark that surrounded her. A dog pack barked in the distance, making the hair on the back of her neck stood on end. She looked up at the full moon, thankful for some sort of light, no matter how small. This was the fastest way home, but Gina began to regret not following the road to the highway. *Though with my luck, I'd probably get run over or something,* she thought. Gina hummed quietly to herself to drown out the sounds in the dark as she approached the barbed-wire fence that connected the field to the Wilsons' pasture. She'd passed through here many times on weekly grocery trips or the occasional run to the Piggly Wiggly for odds and ends. Sliding under the lowest wire, she resumed the trek home, not even taking the time to brush the hay off. She slunk through the pasture on a hill, hunkering low so that if for some reason Mr. or Mrs. Wilson were to look out their bedroom window, she wouldn't be spotted trespassing. She crept past a few sleeping cows, hopped over cow patties, and sweet-talked the resident old bull, who didn't even stop chewing his cud long enough to consider her a threat.

Finally, she made it across and slipped under the fence. Gina smiled at the expanse of field in front of her, sloped downward as if it was carved especially for her convenience. She took off running, the hot August air blowing through her short mane and billowing her loose blue tank top. Treaten's high school had shut down the track program in the middle of last semester when the team was reduced to three people, and Gina had forgotten just how much she missed running. As the landscape leveled out, she slowed to a trot, and finally to a quick walk. When her feet hit the asphalt of the road that ran past her driveway, she gave a sigh of relief. Almost there!

The gravel crunched as she marched up her driveway. Suddenly, a large furry mass flew at her from the darkness, eliciting a stunned yell from the terrified girl. It barked and wagged its rear end. "Hank! What are you doing out here?" Gina scolded the panting dog after recovering from the initial shock. Hank stood on his hind legs to try and lick her chin. She pushed him down, patted the mutt's black-and-blue-speckled head, and continued up the drive. "How did you get out of the house?" The dog trotted on ahead toward the white farmhouse, and Gina stopped cold. The eighteen-wheeler shone menacingly in the light of the lamppost, its entire lower half spattered with mud. *Oh, no.* Gina took a deep breath and quickly crept the rest of the way to the house, sneaking around to the back porch. She plucked the spare key from its hiding place in the gutter spout, snuck up the porch steps, and unlocked the green door. Mercifully, the hinges didn't squeak as it swung open into the kitchen. Gina cautiously peered around the door into the darkness, listening intently for any sounds of movement. She held her breath as she quickly entered and shut the door behind her. She slipped her boots off and carried them across the wood floor toward the hallway. If she could just get up the stairs-

"Where the hell've you been?"

Gina jumped as the light turned on. She squinted toward the sound of the growling voice, trying to think of a viable excuse. "Dirk! You're, uh, home early. I... I thought your route wouldn't be done 'til Thursday."

The man stepped into the light, glaring. He was slumped slightly, but built like a bulldozer. "I drove fast. Seems like a good thing I did, too." Dirk scowled angrily down at Gina's smeared makeup, short skirt, and hay-covered exterior. "Looks like my dear stepdaughter hasn't been the good girl she's supposed to be." He took a few menacing steps forward past the fridge, stumbling on the last step. Gina swallowed hard, eying the nearly-empty bottle in the man's beefy hand. "You wanna tell me why you're out running around after midnight?" Dirk slurred slightly, taking another step forward. "'Cause that's one thing I'd really like to know. Now."

Gina unconsciously backed up a step and tried to keep her voice steady. "I just went for a walk."

"Do you always dress like that when you go for a walk?"

"Well," Gina faltered slightly, "Actually-"

"LIAR!" Dirk roared, charging forward. Gina gasped and stumbled backwards, tripping over the dining table. Dirk dropped the bottle, shattering it on the floor. He grabbed Gina's shoulders, lifting her small frame up off the ground and slamming her into the wall. "Where were you?" He snarled. The smell of alcohol on his breath was overpowering. Gina opened her mouth to say something, but words refused to form. "Answer me!" He shook her before dropping her back to the ground. "You were with that damn Crawford boy again, weren't you?"

"I – I –" Gina looked to the floor for answers.

He grabbed her face and jerked it up, forcing her to meet his bloodshot eyes. "I want an answer!"

"Yeah I was!" Gina cried, Dirk's grip burning her face. "But nothing happened, we broke up!"

He dropped her immediately, his entire demeanor changing.

"So that's how it is, is it?" Dirk took a few steps back, face unreadable behind his scraggly red beard. They stood in silence for a few torturous moments before Dirk spoke again, low and serious. "You better not have got yourself pregnant. I ain't gonna take care of *two* of your mama's mistakes." He gave Gina one last heart-stopping glare before turning and storming toward the living room. "Also," he added over his shoulder, "That damn dog was stuck in the house. If it happens again, I'll shoot it."

As the door slammed behind him, Gina bolted for the hallway before he could think of something else to berate her for.

Chapter Three

Yonkers, NY
Thursday, Week One

When the man came to, he was lying in a hospital bed with a killer headache. He pressed the nurse call button and a doctor came in, carrying his chart.

"How are you feeling, Mr. Housely?" The doctor raised the bed up slowly until the man was in a sitting position. "I'm Doctor Mitchell. You're at Yonkers' Mercy Heart Hospital with a broken leg and head trauma. You'll need to be in here for a few days. We obtained your personal and insurance information through the contents of your wallet. I hope that's alright."

"Yeah. When can-" Housely started to say, but stopped, raising a hand to his head. "Ohh… I'm dizzy."

"That's perfectly normal after fainting. We ordered some bloodwork, and found that you were severely anemic and dehydrated, which could have contributed to you passing out and crashing. We're giving you a blood transfusion and fluids now."

Housely looked from the tubes in his arm to the bag hanging next to him and nodded dazedly. "Can I go back to sleep now? I'm really tired."

Dr. Mitchell frowned and moved closer, pulling something from his coat pocket. "You shouldn't still be…you've been out for almost twelve straight hours." Housely yawned as the doctor shined a flashlight into his eyes. "The transfusion should have replaced enough platelets to give you your energy back…" Dr. Mitchell backed away suddenly, face unreadable. "I'll be right back." Housely looked over to the metal pole that the blood bag was suspended from to catch a glimpse of himself. Staring back from the distorted reflection was a pair of yellow eyes sunken into a deathly pale face.

"Right back" was less than truthful; Dr. Mitchell didn't return for over an hour. A nurse came in to check Housely's blood count and found him deep asleep. She ran the test anyway, and found that even with the transfusion, the number was dangerously low. The doctor ordered an emergency transfusion to try and stabilize the still-dropping count. He conferred with some of the other doctors in the hospital, but they were just as baffled about the mysterious disappearing blood cells.

At the nurse's station, Marianne Nanton – the graying nurse that had originally admitted Housely – absentmindedly stared at the wall, mentally prepping for the upcoming family reunion at her sister's house on Saturday. She'd been asked to bring pie, and debated silently if she would make them from scratch or give up and buy them from the store. One of her fellow nurses finally told her to just go home, that they'd cover her shift. She thanked them all and left, stopping by the 24-hour grocery store on the way home. There, she purchased 5 family-sized frozen apple pies and paid with three $20 bills, but not before habitually rifling through all the magazines at the end of the checkout stand. Some of the pages stuck together and she licked her thumb absentmindedly to separate them.

In that one trip to the store, she left microscopic gifts for 76 people that would be grocery shopping the next day. One of those people was Kendra Bennett, lead counselor at nearby Camp Sunshine, an overnight camp for girls aged 10-18. Camp Sunshine was renowned for its unique activity offerings, and housed around 250 girls from all across the nation in one-week blocks. Kendra went to the store early that morning to buy ice cream for closing ceremonies that were to be held that afternoon before the girls went back to their respective homes. She bought six 3-gallon tubs of ice cream and a tabloid magazine from the end of the checkout lane. By the time Kendra was done hosting closing ceremonies, nearly every camper plus 20 or so of the staff was infected.

Chapter Four

Watertown, NY
Monday, Week Three

"Yoo-hoo, Zach!" Connie, Zach's bubbly neighbor, had an unmistakable sing-song voice that now called to him as he entered to the trailer park. The older woman smiled and waved from where she was watering her plants outside her tin double-wide. Zach returned the smile and walked over to say hello. "It's been a while since I've seen you!"

"I guess it has. How've you been, Ms. Connie?"

"Pretty good, pretty good." She beamed. "This new fertilizer I got from the Home Depot is doing wonders for my Begonias! How's your mama?"

"Good. She changed doctors again and is feeling a lot better."

"Oh, good. I got real worried about her when that ambulance came a while back," Connie said sympathetically. "That must've been so scary for you."

"It was a rough couple of days for sure. Thank you again for that casserole, it was delicious." Zach glanced down the road toward their home. The maroon beater wasn't in its usual parking spot. "But you know Mom, she doesn't let anything keep her down for long. She's on her feet again and back at work now."

"I'm so glad! Is she still working at the laundromat?"

"Yes ma'am, they've got her on nights right now."

"I'll have to stop by sometime and say hello!"

"I'm sure she'd like that."

Connie smiled and reached up to move a stray strawberry-blonde hair out of her face. "Out of curiosity, would you be going to see Shannon later?"

"Shannon…" Zach frowned, confused. "Oh! Right." It had been a long time since Zach had heard someone use Oleson's first name, and for good reason. The old man forbade most people from using it, saying that it made him sound too much like a lawyer. "Yeah, I was headed over there now, actually."

"Oh, good! Can you take him something for me?" Connie disappeared into her house without waiting for an answer. Zach glanced around at the flowerpots surrounding her walkway. Connie was back almost as soon as she left, carrying a pie dish. Her blue eyes lit up as she held the pie out to him. "I felt like baking this morning but I don't need the calories in the house, so I thought who better to give it to than Shannon Oleson!" Zach adjusted his backpack and took the pie from her.

"Thanks, I'm sure he'll like it. Are you sure you don't want to give it to him yourself?" Zach raised an eyebrow and smiled.

"Oh, no," Connie giggled, putting a hand to her cheek. "I can't do that right now." Her rosy cheeks deepened in color.

Zach chuckled. "Well okay. I'll let him know that you made it especially for him."

"Thank you, Zach. And if you feel like putting in a good word for me, I'd appreciate it!" She winked at him and turned to go back inside.

"Will do," Zach said and turned to leave. As he approached Oleson's trailer, a boisterous laugh erupted from inside. *What's he got himself into this time?* Zach knocked on the door and pulled it open.

"Bub! C'mere!" A gnarled hand shot up and motioned over the backrest of the tall swivel chair in front of the radio station. Zach stepped up into the trailer and set the pie on the counter next to Oleson's minifridge. The trailer was old, but the old man patched up any holes that appeared in the wood panel interior throughout the years with brown duct tape. Zach dropped his black backpack to the floor.

"Hey, Dave. Would you mind holdin' for just a moment?" Oleson spoke into his microphone.

The radio crackled. *"No problem. Standing by."*

Oleson turned the mic off and set it down. He swiveled his chair around to Zach with a toothy grin. "Hey, Boy! How's work?"

"Ah, y'know," Zach said, leaning against the wall. "Crates and dead fish, the usual fun stuff. Who's on the radio today?"

"Some Canuck named Dave," Oleson replied, leaning his chair back a ways and glancing at the clock above the sink. "We've been talkin' for a few hours now." He suddenly stopped and lifted his head. "What's that smell?"

"Dead fish."

"No, the not-usual one."

"Oh, yeah. Connie baked you a pie." Zach pointed to the counter.

"Who?" Oleson hopped out of the chair and scurried over to the source of the smell.

"Connie. Our neighbor?" Zach paused, trying to figure out how to describe her. "The redhead who laughs a lot and has all those plants."

"Oh, her! Yeah, I know her." Oleson stared at the pie, licked his lips, and fished in the cabinets above the counter. He pulled out two mismatched plates and set them on the counter. "Why'd she make me a pie?"

"I think she likes you."

Oleson whipped around and gave Zach a bewildered look. "What? Now why on earth would she go and do a thing like that?"

"Beats me. Maybe it's your rugged charm," Zach said, folding his arms. Oleson cackled and fished a knife and two forks out of his clean-dish-holder.

"Ah, that's a good'n. But I ain't got time for women, Bub." Oleson cut two generous slices of pie, put them on plates, and handed one and a fork to Zach.

"Why not?" Zach slid into his chair next to Oleson's at the radio station. The cherry filling oozed out of the golden crust, filling the room even further with its mouth-watering aroma. "What exactly do you do all day?" He asked as Oleson sat down.

"Well, I tinker with my radio and go fishin' and check the mail for my retirement check and go to The Diner and talk to radio people…" The old man went silent for a minute and picked up his fork. "Nope! No time for women!"

"What if it was just Connie? One wo*man*, not multiple wo*men*. Maybe just ask her to The Diner one day? Who knows," Zach added with a smile, "It might be a good thing."

Oleson stuck his lower lip out in contemplation. "Eh. I'll think about it." The old man took a bite of pie and his eyes shot open. "Mmrrph!" A look of delight floated across his scraggly face as he swallowed. "Jumpin' Jehosaphat!" He took another giant bite and chewed slowly, his eyes half-closed in contentment. Zach grinned and scooped up a forkful. Oleson finished the first slice in record time and immediately got another. "Y'know, Bub, maybe I should get to know Connie a mite better after all." Oleson said, cutting another bite-sized piece with his fork. He reached over to turn the speaker back on and grabbed the mic.

"K2OLS here. VY1FRD, you still around, Dave?" Oleson asked.

"Sure am, Oleson."

"I've got my buddy, Zach, here, so he'll be listenin' in." Oleson grinned at Zach. "But more important, we got some durned good pie!"

Oleson and Zach talked with Dave for an hour. Zach learned that Dave was from Ross River, Yukon, and had been primarily using this frequency for about a year to try and run into the same people more often than not. Oleson and Dave talked at length about the importance of a good pie; Dave mentioned that his brother, who works in a morgue, used to compare their mother's pies to the inside of a corpse. They agreed that a good handmade pie is hard to come by, and Zach and Dave persuaded Oleson to talk to Connie awhile next time he saw her. Finally, Dave's wife called him for supper and he signed off.

"I like that Canadian," Oleson said with a yawn after keying the mic off. "Think I might add him to the Map!" Oleson gestured to his "Map of Friends" attached to the corkboard on the wall beside him. The map was spattered in tiny pins, each one holding a piece of paper with a callsign and name on it. The more interesting friends had a green sticker flag by their pushpin, and the least interesting had red flags. A running goal of Oleson's was to turn all the red flags green.

Zach stood up and stretched. "That's the fastest I've ever seen you befriend someone."

"Maybe that'll be my new challenge, to see how fast I can friend people!" Oleson said.

"I know who you could start with." Zach nodded at the empty plate on the table in front of Oleson. The old man cackled and reached up to scratch his beard. He yawned again, setting off a coughing fit.

"You okay?" Zach asked, slapping him on the back.

"Yeah," Oleson said, blinking and opening his eyes wide. "I'm just old and tired."

"Maybe you should sleep more." Zach took Oleson's plate from him and rinsed both plates in the sink.

"Maybe so," Oleson shrugged, swiveling his chair around.

"Well, I'd better head home," Zach sighed. "Gotta check on mom and deal with some stuff."

"Alrighty, Bub." Oleson smiled blearily up at Zach. "See ya tomorrow!"

When Zach got home, the car was gone and the house was empty. He dropped his backpack on the floor by the door and looked around the room. The mail lay opened on the kitchen table, and the TV across from the couch buzzed static. Zach grabbed the remote off the kitchen counter and hit the power button. Glancing at the refrigerator, he saw a note taped below the picture he'd drawn in fifth grade that'd never made it off the fridge.

Gone to work. Thanks for the leftovers, the lasagna was good. Still some left if you want it. Love you, mom.

Zach tossed the note into the trash can beside the closet that housed their washer and dryer. Opening the fridge beside him, he grabbed the cardboard container of store-bought lasagna. He removed the foil and tossed it in the trash, opting to slide the entire container into the microwave to reheat. Three minutes later, he sat at the table and stared into space, chewing and listening to the silence of the house.

***

Isherwood, PA
Monday, Week Three

"Now boarding terminal 17, flight 210 to San Francisco."

"Hurry, quickly now, Timothy!" Nana was a good thirty feet ahead of Millie and Dad as they ran through the airport. "They're boarding now!"

"Remind me again why they haven't recruited her for the Olympics," Dad wheezed, awkwardly hugging Nana's pink carryon to his chest. He ducked his head to either side to see around the questionably stuffed bag as he sprinted.

"Forget the Olympics; at this rate she could just run to California," Millie quipped. She shifted Nana's heavy leather bag on her shoulder and dodged a small boy playing on his Nintendo.

"Or replace an entire team of sled dogs in the Iditarod!" That mental image made them laugh so hard that they almost had to stop running altogether.

When they finally reached the terminal, Nana was already in line to board.

"About time, Timothy. I thought I would have to fly without my belongings!" Millie handed Nana her purse. "Thank you, Amelia. Keep this one in line while I'm away."

"I will," Millie smiled, hugging her. "Have fun on your trip, okay?"

"I plan to," Nana patted Millie on the back and the two separated.

"Take lots of pictures," Dad said, "And bring me back something shiny."

"Be good or I'll bring you back lumps of coal!" Nana picked up her luggage and moved up in the line.

"Then we could have a barbeque," Dad mused. Millie swallowed hard to fight the rising lump in her throat as Nana handed her ticket to the flight attendant. Nana paused in the doorway and looked back at the pair. She winked and waved before continuing through the gate.

"She'll be back in no time," Dad put his arm around Millie.

"Yeah…"

As they made their way toward the airport's exit, Dad spoke up. "I don't know about you, but I'm in no mood to cook tonight."

"Me either."

"The one good thing about Nana being gone is she can't get onto us for getting pizza delivered…"

"I'll order if you'll pay."

"Deal!"

Thirty minutes later, they were home and waiting rather impatiently for the pizza's arrival.

"I think I'll dust off the old treadmill tomorrow," Dad said, checking out the kitchen window for the third time. "Being outrun by an 80-year-old woman damages the ego something fierce." He drummed his fingers on the granite countertop.

"I don't mind. At least I can out-violin her…kinda." Millie replied, spinning around on the barstool. "You know, they say a watched pot never boils."

"Irrelevant," Dad replied, looking over his shoulder at her. "This is *pizza* we're talking about, the king of food! Not lowly water in a pot." Millie stopped spinning and glanced at the window as a Pizza Palace van drove by. Dad turned back to the window. "It's *here*." He grabbed his wallet and jogged into the living room.

Millie's phone buzzed. She picked it up and read the message from her friend Hannah.

"Hey, M! A few of us orch-dorks are going to go see 'The Hungry Dead' tonight and I wanted to see if you wanted in on it. So far it's me, Kim, Jade, Austin, and Ryan, but I'm going to try and get Lucas and Leah in if I can. Last hurrah before school starts kinda thing. Let me know!"

"What's up, Mil?" Dad appeared in the doorway with the pizza.

"Hannah's trying to get a group together to go to the movies tonight."

"You should go!" Dad smiled. He slid Millie the box and opened the fridge.

"I don't know if I want to," Millie said, opening the box. "It's the orchestra kids which is a fun group, but it's one of those slasher zombie flicks, and I don't think I'm up for that much gore."

"Says the kid who spent every waking moment in the operation observatory when she was twelve." Dad pulled back from the fridge with a can of pineapple chunks.

"That was different," Millie replied, quickly moving two slices to her and dad's respective plates. "Besides, the whole apocalypse genre is so overdone. They're just beating a dead horse at this point."

"A dead horse or a *zombie* horse?" Dad made a purposely dramatic face as he pulled the pop-top lid off.

Millie rolled her eyes. "That one physically caused me pain."

"You know you love my dad jokes." He scooped a few pineapple chunks out of the can with a fork.

"I'll never get over that." Millie wrinkled her nose as he arranged pineapple chunks on the pizza.

"Cold pineapple and warm pizza are like Harry Potter and Voldemort, neither can live without the other." He moved three pineapple bits into the shape of a lightning bolt with his fork.

Millie shook her head. "It's 'neither can live while the other survives.'"

"I was just making a reference to your childhood in an attempt to stay relevant." He shrugged. "Besides, just the fact that you remember the exact wording of that prophecy means that I succeeded in my parental efforts to turn you into a nerd."

"Intellectual pop culture enthusiast, not nerd." Millie picked up her pizza and blew on it.

"You sure you don't want to go tonight?"

"Yeah. I'll text Hannah in a bit and let her know I'm not coming."

"Well…since I'm off tomorrow, do you want to marathon the first few Harry Potter movies? It's been years since we went through them."

"Pizza and Potter. Sounds like a plan!"

Chapter Five

Treaten, TX
Tuesday, Week Three

The rain was a welcomed change for the parched landscape, though Gina wished she'd had an umbrella when the darkened sky opened up. She skidded slightly on the wet concrete in the middle of the Piggly Wiggly's parking lot, clutching Hank's frayed red leash tightly as he charged ahead. After the incident with him and Dirk, she didn't want to leave the pup at home if there was even a small chance that Dirk was going to be there.

When they reached the Piggly Wiggly's awning, Gina tied Hank to a dry post and gave his soaking head a pat. She walked to the entrance, sucking in a breath as the automatic doors squeaked open, blasting her with cold air. She blinked into the bright light that contrasted dramatically with the outside.

"Hi and welcome to Piggly Wiggly. If you need any help, don't hesitate to ask." The clerk at the front seemed especially bored tonight, her blue-black hair pulled back into a messy ponytail. She caught sight of Gina, dripping on the floor, and stopped chewing her gum long enough to tell her, "Paper towels are on aisle seven."

Gina grimaced, ducking down the nearest aisle as the cashier yawned and leaned on the counter. She quickly found what she needed – a loaf of bread, package of bacon, and a jug of milk. The cashier's voice came on over the PA as Gina made her way back to the register.

"Attention shoppers, the time is 9:50, the store will be closing in 10 minutes. Please bring all purchases to the front. Thank you." Gina glanced around as she set her items on the conveyor belt, but saw no other customers. The cashier sighed and rang everything up, glancing out the glass doors.

"You got an umbrella or something?" She sniffed, raising an eyebrow.

"No..."

"You should invest." The cashier gave Gina the total.

Gina fished the money out of her pocket and laid it on the counter. The cashier raised her other eyebrow, picking the wet bills up between two fingers. She cleared her throat and slid the money into the drawer, dropping a few coins into Gina's hand. Gina gave a quick smile as she grabbed the plastic bags and tied them off so the groceries wouldn't get wet.

"Thank you and have a nice day." The cashier deadpanned as Gina left.

Outside, Hank lay happily panting on the concrete, his brown eyes half closed in contentment. He hopped to his feet and wagged his tail as Gina approached. She untied the knot quickly and pulled him reluctantly out into the rain.

By the time they got home, the sunken dirt driveway was a muddied creek. Gina tied Hank to one of the posts holding up the back porch's overhang and slipped her boots off. Hank whined as she opened the back door.

"It's okay, boy. Shh," she whispered, shaking as much water off of her as she could before stepping inside. Shutting the door behind her, she put the bag of groceries on the kitchen table and quickly tiptoed down the hall toward the bathroom behind the stairs. She opened the cabinet across from the sink and grabbed four clean towels, careful to leave three in case Dirk decided to shower sometime this century. When she'd left that afternoon, Dirk had been passed out in the living room in a rare snoreless slumber, probably brought on by whatever was in the empty bottles beside the couch. As she quietly made her way back toward the kitchen, she glanced into the living room. Sure enough, he was exactly where she left him. He was due to leave on a new route in a half-hour, but Gina knew from experience that waking him too early in the evening could be disastrous. She watched him in disgust for a moment before slipping across the kitchen to the outside.

When Hank was sufficiently dried, Gina untied him and went back inside to change. She always habitually locked her bedroom door whether or not Dirk was home, even if she was only going to be in the room for a second. She slipped into a black t-shirt and jean shorts and went back downstairs to drop her wet clothes in the laundry room. She glanced at the clock. 10:45. 15 minutes until Dirk was to leave. She grabbed a broom and went into the living room.

"Dirk, wake up." Gina flipped on the light and approached the sleeping mass, broom handle at the ready. "Time to go to work." She gently jabbed the broom handle into his arm a few times, the standard wake-up call that normally brought him snorting into consciousness. He didn't move. Gina brushed her bangs out of her eyes and flipped the broom. "Must've been some brew." She rubbed the bristles against his bare foot, hanging off the couch uselessly. "Dirk. You've got to get going." *Hungover or not.* His form lay still, unmoving. Gina frowned. "Dirk..?" She cautiously moved closer, within the arm's length safe distance that she normally kept. Reaching out a hand quickly, she patted the pale, unshaven face and jumped back. Nothing. Gina stood silently, watching, waiting for his chest to rise. Nothing. The slowing rain tapped lightly on the window, the only sound in the deathly quiet room aside from the pounding of her heart.

She sat against the far wall with her knees to her chest, staring wide-eyed at the body on the couch. So he'd finally done it. She always figured that one day he'd drink himself out, she just never thought it'd be on her watch.

Dirk was dead. Gone. There would be no more yelling, no need to walk on eggshells to avoid provoking him. No drunken tirades, no more broken dishes. But more importantly, there was nothing to keep her in Treaten.

It was as if a calming fog settled over her as she went up to her room. She pulled the thrift shop Red Cross duffel bag out of her closet and put it on the bed. Slowly, methodically, she began to pack her essential belongings. She didn't know where she was going; all she knew was that she couldn't stay in the house. Dirk was far too heavy to move by herself, and if she called the coroner, she figured there'd be police, lawyers, and eventually, a foster home or local girls' shelter where she'd stay until she was eighteen, when she'd be thrown into the world by herself.

Gina turned to the pillow on her bed, stripping it of its case. She flipped it over and removed the safety pin holding the pillow's seam together. Carefully, she fished around inside until she found the small plastic baggie of money she'd earned over time doing odd jobs around town when Dirk was away. That, plus whatever was in Dirk's money box, would probably last her two months. Three, if she was extremely careful with it.

After packing a week's worth of clothes, she carefully removed the butcher knife from its place under her mattress and slid it in between two shirts. She pulled a large yellow envelope from the bottom drawer of her nightstand and packed it with everything else.

When she went to get Dirk's money box, her feet refused to move past the doorway. She had only ever gone in his room once, and could still feel the bruises from when he discovered her in there. Glancing down the stairs, she finally pushed past the doorway and went straight to the box hidden under the unmade bed. She'd seen him remove the shoebox many times before going on a booze run, but had never ever seen the contents. She was astonished to see rolls of tens and twenties stacked on top of each other. Dirk's paranoia and distrust of banks had finally paid off. Gina opened a zippered compartment inside her duffel and proceeded to dump the box's contents inside, glancing behind her habitually. As the last roll landed in the pocket, an envelope fluttered to the ground. Gina set the box aside and picked up the envelope. It was addressed to Dirk, with a Greenville, Alabama return address. Intrigued, Gina opened the envelope. Inside was a letter written in loopy cursive, dated eight years ago. She skimmed the letter, eyebrows furrowing at the indecipherable words. Finally, she reached the end, where she was just able to make out the end of the last line: "…always welcome home. Love, Aunt Rita."

Aunt. Ain't that convenient, she thought, taking another look at the address. *Guess I'm going to 'Bama.*

After stuffing the letter and envelope into the bottom of her bag, Gina went downstairs. The rain had stopped, and the house was deathly quiet. Gina set the duffel on the kitchen table before walking back into the living room and leaning against the wall. The more Gina stared at it, the more the body resembled a beached whale. A whale that didn't deserve the proper burial that it would get when found. Gina saw only red as she went to the kitchen.

She emptied the cabinets of alcohol, carrying it all into the living room. The hairs on her neck stood on end as she got closer to the body. She spilled two bottles of cheap tequila over the carpet littered with cigarette burns and dropped the empty bottles near the pile that Dirk already made. She threw one bottle at the wall opposite the couch, shattering it on the wood paneling. She dumped the remaining bottle on the couch and corpse. As she glared at the body, a wave of nausea came over her suddenly and she stumbled back out of the room. Her hands shook as she sat down hard in the nearest chair.

"What am I doing? I can't do this. I can't," she muttered to herself. She nervously reached up to rub the back of her neck. There, she felt it. The scar where Dirk had "accidentally" burned her with a cigarette when she was seven. She ran her fingers over the raised circle for a moment before shoving the chair back away from the table.

She retrieved a cigarette and lighter from the drawer Dirk kept them in, and went back into the living room. She fiddled with the lighter for a moment before figuring out how to work it. She tried to light the cigarette a couple of times, but it wouldn't catch. She realized the problem, and stuck the filtered end in her mouth. She touched the flame to the other end and sucked in a breath; as soon as the smoke entered her throat she began coughing so hard that she was sure she was going to choke up a lung. Still hacking, she threw the lighter and lit cigarette at the base of the couch. The alcohol caught fire quickly, spreading rapidly around the room.

By the time that she'd gotten to the end of the driveway with Hank and the bag, the entire living room was aflame. As she made it to the hill, the fire crept up the walls to the second story. When she sprinted through the Wilsons' pasture, the fire waltzed into the upstairs bathroom and the kitchen. When she passed by the Piggly Wiggly, the flames snuck under the door into her room. When the entire house was ablaze, Gina was sitting with Hank at the bus stop next to a lady in a skirt and man with a suitcase, both oblivious to what she'd done.

When the eastbound bus finally arrived at midnight, the man and lady climbed on first, and Gina picked up Hank's leash and started to follow.

"Uh-uh," the driver stopped her. "No dogs." Gina mentally slapped herself for not remembering that public transportation wouldn't allow pets. "Unless," the driver continued, pointing at a sign near the door, "it's a service animal."

"He is," Gina lied. "I have… attacks. He alerts me when one's coming." She patted her Red Cross bag.

The driver looked at Hank. "Where's his vest?"

"'Scuse me?"

The driver blinked slowly, exaggerating the bags under his eyes. "His vest, his ID. Something that proves he's a service dog."

"Oh." Gina nodded slowly. "He doesn't have one yet. It got lost in the mail. They're sending a new one." The driver raised an eyebrow. Gina glanced up at the passengers. "But if you want, I could call my doctor and the service dog registry. They can prove it, and it'll only take a half-hour or so." Some of the passengers groaned.

"Just let the dog on," somebody said loudly.

The driver looked back at the few passengers, then at Gina. "Fine, but you clean any of his messes."

"Yes sir," Gina nodded solemnly and climbed into the bus.

An hour later, the bus was rid of all late-night passengers except Gina, Hank, and the lady in the skirt. Gina continued looking out the window until she saw the lady sit in the seat in front of her.

"Cute dog," she smiled at Hank lying in the aisle.

"Thanks," Gina replied.

"Where are you headed?" The lady asked.

Gina replied with the first town that came to mind. "Dallas."

"Wow, sounds like you've got quite the journey ahead of you."

"Guess so."

"You know how to get there…right?" The lady gave Gina a sideways look.

"Yeah, sure." Gina lied, turning more toward to the window.

"So I guess you'll be getting off at the stop after next, since you missed the first connection to I-20 forty minutes ago."

Gina looked back at the woman, who had a concerned look on her face. Gina stared at her a second. "Uh, yeah, I will."

The lady nodded slowly and leaned forward. "Listen, if you're in some sort of trouble…"

"No, I'm fine." Gina lied. "My grandparents are in Dallas. I'm visiting them and got lost in thought." She gave a quick smile and turned pointedly away from the woman.

Two hours later, the bus stopped at a small bus station next to a diner where Gina picked up a map of some of the Texas bus routes. She found that Interstate 20 went all the way to Birmingham – two hours north of Greenville – and that the Whippet Line had a bus running on it daily at 9 AM. The lobby was deserted, so she lay down on one of the benches to try and catch some sleep.

At 8 AM, the desk clerk came in and found Gina and Hank. Gina gave the same story about Hank being a service dog, adding that he had signaled her to lie down and she accidentally fell asleep. Gina then bought a ticket and sat outside the brick building on a bench to avoid any more questions. She watched the cars pass by on the highway, counting the trucks, but after checking the clock on the wall five times in twenty minutes, she realized she needed something else to pass the time. Her stomach rumbled loudly just as the next-door diner's lights flipped on.

Chapter Six

Yonkers, NY
Saturday, Week One

On Saturday evening, Housely's condition worsened by the hour. Upgraded to the ICU, he was lethargic, jaundiced, and his blood pressure was dangerously low and dropping. An assembled team of doctors worked feverishly to try and figure out the cause. They ran test after test, tried treatment after treatment, but nothing worked.

In a borrowed conference room, one of the doctors cursed and slammed his hands down on the table. "It can't just disappear! The blood has to be going somewhere," he exclaimed. His large forehead was spattered with beads of sweat.

"Don't you think we know that, Foster?" A bearded doctor named Renshaw stood angrily. "We've done everything there is to do! There aren't any more tests to run, there's no disease, illness, or parasite that fits his symptoms."

"Has anyone tried talking to him lately?" A petite blonde cardiologist named Hill asked exasperatedly. "Or tried to locate his family?"

"He's been practically comatose since the first day, drifting between delusional mumbling and catatonia." Foster stood and began pacing, running his hands through his brown hair. "A brick wall would give more information than him right now."

"Alright, enough," Mitchell pinched the bridge of his nose, "Somebody go personally run another CBC. I want to know what his count is."

"Got it," Foster muttered, swooping out of the room.

When he got to the ICU, Housely was staring blankly at the wall through half-lidded eyes. The only noise in the room was the soft beeping coming from the stat monitor. "Hello," Foster smiled. "I'm Dr. Foster. I'm assisting Dr. Mitchell with your case. We need some more blood to run a test to see how you're doing." Housely continued to stare directly ahead. "I bet you just love these needles by now. Yeesh," Foster joked lightly, retrieving a sterile syringe from a drawer. No reaction. "…Alrighty. On the count of three…" He tied off Housely's arm with a band right above a vein, and stuck the needle in. As Foster began to draw in the plunger, he immediately knew that there was something very, very wrong. The blood that should have been the consistency of water was as thick as pudding. "Oh, God," he pulled the syringe out in horror. Just then, the machine started going crazy, beeping wildly as the heartbeat graph dropped. Foster slammed the emergency button on the wall, threw the syringe in the biohazard bin and ran into the hallway. "We need a crash cart in here!"

***

Watertown, NY
Tuesday, Week Three

On Zach's way home from work he passed through the alley behind the old shopping strip, kicking a rock absentmindedly. As he passed the electronics store, something shiny in one of the trash bins caught his eye. Moving closer, he saw that it was a discarded radio transmitter. It seemed fully intact, the only problem being the destroyed packaging. Since it was being thrown away anyway and Oleson's transmitter was tin foil and old batteries, Zach slipped it in his pocket and continued toward home.

"Hey, Oleson?" Zach rapped on the trailer door. No answer. Zach glanced over and saw that the Olesmobile was parked in its usual spot. He knocked on the door again. "Oleson, you home?" A faint thud and pained groan answered back. Zach opened the door quickly and jumped the concrete step. "Oleson!" Zach looked toward Oleson's room. The old man was lying on a crumpled blanket in blue pajamas beside his bed. Zach kneeled beside him and rolled him over slowly on his back. His face was pale, his eyes squeezed shut.

"That you, Bub?" his voice was weak.

"What happened to you?" Zach searched the man's face for signs of anything other than pain.

"I think this old body's finally beginning to quit on me," Oleson squinted up at Zach. "I'm real tired is all. Feeling right like a weakling."

"Come on, we've got to get you to a doctor," Zach slipped an arm around the old man's shoulders, gently lifting his head off the ground.

"No!" Oleson's eyes shot open, and for the first time Zach could see that they were yellowed and bloodshot. "No," he reiterated quieter. "No doctors…They scare me." Oleson looked up at Zach with helpless fear in his eyes. The old man had never been anything but smiles, so seeing him act like frightened child was terrifying.

"But we've got to get you help," Zach said again, glancing to the door. "I'm not going to just sit here and do nothing."

"I think I ought to just rest now. I'm awful tired." The older man sighed and yawned.

"But-" Zach protested before Oleson cut him off.

"-I'll be fine in the morning. Just need sleep. Help me up, will you?" Zach stood slowly, raising Oleson up onto the bed. He helped him get situated and picked his blanket off the floor, before stepping back hesitantly. "Bub?"

 "Yessir?"

"Pretty strange weather we've been havin', innit." Oleson's eyelids drooped slowly.

"Sure enough." Zach eased down onto a wobbly chair near the door.

· "Them Canucks said it's snowing up there. But I think…" His voice wavered as another yawn interrupted him. "…they's fooling."

"Yeah?"

"Makes sense that it'd be summer there too, right?" Oleson feebly drew the blanket up to his chin, his eyes rolling back a bit as his lids shut.

"Makes complete sense." Zach smiled, eyebrows knitted.

"Good… I like making sense…" Oleson's head lolled to the side, his breathing slowing slightly.

Zach waited for what seemed to be hours to make sure he was sleeping soundly before hesitantly standing up. Slowly, quietly, he pulled Oleson's bedroom door shut. "See you round, Oleson."

*

Zach numbly watched the coroner load the stretcher into the ambulance.

"Son?" Zach looked to the police officer standing nearby. He grasped a notepad and pen, watching Zach carefully. "If you need to sit down or something…"

"Nah. No…I'm okay. What was the question again?" Zach crossed his arms in front of him.

"I need a statement of what happened this morning."

"I woke up on his couch around 5:30 and went to check on him…and he was…wasn't breathing, he was cold and…" Zach swallowed hard.

One of the other policemen called the first officer over to the yellow tape surrounding the house. "Wait here, I'll be right back."

The officer returned as the ambulance pulled out of the trailer park, its lights illuminating the gravel in the early morning darkness. By then, some of the residents were peeking out of their doors and looking out windows trying to get a glimpse of what was going on.

"Did he have any family?"

Zach shook his head and cleared his throat. "Nah, it was just him."

The officer made some notes on the pad. "Alright. Well, the coroner says that it was a straightforward passing of natural causes. We'll have somebody run his name through the records and see if we can find any family. If not, somebody will be by next week to collect his things." The officer glanced at the Olesmobile. "So if ah, if there's anything of yours or anyone else's in there, you might want to get it out. I'm sorry for your loss."

When the officers left, Zach slowly made his way to the yellow tape. Slipping past it, he opened the trailer door and stepped inside. He sunk into his chair at the radio station and stared at the empty seat next to him. All the memories Zach had of Oleson suddenly came rushing back; from the hours spent creating secret languages to the afternoons spent fishing at the lake to the evenings chatting with people halfway around the world.

Zach blew out a long, slow breath of air, glancing up at Oleson's fire hazard of a kitchenette. There, tacked up on the wall above the mini fridge, was a framed picture. Zach had taken it with the disposable camera Oleson gave him for his birthday one year. A grinning 10-year-old Zach and laughing Oleson were crookedly framed in the snapshot, and scrawled at the bottom was the caption "Oleson and Bub, best friends."

Zach's vision blurred.

***

Isherwood, PA
Thursday, Week Three

Millie was dozing on the couch when her dad burst through the front door and ran into the living room, startling Millie from her nap.

"Channel 7. Quickly!"

Millie sat up, grabbed the remote off the coffee table and flipped over to the news station. "What's the matter?"

"Shh!" Tim slid into the chair in front of the coffee table as the president appeared on the screen. He looked as though he hadn't slept for days, yet his presence was commanding as always. The mob of reporters seated in front of him went silent as he stepped up to the microphone.

"My fellow Americans, I've come here today to address a very serious issue that has come to my attention. There has been an outbreak of a viral infection that has spread over part of this great nation, and today I am setting in motion a series of events that will contain this virus before it can spread further. A quarantine of many sections of the United States will be instated effective immediately; we'll detail exactly where those quarantine zones will be in just a moment. Cancel any and all public gatherings, summer schools, and non-essential public outings. Enforce social distancing in the workplace, and increase sanitization efforts by 300% in all aspects of life."

"What does that even mean?" Millie muttered to herself.

The President continued. "Only visit the hospital or your medical caregiver if there is a genuine emergency. The United Department of Health and Human Services and the Center for Disease Control and Prevention are working overtime to bring more information to you, the public, at this time." The crowd of reporters erupted into a frenzy, hands and microphones waving wildly as their questions piled on top of one another. The President pointed to a female reporter in a gray suit and the voices went silent.

"Mr. President, what are the symptoms that people should be watching for?"

"I'm unable to discuss that at this time."

"Sir, what is this virus?" Another reporter jumped in.

"Once again, I cannot discuss the particulars at this time. But I can assure you, with the efforts of the UDHHS and CDCP and with proper quarantine and sanitization efforts, this problem will be solved in a short period. Please, there is no need for panic. Thank you."

As soon as the President stepped off the podium, the reporters erupted into a frenzy until the screen went suddenly black.

Millie turned slowly to her father, jaw hanging open slightly. "Dad...?"

Tim's lips pursed into a fine line as he stared at the blank screen. "He shouldn't have done that," he said, shaking his head slightly. "By saying 'don't panic' he's inadvertently going to send everyone into a panic." He dropped his head back onto the chair and sighed. "Things are about to get really bad." His pocket beeped loudly. Tim retrieved his phone and looked at its tiny screen. "Well, that was fast."

"What is it?" Millie asked.

"Emergency meeting at the hospital." He looked to Millie and stood up. "I gotta go. Lock up and keep your phone nearby, and I should be back sometime tonight." His phone beeped again, and Tim glanced at it. "...make that tomorrow." He leaned down and kissed Millie's forehead quickly, disappearing through the door. "Oh, and Mil," he stuck his head back in quickly, "Call Nana and check on her, would you?"

"Ok." Millie nodded.

Tim smiled and vanished from the doorway.

Millie fished her phone out of her pocket and dialed Nana's number. It went straight to voicemail.

"Hey, Nana, it's Millie. I just wanted to call and check on you." Millie paused. "If you could just call me back when you get a chance, I'd really appreciate it. Love you."

She hung up the phone and flipped over to her internet app, typing "USA virus" into the search bar. She tapped the first link that popped up, the CDC website, and was met with a "temporarily closed for maintenance" message. Frowning, she tried the Puffing Host's website, but a "404 error" popup blocked out the screen. She tried three more links, but hit a wall each time. Frustrated, she closed out the browser and set her phone on the coffee table. She flipped TV channels to try and distract herself, but soon felt her eyelids drooping. She fought it as long as she could, but exhaustion blocked out everything.

Brrring. Brrring. A dull ringing roused Millie from her deep sleep. Her hand fumbled for her phone on the table, eyes not quite ready to open.

"Hello?" She answered sleepily.

"Millie! Thank God. I was starting to get worried, I've called six times." Dad's voice was tight.

"I'm sorry. I didn't even hear the phone." Millie opened her eyes and sat up slowly, joints aching a bit.

"It's alright; I'm just glad to know that you're okay." He paused.

"What is it?"

"Ca-" The sound of loud frantic voices cut him off. A door slammed loudly in the background. "I don't have much time to talk, so I have to make this fast."

"Dad, what's going on?"

"Nothing, it's okay." His voice was strained. "I... I can't come home right now. I'm not sure when I'll be able to." Millie nodded slowly to herself, brows furrowed.

"Can I come up there to-"

"No. I need you to stay put. It's hectic up here, and you're safe at home." A loud crash and scream coupled with yelling and thundering feet emphasized what he said. "I gotta go. I love you, Mil."

"Love you too. But Dad-" The line went dead suddenly. Millie stared at the phone's screen a moment before hanging it up. 1 AM. She had slept for well over 13 hours. She felt feverish, achy. Her mind went immediately to the earlier broadcast. Raising slowly off the couch, her knees almost buckled under her. She slowly made her way down the hall to the bathroom, leaning against the wall to steady herself.

Nothing looked especially out of place as she examined her face in the mirror, except her dark eyes looked slightly yellow in the vanity lighting. Then again, the President hadn't said what the virus's symptoms were. Maybe she just had a cold. Whatever it was, it was draining her of energy. She turned the light off and stumbled across the hall to her bedroom where she collapsed.

Chapter Seven

Somewhere in Texas
Wednesday, Week Three

After tying Hank's leash to a post in the shade outside the diner, Gina went in and was immediately hit with the smells of breakfast. A bell above the door tinkled.

"Come on in and sit where ya like! I'll be with you in a minute." A cheerful voice rang out from the kitchen. Gina looked around at the home-style diner, complete with checkered tile floor and jukebox, and slid into one of the red booths in the corner next to one of the windows. A middle-aged lady with a bright red beehive of hair atop her head came waltzing out of the door behind the counter. "Well, hi there!" The lady pulled a menu out of her apron and dropped it in front of Gina. "My name's Pauline and I'll be serving you today. What can I start you off with?"

"Just water, thanks. And also," Gina added, "Could I get a bowl of water?"

"We've got restrooms if you want to wash your hands, dear," the lady smiled wide, sporting a missing molar.

"It's for my dog."

"Dog? Are you hiding him in that bag of yours?"

"He's tied up outside," Gina replied, pointing out the window.

"Oh, I see. Be right back." Pauline disappeared behind the counter again, returning quickly with Gina's order, and two biscuits. "Here you go, hon. Something for your pup to snack on!" She winked at Gina. "I'll take your order as soon as you're ready."

Gina ordered a sausage and egg sandwich with grits, and took the bowl and biscuits out to Hank.

Shortly after returning inside and receiving her food, a group of bikers roared into the parking lot. Gina watched them dismount and head for the door, holding her breath slightly as they passed Hank. A couple of them reached down to pat him on the head or scratch his ears. The chimes above the door tinkled as the group thundered in.

"Hey, Pauline!" One burly man with a beard and bandana on his head called, "How about some food for weary travelers?"

"Depends on what you're paying with," Pauline stuck her head out of the kitchen door. "It's about time! I was starting to worry about you, Bruce."

The burly man crossed to the counter and leaned over it to give Pauline a kiss on the cheek. "You know we'll always come back for the amazing cooking and your sweet disposition." He glanced over his shoulder and gave one of the men a wink.

"Oh shut up," Pauline laughed. "You can sweet talk me as much as you want, but you've still got to pick up the tab," she poked his shoulder. The bikers settled at the counter and into the booths on the other side of the restaurant as Pauline passed out menus. "So what'll it be?"

One of the bikers snorted. Gina looked over to see him rubbing his eyes as if he'd just woken up.

"You okay, Lon?" One of the bikers asked the snorter.

"Yeah, yeah I'm fine. Just tired."

"You'll be fine after we eat," one of the others said. Gina glanced at the clock. The bus would arrive in ten minutes. She quickly finished eating the grits, walked up to the register that Pauline was leaning next to, and paid the bill.

"Thank ya much. Y'all come back sometime!"

Gina took Hank around the back of the diner to do his business, returning right as the bus pulled up. Gina gave the service dog story again, and the driver let her on without a second thought.

Five hours and seven rest stops into the drive, Gina was dozing in the farthest left rear window seat with Hank at her feet. She was suddenly thrown into the back of the seat in front of her as the bus screeched to a stop.

"Hey there folks, sorry about that," the driver said over the intercom. "We're about fifteen miles outside Kilgore, and we seem to have just hit a solid wall of traffic. It looks like we might be here a while." Some of the passengers groaned over the delay, others strained to see what lay ahead outside.

After a solid hour of sitting at a standstill, the bus driver's voice came over the intercom again. "Alright, folks, I'm going to step outside for just a moment to see what's going on." The bus shuddered and turned off.

Gina glanced around the cabin at some of the other passengers. A few were trying to sleep, their chairs reclined the full four inches backward. Others talked quietly to each other or played on their electronics. One boy a few rows ahead who looked to be around Gina's age and had gotten on at the last stop was speeding through a book, flipping pages faster than Gina could read a paragraph. The driver returned after ten minutes, turning the bus back on so he could talk over the intercom again.

"Well folks, it looks like we're going to be here a while. I'm told there's been a wreck involving an oil tanker about two miles up the road. I suggest getting comfortable, it could be a while before they manage to get things moving." The majority of the passengers sighed and mumbled to each other. "I apologize for the delay," continued the driver, "But you are all welcome to stand up, stretch, walk around. And if any of our four-legged passengers need to take a walk, now would be the perfect opportunity." The driver's joke sparked a few chuckles and glances toward Gina. She grimaced slightly and looked to Hank, happily panting as usual.

Two hours later, the passengers were getting very agitated. Most were well past due at their respective drop-off locations, many were exhausted, and all were tiring of the heat. Since he wasn't sure how long they would be stuck in traffic and the bus's fuel tank was low, the driver told everyone that he could only turn the bus on intermittently. The bus would turn on, blast everyone with freezing cold air for seven minutes, then turn off and roast the passengers for fifteen. The shades on the windows had long been lowered to try and beat the heat, but by 4 o'clock some of the passengers had had enough.

"I can't take it anymore!" A very sweaty man in the middle of the right row stood up. "How long would it take to walk to the nearest town?"

"Well, ah," the bus driver stood and took off his hat to scratch his bald head. "Tyler's the closest, and that's still fifteen miles out. I can't let you attempt that in this heat, sir. You're much safer in the bus."

The man sat down hard, shaking the whole bus. Gina rested her head on the back of the chair, looking to the call buttons attached to the roof. She could swear the heat shimmered above her. She rolled her head to the right and noticed that she was no longer alone on the row: the fast-reading boy who had gotten on at the last stop was perched a few seats over. His dark eyes were abnormally large for his face, giving him the look of a perpetually stunned owl.

"Hello," he said, smiling quickly. "I uh, just finished my book and was admiring your dog and just thought you looked a bit lonely sitting back here by yourself. But I guess you're not really by yourself because your dog is here, too." He blinked a few times in rapid succession. Gina's face remained blank. "So um, my name's Louis, what's yours?"

"Gina." She straightened her neck.

Louis nodded at Hank. "And who's this?"

"Hank," Gina replied.

"Like *Hank the Cowdog*?" Louis grinned.

"Yeah, I guess," Gina said.

"That was one of my favorite series when I was younger," he said. "Well, that and pretty much any scary story I could get my hands on. Gotta love those!"

"Interesting." Gina leaned her head back on the headrest.

"So," Louis continued, "Where are you two heading?"

"Alabama," she replied absentmindedly.

"Visiting family?"

"Sure."

"Me too!" Louis' face lit up.

Gina looked at the boy from the corner of her eye. "Really?"

"Uh-huh!" Louis nodded. "My grandparents live just outside of Birmingham. My mom used to live in Alabama, but moved to Seattle for work where she met and married my dad. Fun fact, I was born while my parents were vacationing in Canada, so I'm technically Canadian. Eh," he added with a grin. "But I do have a dual citizenship, so I'm American, too! My parents were just going to fly me to Alabama, but I thought it'd be more fun to bus it. You can see a lot more sights this way, and you can stop at all the iconic places along the route!" His voice had been growing progressively louder, ending the last sentence in an almost shout. "Am I talking too much?"

"Yes!" One of the passengers three rows up said exasperatedly.

"Oh. Sorry," he whispered, ducking his head slightly.

The corner of Gina's mouth twitched upward in amusement. "So, Seattle?"

For a while, Louis and Gina swapped stories. Louis did most of the talking, resetting his volume every so often so to not anger the nearby passengers. The conversation was sporadic, never lingering on one topic too long.

"…So yeah, I prefer sifting through my dad's library instead of modern books and films. Everything nowadays just sounds the same," he waved a flat hand dismissively, 30 minutes after beginning his latest monologue. His slightly-too-large head and jerky gestures reminded Gina of a marionette.

"Alright folks," the driver's voice echoed overhead, "Traffic's started moving again." A few of the passengers cheered as the bus jolted to a crawl.

Gina awoke the next morning to Hank's whimpering. The bus was parked at a rest stop, so she grabbed the leash, her bag, and took the mutt outside to a nearby tree. After he did what he needed to do, Gina took him with her into the building. Inside was a small seating area with various vending machines, and the passengers of the bus sat around eating and chatting. Louis spotted her from his table against the wall and waved frantically for her to come over, looking a bit like a drowning man. Gina bought a sandwich from the vending machine and slid into the chair in front of Louis.

"Good morning, Gina!" Louis chirped. "Looks like we won't be in Alabama until Friday night at this speed, but that should be fine, right? I mean, at least we're moving."

Gina unwrapped one of the sandwiches and gave it to Hank. "Why didn't anyone wake me?"

"Oh, sorry, that was my fault," Louis replied, "You were sleeping so hard and looked so exhausted yesterday that when the driver turned on the lights and most everyone left and you and a few other people were still sleeping, I didn't want to wake you." Gina raised an eyebrow. "Sorry, that sounded creepy, didn't it?" Louis grimaced. "I didn't mean for it to, I swear."

The corner of Gina's mouth twitched upward. "Could you hold him for a minute?" She held the leash out to Louis. "I'll be right back."

"Sure!" Louis took the leash and scratched behind Hank's ear. Gina stood, picked up her bag, and made her way to the bathroom.

After washing her hands and face and reapplying deodorant, Gina stared at her reflection in the mirror. Her green eyes had dark circles beneath them and the spattering of freckles across her small nose seemed more prominent than usual. For the first time since leaving Treaten, doubt crept into her mind. *What if the police find out I set the fire? What if they think I killed Dirk? What if they try to find me? What if Aunt Rita won't take me in? What if...* She shook her head, snapping out of it. *Deal with those problems when and if they happen.* Stepping into the main room, she could've heard a pin drop. Gina followed everyone's gaze to the glass door. Outside, the driver paced back and forth, talking into his shoulder radio.

"What's going on?" Gina asked, sliding back into her seat. Louis' lower lip was sucked into his mouth, his brows knitted together.

"The President's ordered a national lockdown," Louis stated, his eyes never leaving the driver.

"What?" Gina frowned. "Why?"

"There's been some sort of virus outbreak, and he's declared a state of emergency. Only fuel and food trucks are being allowed in and out." Louis turned to Gina, his face grim. Hank put his head on Gina's knee and sighed, earning a scratch behind the ear.

"Who's he talking to?" Gina looked to the driver, still mumbling into his radio.

"His supervisor, I think." The driver adjusted his hat, yawned, and glanced over his shoulder to the waiting passengers. He talked into the radio a bit more before walking back into the rest stop. The smile he offered looked forced as he wiped the dampness from his forehead.

"Alrighty, folks, sorry for the wait. My supervisor says that since we're inside the quarantine zone, there's really nothing we can do except journey on. I've been told that whoever wants to continue on the route will be welcomed to do so, and anyone who wants to stay will be refunded half of their ticket's purchase price. The President says that they're working on figuring out the problem, so I think we should just let them handle things-"

"Let them handle things?" One of the men spoke up, his face pale and sweaty. "How do we know that they didn't cause this? They're always doing who knows what with genes and stuff, who's to say they didn't create it just so they could make us pay them for a vaccine?" A few of the others muttered in agreement.

"I don't know." The driver looked calmly at the man. "I'm just telling you what I've been told, sir."

"I don't know about you all, but I'm sure as hell not getting back on that bus," the man folded his arms and settled into the chair.

"That's fine, sir, the company is more than willing to reimburse you. But because of our schedule, I'll need to ask that anyone who plans on continuing the trip to board as soon as possible for departure in thirty minutes." The driver turned on his heel and went out the door.

People started whipping out their cellphones to contact relatives and friends and let them know of the change in plans.

Louis looked to Gina. "What are you going to do?"

It's not like I can turn around and go home. At this point, there were only two options; stay in whatever poor excuse for a town they were in or ride the bus to the end of the line.

Gina glanced at Hank. "I'm going."

Chapter Eight

Yonkers, NY
Saturday Night, Week Two

The doctors and attending nurses tried for fifteen solid minutes to stabilize Housely.

"Charging… Clear!" Mitchell pressed the pads into the man's chest. His body twitched as the electricity coursed through it, but the heart monitor continued to slow. "Come on!" Mitchell yelled in frustration as the machine flatlined. "Charging… Clear!"

Renshaw laid a hand on Mitchell's shoulder. "Let it go, Steven. He's gone."

Mitchell stepped back, slamming the pads into the cart and glancing at the clock. "Call it."

"Time of death, 12:14 AM."

Mitchell wiped his forehead on the back of his sleeve and left the room. The other doctors followed him out just in time to watch him slam his fists into the wall.

"It doesn't make any sense! He was fine two days ago. What the hell could have done that to him?"

"There was something seriously wrong with him before he even got here." Foster said. "Whatever this was, it caused his blood to thicken."

"Coagulation? Like a clot?" Hill asked.

"No, it was like someone had drained all of his blood and replaced it with Jello."

"What?" Mitchell put his hands on his hips. "That's not possible. He would have died long before it could get to that point."

"I know it's not possible, but it happened," Foster said, shaking his head. "Go see for yourself."

The team went back into the room and tapped a vein. Sure enough, the blood was just as Foster had described. Mitchell transferred it into a vial and the team rushed it to the lab. When Mitchell got a sample under a microscope, even more red flags went up.

"He's got a third of the white blood cells that he should, and more than three times the concentration of red blood cells." Mitchell sat back in the lab chair. "The hell does this mean?"

"Who knows," Renshaw yawned. "There's nothing else we can do for him now. I think we should sleep on it. I don't know about you all, but I've been running on overtime for the past five hours."

"I'll send the body to the morgue and order a final search for friends and family members," Hill stated.

"You guys go ahead," Mitchell rubbed his eyes. "I'm going to stay just a little longer."

When the team returned to the hospital late Sunday morning, Foster found Mitchell asleep on one of the couches in the break room.

"Mitch?" Foster shook his shoulder. "Did you stay here all night again?" Mitchell rolled over slowly. He was uncharacteristically pale, his five-o'clock shadow and dark circles giving his face a sunken, ghostly appearance. Foster took a step back in shock. "Geez, man, you look like death."

"I'm fine," Mitchell sat up, blinking wildly. "What do we have on Housely?"

"Nothing yet." Foster sat on the couch across from him. "Mitch, why don't you go home? Take a couple days, spend some time with Audrey and the boys. We'll call you if anything turns up."

It took some convincing, but Dr. Mitchell did finally leave. But by the time he got home, he was too tired to do anything but sleep. On Monday, since no family had been located for the deceased, the team – minus Mitchell – ordered an autopsy. Shortly after the coroner started the procedure, the team was called down to the morgue. The coroner met them at the elevator, explaining as they walked that the body wasn't acting like a normal cadaver. Instead of the blood settling, it had frozen. Somehow, the blood had hardened to glass. To add to the confusion of all present, the body seemed to be mummifying itself.

"Compare his skin to how it was when he first came down here," the coroner licked his dry lips as the team stood around the autopsy table, "The skin's developed wrinkles that weren't there before. And more than that," he adjusted his goggles and pointed into the abdominal cavity, "His internal organs are shriveled and drying. It's as if all the moisture has evaporated from the body."

On Monday afternoon at the Nanton house, Nurse Marianne was just waking up. On Saturday, she was so worn out from the reunion that she slept for 12 hours. Her husband tried to convince her to make a doctor's appointment to see if her thyroid was acting up, but she insisted that as a nurse, she would be the first to know if there was anything wrong. He muttered that she should listen to him, and when Marianne managed to drag herself out of bed, she wished she had. She stumbled into her bathroom, and was shocked when she caught sight of herself. She called for her husband and collapsed onto the floor, unconscious. Mr. Nanton rushed her to the emergency room when he couldn't wake her. They did everything they could, but much like Housely, it just wasn't enough. Four days after contracting the disease, Marianne Nanton was dead.

Mercy Heart and the surrounding hospitals soon found themselves with an influx of anemic and jaundiced patients. Neither ailment was contagious, so it was just brushed off by the medical staff as coincidence. It was only after every person who came through with those symptoms died that anyone realized there was a serious problem. It took three days after that for anyone to alert the authorities, who then alerted the CDC, and on up the ladder to the WHO.

A month after the unwitting Housely landed at the California airport, it was over.

***

Watertown, NY
Thursday, Week Three

The next day, Zach was back at Holt's. He clocked in as usual, dropped his backpack off at his locker, retrieved his hard hat, and was headed for the warehouse floor when the supervisor called him over.

"Carter! I told you to take a day off." The supervisor was a red-faced man who always seemed to be carrying at least three clipboards.

"I did take a day off," Zach replied.

"No, you called yesterday and I told you to take a mandatory bereavement day."

"Yeah, and I didn't come in yesterday, did I?"

"Grief-stricken employees make mistakes that we can't afford to happen," the supervisor said.

"Is that quote *directly* from *The Supervisor's Handbook?*" The supervisor's eyes narrowed and Zach sighed. "I really need the hours, Mr. Flannigan. Please."

The supervisor's face softened for a moment before toughening back up. "Fine. But if you screw up…" He let the threat trail off, presumably to let Zach imagine what might happen.

"Got it." Zach turned on his heal and headed for the floor. There was a new shipment to unload at the far end on the warehouse, and it was Zach's job to unpack the crates from the even bigger crates.

"Hey, Zach!" Zach looked to the left to see Garret Jensen jogging toward him. Garret was shorter than Zach – at 5'3 only coming to his chin – and armed with muscles far too bulky to belong to an 18-year-old. "Heard about Oleson."

"Yeah."

"Look, if you need a day off or something, I can cover your shifts…"

Zach shook his head. "Nah, man, it's fine. It'll get my mind off it. 'Sides, I've got boots to replace." He halfheartedly grinned, slapped Garret's arm, and continued toward the awaiting boxes.

"Yeah, okay," Garret nodded, following alongside.

Around 11 o'clock, the emergency alarm suddenly sounded. Zach immediately set down the crate he was carrying to stack on the back of a truck and headed briskly for the front door along with everyone else. Once everyone was gathered outside, the alarm shut off. The 30 men began to talk amongst themselves.

"What's going on?" Garret appeared at Zach's elbow. Flannigan stepped forward from the crowd, holding a clipboard and wearing a somber face. A hush fell over the crowd.

"I think we're about to find out," Zach replied.

"We're closing up early today," Flannigan began. "There's been an outbreak of some sort and the President has told everyone to sit tight until the CDC finds a solution to the problem. Mr. Holt called me ten minutes ago and told me to send you all home early."

"What about our pay?" One of the men asked. "We've got families to support, man."

Flannigan nodded with a yawn. "I know, and Mr. Holt is fully aware of that, so that will be dealt with next payday. However, until he tells me otherwise, we're shut down."

When Zach got home, the car was gone from the driveway. He went inside and dropped his backpack on the couch. "Mom?" He walked down the hall, but her room was empty. "Huh." He glanced at the fridge to see if she'd left a note, but there wasn't one. "Must've gone to the store," he said to himself, glancing at the pile of dishes in the sink. Retrieving his lunch from his backpack, he sat on the floral couch and flipped the TV to the 24-hour news station. An overly-tanned brunette was mid-sentence when Zach finally found the correct channel.

"...having to turn people away because there simply isn't enough room to keep up with the influx of patients. Coming up next, what exactly are the symptoms of this pandemic, and what can you do to avoid exposing yourself to it? Later on, we'll list the top ten germ-killing cleaning agents, and how to use them." Zach looked out the window beside the TV and ate his sandwich as a pair of poorly-animated CGI lions tried to convince him that their toilet paper was better than their competitors'. He glanced at the clock on the wall, unsure of what to do with the foreign amount of free time. His eyes wandered around the room absentmindedly, stopping on a basket of laundry at the end of the couch. He stuffed the remainder of the sandwich into his mouth, dusted his hands off on his pants, and reached for the basket.

By mid-afternoon, Zach had deep-cleaned the entire house. After folding the laundry and taking care of the dishes, he turned on the radio and got so lost in the music that he forgot that he hated vacuuming. It was only when he heard a loud knock at the door that he snapped out of it. Zach opened the door to Connie standing at the bottom of the stairs. Her face was red and her eyes were almost swelled shut. She held a pie in her hands.

"Hi, Zach," she said, sniffing slightly. "What are you doing home so early?"

"Work got canceled," he replied. "Pandemic scare."

"Oh," she said with a nod. "Is your mama home?"

"No ma'am, I'm not sure where she went," he replied. "I could call her if you want, though."

"No, no. That's okay. I just thought I'd stop by and bring her this." She lifted the pie slightly. "I've been baking a lot lately. It keeps...keeps my mind off..."

Zach shifted on his feet. "Hey...would you like to come inside? My mom should be back soon."

"I'd like that," she said, wiping a tear off her cheek.

Zach and Connie reminisced about Oleson for an hour, in which time all but one slice of apple pie went missing. Connie tearfully recalled when Oleson brought her pie plate back to her, and how he'd actually combed his hair for the occasion. Zach then brought up Oleson's experimental self-inflicted bowl cut – "the Bowleson" – sending them both into a fit of laughter.

"I'm going to miss him," Connie said softly, a small smile resting on her lips. "He was a good...a great man."

"He was that."

"I still don't know how...he was so..." she trailed off and looked up at Zach, whose face fell. The puffiness in her face had gone down considerably, and Zach suddenly noticed how yellow her eyes were.

"Well, I'd better get home now," she said, yawning. "Tell your mama I stopped by, and that I'm sorry I missed her."

"Will do."

After Connie left, Zach grabbed the home phone and called his mom's cell, leaving a message asking her to call him at Oleson's.

When Zach reached Oleson's trailer, he went straight to his chair. He looked at the Map and quickly found Canadian Dave's pushpin. He flipped the switches, and tuned to Dave's frequency.

"...not sure what to think, honestly. Facepage is down, Tweetser is down, hell, even my kid's Animal Playhouse site is down."

"Sounds like the Feds don't want us talking about it. Everything goes through the internet these days so why would the phones still work but not websites?"

"Always knew something like this would happen. Me and mine are holed up in our cabin, got plenty of supplies."

"My family is stuck in the quarantine zone and I can't get to them. What do I do now?"

Zach stared at the microphone. Licking his lips, he picked up the mic. "K2OLS listening."

"K2OLS, welcome to the freak-out zone. Call me Al, I hate my call sign."

"We're not freaking out, we're debating! I'm Sandra," came another voice.

"Wait... you're not Oleson. Who is this?"

"My name is Zach. Oleson...Oleson died two days ago."

"Ah, man... I'm so sorry to hear that."

"I think..." he paused. "I think he might have had the virus."

"Holy-"

"-my god."

"...no."

Zach shook slightly. "He was fine one day and the next he couldn't move. I found him...he didn't look the same. They said it was natural causes, but people who just die, they don't go all yellow and pale, right?"

Suddenly, a new voice sounded. *"VYIFRD speaking. Zach, right? I think we talked the other night. It's Dave."*

"Dave! It's good to hear you."

"I think you may be right...We haven't had any incidents here yet, maybe because we're so isolated...who knows? But my brother works in a morgue in Whitehorse and he said they've had fifty deaths, and they happened exactly like you described."

Zach swallowed hard. "Do they know what's causing it?"

"...no."

"Ok, thanks. I gotta go, now. K2OLS signing off."

Zach spent what felt like hours scanning the airwaves and listening to what other HAMs had to say. He used the Map, putting a red flag on every pushpin that reported at least fifty deaths. It was 2:00 AM by the time he ran out of flags. He stepped back from the board, now almost completely covered in red.

"Oh, God," he swallowed hard, mouth dry. "It's an epidemic..."

Chapter Nine

On the Road, TX
Thursday, Week Three

Of the original passengers, only nine re-boarded the bus. Most spread themselves out so that each person had a couple of rows between them, except for Gina and Louis, who took the back row again. By late-afternoon, the heat had put half of the passengers to sleep with the other half staring vacantly out the windows.

"What do you want to be?"

Gina snapped out of her daydreaming and looked to her right. Louis was looking at her intently, bottom lip sucked into his mouth, patiently waiting for a response.

"What?" She asked.

"When you get older, I mean. What do you want to be?" He blinked rapidly. "Everyone's got that one thing they wanna be, right?" Gina frowned slightly. "...or at least they did when they were younger?"

"I don't know," she said finally, picking at her fingernails. "I mean, when I was a kid..." she trailed off, suddenly self-conscious.

"Yeah?" Louis looked at her hopefully, giant eyes focused like search lights on her.

"When I was a kid...I wanted to be an animal doctor."

"Ooh!" He said giddily. "Dr. Gina, veterinarian extraordinaire."

"No...it's silly." She said flatly.

"No it's not! You'd be great at it." He smiled.

"I think I mostly just wanted to be an anim – a veterinarian because I've always loved animals." She absentmindedly reached down to pet Hank as she talked. "I always wanted to have a lot of them and love and take care of them so nothing bad would happen to them. Once I found this baby bunny-" she stopped cold as the memory of the rabbit she tried to rescue came back to her. She'd managed to hide it for three full days until Dirk found it under the porch, and then...she felt herself sink down into the seat and her body went numb as the memory sucked her in.

"Are you okay?" Louis asked. Gina's chest tightened and her head began to pound. She felt like she was on fire. Suddenly, she felt something cold and wet nudge her hand insistently. Hank whimpered, put his front paws in her lap and licked at her face, bringing her out.

"Do I need to call someone?"

Gina glanced at Louis. He frowned, wringing his hands.

"No," she said. "I just…what…what do you want to be?"

"I want to work with alternative energy sources. Are you *sure* you're okay?"

"I'm fine!" She snapped. Louis sat back a little. "I'm fine."

They sat in silence a moment before Louis spoke up quietly. "I'm sorry for pushing you, I didn't mean to go somewhere off-limits."

"It's okay," she said after a moment, "Thanks for apologizing. What do you mean 'alternative energy sources'?"

Louis brightened up. "Like hydroelectric and wind power and solar! I find it fascinating. I've even got my own solar charger, see?" He pointed to the other side of the aisle. Stuck to the window was a small black box with a cord running into his backpack on the seat. "It powers my devices. It's really handy!" Gina nodded. "So," Louis yawned and glanced ahead at the other passengers, lowering his voice. "Do you think anyone on the bus could have the virus?"

"I don't know. I guess we'll just have to wait and see."

Around midnight, Gina was still awake. The "what ifs" were back, and angrier than ever. She shifted to look out the window, careful to not disturb Hank's head in her lap. The dog had taken Louis's seat when he'd moved to the other side of the bus earlier to sleep. Images of the incinerated house flashed in and out of her mind. She imagined that by the time anyone noticed the smoke in the clouds and called on it, there would be very little left for the local police and firemen to salvage. Maybe there'd be only the collapsed shell of a house. If she was lucky, the sheriff would find the bottles and cigarettes and automatically rule it an accident. If she was even luckier, the police might be just lazy enough to forget she ever existed.

A sudden rumbling from the right side of the bus knocked Gina out of her thoughts. She glanced up and noticed the bus veering onto the highway's textured shoulder, heading straight for a metal guardrail. Alarmed, she looked to the driver's seat and saw him slumped against the side window.

Gina instinctively threw her seatbelt on and wrapped her arms around Hank's middle. Before she could yell to the driver or other passengers, the bus smashed through the guardrail, throwing her forward against the strap. She glanced to her right and saw Louis pinned by his seatbelt. His head was drooped against his chest, eyes closed. As the bus careened off the road, Gina ducked her head down over Hank, squeezed her eyes shut, and held onto him for dear life. *THUD*. The bus hit a ravine and rolled, flipping completely. Hank yelped as the whole world turned upside down. Gina tensed every muscle in her body to keep from being flung about. The dog cried out and struggled as Gina tightened her grip on him.

When the bus finally stopped moving, Gina opened her eyes. She was suspended upside down by her seatbelt, and her neck hurt. She immediately set the struggling Hank down on the new floor above her head, who ran down the aisle barking. He stopped to sniff and paw at one of the other passengers who hadn't had her seatbelt on and was now lying face-down on the floor. Gina ducked her head and tucked herself into a ball as best she could before unhooking her seatbelt. *Thump!* She landed square on her spine. Groaning, she rolled over. There she saw Louis, dangling limply by his seatbelt. Blood dripped from his open mouth and his arms hung down above his head, swaying slightly.

"Louis!" Gina went to him and grabbed his shoulders. She unhooked the seatbelt with some difficulty and tried to catch him as he hit the ground. When he was laid out, she dropped to her knees next to him. "Louis, can you hear me?" She gently slapped his face. "Come on…" She watched his chest, willing it to rise. It didn't. She sat back slowly and stared numbly at him. The face that was so full of happiness earlier that day was expressionless. His characteristically rosy cheeks were deathly pale as blood continued to leak from the corner of his mouth.

Suddenly, sirens echoed in the distance. Gina's heart pounded. *Police.* If the police found her as the only survivor, there would be questions. Gina clambered quickly to her feet and ran down the aisle, stopping only to grab her duffel off the floor where it had skidded to. She carefully stepped over the woman lying in the aisle, her boots crunching on the glass from the shattered front window. She reached up and pulled the lever to open the door. Hoisting

Hank over the shattered glass, she hopped out of the bus. Gina looked around wildly for an escape. A single car had pulled over on the highway, and the driver was on the phone but not watching the bus. The bus had stopped skidding a few yards from a sloped valley, and Gina could just make out a road at the bottom. She put Hank on the ground, grabbed his leash, and took off running down the hill.

Chapter Ten

Isherwood, PA

Millie awoke suddenly. She was lying in her own bed, with no recollection as to how she got there. She sat up slowly, joints popping. She rolled her neck and stretched everything that ached. She grabbed for the lamp on her nightstand, but just knocked it onto the floor. She picked up the watch on her nightstand and moved it closer to her face. 11:20.

"Dad?" She called, throat dry. Water, she needed water. When she slipped out of bed, her knees gave out immediately. *Thud.* "Ow…" She grabbed at the bed's baseboard and managed to pull herself to a wobbly stand. She carefully took a few weak steps toward the bathroom door in the corner. She held onto the sink for dear life and flipped on the tap, bypassing the plastic water cup and sticking her mouth directly under the stream. When she finally had her fill, she turned back to the door.

"Dad? Are you home?" *Maybe he's still at work,* she thought, moving through her room toward the hallway. The house was dark and quiet, despite it being in the middle of the day. She flipped the hall light switch, but the light didn't come on. She frowned at it and continued into the living room. "Hello?"

After checking the kitchen and home office, Millie circled through the rest of the enormous house on the hunt for Dad. She made her way back down the hall and knocked on the always-closed door to her father's room. "Dad, you in here?" She turned the knob and pushed the door open. Instantly, the smell of mothballs and Old Spice struck her nose. The room was dark, the only light coming from under the closed blinds on the far wall. Like in the hallway, the light switch didn't work. As her eyes adjusted, Millie saw him lying asleep in bed. *At eleven?* Millie thought to herself, *the man never sleeps past eight, especially not on a work day.*

"Dad?" She moved closer. "It's after eleven, sleepyhead. It's long past time to start the day." She opened the blinds slightly, just enough to let in enough light to see by. "Also, let's get some air freshener in here STAT." She chuckled lightly and turned toward the bed. Millie gasped and fell back into the window. Her father's face was sunken, his skin wrinkled and leathery. "…Dad?" She reached across the left side of the bed to put a hand on his face. It was cold. Her heart pounded audibly in her ears. She felt his stiff neck for a pulse. Nothing. "No…" She took a step back, shaking her head. "No, no no no. This isn't- this-" She began to shake uncontrollably. "Daddy, please wake up!" She pleaded, not daring to touch the still form again. "Da…Dad, *please!*" She screamed at him, knees buckling.

This wasn't, *couldn't* be real. Any moment now Millie would wake up from this nightmare and Dad would be there, singing along to the car radio or burning pancakes or telling her a story he made up on the spot. The room was spinning, spinning… she collapsed into a ball on the floor and retched, a guttural wail escaping her dry lips. She sobbed hysterically into the carpet for hours, until there was nothing left in her.

When she was finally able to lift herself off of the floor, Millie stepped numbly out into the hall. She glanced into her room, eyes glazed. There, tacked up on the corkboard behind her bed, was a sheet of notebook paper. She moved closer and saw the unmistakable physician scribbles. The lighting was too dim to make out the words, so she took it into the living room.

My dear Millie,

I'm so sorry. I fear you'll never have the opportunity to read this, but I need you to know that I love you more than anything. You're my whole world. I only wish I could have done something to save you.

I'm dying. Everyone is. They couldn't do anything to stop it because it's unstoppable. There hasn't been a single person admitted to the hospital that hasn't died or gone into a coma from this unknown virus.

I estimate that I have about twelve hours left before the catatonia sets in. Already my muscles are beginning to spasm and fail on me. I don't want to die in this house, but I also don't want to leave you alone. You've already lasted longer than any of the other patients, so I can't help but hold out hope that you might pull through. Though, at this point, I wonder if it'd be better if you just stayed asleep.

It's absolute chaos on the streets. As I predicted, the message from the President only made the people panic and try to run. There have been countless car wrecks, nearly all involving people falling asleep at the wheel. They just don't seem to get that there's no outrunning whatever this is.

Honey, if somehow you pull through this, please be careful. If you survive, others will too. And while some will be good people, many won't. You'll have to be very discerning, but I have faith that you'll make the right choices. Use your strengths to your advantage. Be careful, stay safe, and don't ever give up.

I'm so tired. Guess I'll curl up with a good book and wait.

I love you so much. Never ever forget that.

Dad

Millie slowly re-read the letter three times. *There hasn't been a single person admitted to the hospital that hasn't died...chaos on the streets...* Sitting motionless on the couch, she was suddenly aware of how deathly quiet the house was. "What do I do now?" She asked the room hoarsely, stuffy nose muffling the words. *If you survive others will, too...* Millie looked to the front door.

*

The streets of Downtown were jammed with cars and their deceased passengers. The tall buildings lining Main Street looked on wearily as Millie numbly passed them. Some of the store windows were broken, the insides ransacked. One of the buildings had a minivan jutting out of it. Millie looked into one of the car windows and saw the remains of an elderly woman still strapped into her seat glassily staring back at her. She turned away quickly. As she made her way down the empty sidewalks, the eerie quiet that blanketed the town made her feel incredibly lonely. A canister of wasp spray she snagged from her garage hung limply at her side as she stepped over an overturned newspaper stand. Dad kept a shotgun in his closet but Millie had been too afraid of it to try and carry it with her. Passing a shadowy alley, she wished she'd brought it anyway. *What if I run into some crazy person who tries to kill me? What if the bodies reanimate while I'm out wandering around?* "Stop thinking like that," she told herself, carefully crunching on the glass from the corner pharmacy's shattered front window. Suddenly, something clattered to the floor inside, setting her hair on end. She spun to face the window.

"Hello?" Millie asked, gripping the wasp spray tightly. Another bout of shuffling in the store sent her heart racing. "Is someone there?" Her voice was weak and scratchy, far from intimidating. *Zombies.* She fought the urge to run as the sound of crunching boots got louder. "I'm armed!" She cried, holding the can out in front of her.

"I'm not." A pair of hands eased out from the shadows, followed by half of a face. Millie tensed as a boy with messy light hair stepped into the light of the window, hands raised level with his head. He scanned the area and looked Millie over quickly.

"You're a live person," Millie relaxed slightly.

"Last time I checked," he said, green eyes settling on the wasp spray. "You gonna bug spray me to death?"

"It's wasp killer and has a spray range of ten yards. It can blind and poison a grown man. It's super deadly," Millie snipped. The boy raised his eyebrows. "…and it was the only long-range weapon I could find on short notice."

"Ah, I see." They stood in silence for a moment before he spoke again. "I'm not going to hurt you, just so you know."

Millie shifted her feet and searched his face for insincerity. "Are you a drug addict?"

"No? Not too fond of drugs, myself. Nyquil's about the biggest buzz I can tolerate," the boy shrugged.

"Then why are you raiding a pharmacy?"

"I was looking for a first-aid kit, but they're all out."

"Are you hurt?" Millie glanced him over. No visible wounds, though the sleeve of his black t-shirt was ripped at the shoulder seam.

"Nah. Just thought it might come in handy during the end of the world."

"It's not the end of the world... is it?"

"Dunno," he shrugged again. "Though, there's a distinct end-of-the-world vibe going on here." He dropped his hands. "I'm Zach Carter." He seemed harmless enough. Millie lowered her arms to her side and introduced herself. "So," Zach asked, "Where you headed?"

"I wasn't really headed anywhere," Millie replied, "I just wanted to see if there was anyone left."

"You're the first person I've run into in days."

"Days?" Millie's mouth fell open. How long had she been asleep?

Zach nodded. "I left Watertown like a week ago, and the only other people I saw after that were a kid ransacking a jewelry store who tried to shoot me and this really old lady who thought I was her son back from the war."

"How long has it been since the President made that speech about the virus?"

"Let's see." He looked skyward and silently counted on his fingers. "Two weeks yesterday."

"That's not possible," Millie shook her head, stunned. The human body can only live without water for an average of four days; three weeks without food. She should be dead by now.

"Are you okay? Do you need to sit down or something?"

"No- I mean, the President made that speech and I fell asleep, and when I woke up my dad was... a-and I found this note he left me, so I decided to try and come look for people, but... two weeks?"

Zach studied her curiously as she sputtered. "Woke up?"

"Yeah?"

"So, you *slept* through the apocalypse." Zach cocked an eyebrow. "I thought that was just a cliché used by lazy authors." Millie blinked, still processing the day's revelations. "Sorry, no time for bad jokes."

The long uncomfortable silence returned just in time to be interrupted by Millie's stomach growling loudly. For the first time all day, hunger pangs shot through her abdomen.

"Hungry?" He asked.

She grimaced as the growling continued. "Haven't really had a chance to eat yet."

"One sec." Zach disappeared into the shadows for a moment, returning with a black backpack. He moved toward the window, fishing through the bag. "Here," he held a large protein bar out to her. "It's not poisoned, I swear." He fished another bar out for himself.

"Thank you," Millie said, glancing over the bar for signs of tampering before unwrapping it. As she took a bite, she accidentally made eye contact with a corpse in a car. "...let's head back this way."

As they aimlessly made their way around and over the blocked roads, Zach filled Millie in on the events in the days following the President's speech. The day after, the Center for Disease Control issued a statement that the vaccine would be available to the general public in four to six days.

"Everybody was tired and angry and dying when day six rolled around and there was still no cure. So when the CDC said that it would be another four to five days, it was chaos," Zach explained. "Then we found out that

France had already released a vaccine, which pretty much sent everyone into orbit."

"Why didn't they just ship some of the French vaccine over here?"

"Turns out that it was just a strong antibiotic. The French government knew that there would be no way to find a cure in time to save everyone, so they were trying to calm everyone down so they wouldn't riot. Last I heard, they were dying off as quickly over there as over here."

"How did they die?" Millie stopped walking for a second.

Zach turned back to her. "They just sorta went to sleep. They weren't in pain or anything, from what I could tell." Millie nodded slowly, eyes on the ground. "Your dad, huh?"

Millie nodded again, fighting the rising lump in her throat. "He's... his body is still at the house. I just couldn't do it yet."

"Yeah..." Zach's expression softened and he rubbed the back of his neck. "Well...if you want, I could help. I've dug my fair share of graves lately."

Millie smiled. "Thank you."

"Yeah. No problem."

Chapter Eleven

Louisiana

Hank gnawed on one of the clothing store mannequin's discarded feet, the rubber making a strange squeaking sound. His tail wagged absentmindedly as Gina perused the shoe aisles. She spotted a pair of brown hiking boots in her size, but hesitated. Was it really stealing if the owner was more than likely dead? She looked down at her tennis shoes; the left's laces were frayed to almost nothing, and the right's sole was reattached with black thread in three places. She grabbed the boots and went to sit in a chair at the end of the aisle, kicking off her shoes as she walked.

The boots were well-made, much sturdier than any shoes she'd had before yet incredibly lightweight and breathable. They fit her almost perfectly, with only a small gap at the end that allowed her toes some movement as she walked carefully around the room in them. Yes, these would do nicely. She clicked her heels together and picked up her duffel, heading toward the clothing section.

The rows and rows of round hanging racks slightly intimidated her at first, but as she browsed, the possibilities began to form in her head. These tan shorts would look good with that green shirt or the purple tee. That long-sleeved, thin white shirt could be worn over a white tank top to keep the sun off, yet not overheat her, and any number of those hats could be great for shielding her from the sun. There were stands of sunglasses next to a round display of jewelry that could be spun to see all sides; as she passed it something caught her eye. She walked closer, reaching out to touch the necklace gingerly. It was simple – a small, silver, diamond-shaped locket with a latch enclosure – but something about it intrigued her, so she slipped it into her pocket.

Gina tried on some tops, slipping them over her t-shirt, and found some that she liked. She folded them carefully and put them in a pile. She held up some shorts and pants, guessing about what her size was, and folded them as well. After gathering all the various items she needed, she realized that it wasn't all going to fit in her small duffel. On the opposite side of the boutique was a wall covered in backpacks and luggage bags. There was a purple rolling backpack hanging on a hook by itself, and Gina looked it over. It was plenty big and the straps looked comfortable enough, so she took it down and loaded it with her new wardrobe.

Sure enough, the wheels worked just fine as she pulled the backpack behind her down the road. Hank trotted happily beside her, mirroring Gina's distinctly springier step. The asphalt bridge they walked across was free of cars, and Gina stopped a moment to look out over the murky lake. Her new sunglasses kept the glare from the water out of her eyes as she stared at a buoy that bobbed in the distance. She leaned against the guardrail, the heat coming off of it warm against her stomach. She glanced over at Hank, who made his way through the grass down to the lake's edge to drink. Judging by the sun, she figured they had about thirty minutes until it was completely dark; that was plenty of time to get back to the deserted bed-and-breakfast where they had been staying. A sudden breeze coming off of the water played with her hair, and she brushed her bangs out of her eyes yet again.

I could cut them, she thought, watching Hank lap at the water. *If I knew how.* Her eyes drifted from where Hank stood lapping at the water, and she noticed a large shape bobbing in the current nearby. The end of it twitched, and her blood ran cold. *Alligator.*

"Hank!" She screamed, voice cracking from disuse as she bolted toward the embankment. The dog looked up at her, ears perked, as the massive alligator floated closer. Its beady eyes were hidden below the surface of the water as Hank cocked his head to one side. "Here, boy! Here, here!" Gina grabbed the butcher knife out of her back pocket, accidentally cutting the seam that held the pocket to her jeans. The dog turned and trotted toward her just as the menacing shape reached the edge of the water. Gina jumped in front of Hank, knife held out. The alligator caught on something underwater, and floated sideways. Gina' shoulders sagged, and she sighed. It wasn't an alligator at all, it was just a very large gator-shaped log. Gina slowly, shakily put her knife back into her pocket.

***

Nowhere

The college campus was deserted. After the President's announcement, the dean suspended all classes and sent the students home, leaving only the staff that lived on or near the campus and their families.

Now, only one remained.

In the administration building's rock garden, the old man laid the last stone on top of the small pyramid. It had taken him two full days to dig the grave, and another to bring himself to bury the small bundle resting on his kitchen table. He reached into his coat and retrieved the small wooden doll that he'd carved for her, running a thumb over its features. The miniature face smiled up at him, tiny wooden hands grasping a lily. He laid the doll gently at the base of the pyramid, blinked tears away, and whispered an amen. Grimacing, he picked up his cane. The hip surgery had been scheduled for last Monday, but by then the surgeon was dead. The old man limped toward the main building.

Inside the small room that functioned as the college radio station, the lights flickered, then stabilized. The generator was working fine, the old man thought. Tomorrow he'd have to go around and turn off all the unnecessary electrical devices, but for now there were other things to attend to. He keyed the microphone and spoke slowly.

"This is Radio Nowhere, in Nowhere, Oklahoma, calling to anyone who has survived this catastrophe. I'll be transmitting every night from 8 pm Central time to 10 pm Central time. This has been a tough time for all of us, but remember…you're not alone." He tightened his fists and said louder and more forcefully, "You are NOT ALONE."

Chapter Twelve

Isherwood, PA

The sun hung low in the sky by the time Millie and Zach finished the burial. The uncompleted pool in the back yard saved them from having to dig a plot, but moving the vast amount of dirt took a lot more time and effort than they'd expected.

Afterwards, Zach went inside to give Millie some time alone at the grave. He set up the windup lamp he'd found in Oleson's trailer on the coffee table in the living room. As he sat on the couch and turned the lamp's crank, his mind began to wander.

*

"Yeah I know it's not much to go off of, but she didn't exactly have time to grab her purse and ID when she passed out." Zach paced in his kitchen, drumming his fingers against the countertop. *"Her coworker just told me that an ambulance picked her up and took her to a hospital after he found her, but for some idiotic reason he didn't think to ask which hospital."*

"Ok, sir," the nurse on the line said with a yawn, *"What did you say she looks like?"*

"She's got longish brown hair and has a tattoo of a bird on her wrist."

"Age?"

"...thirty-six, I think?"

"Just a moment...I'm sorry, sir, but no one recently admitted matches that description."

"Ok. Thanks." Zach hung up the phone and took a deep breath before dialing the next hospital in the phonebook.

"Watertown General, how may I direct your call?"

"Yeah, my name is Zach Carter, I'm looking for my mom, Karen…"

*

"I don't know where my Nana is." Millie appeared in the doorway, startling Zach from his thoughts. The setting sun beamed through the large windows beside her as she crossed the room. "My great-aunt. I don't even know if she's alive." She took the wasp spray out of her back pocket and sunk into a chair by the couch. "But at this point, I'm not sure I want to know…"

"There's a research center in Tennessee," Zach said after a moment.

"What?"

"This lady I talked to on the radio before all communication broke down said that she'd heard rumors that the research center had found a vaccine," he continued, turning on the windup light, "That's where I'm ultimately headed. I doubt they had time to make a vaccine, but I figure the possibility of one would lure people toward the center. I'm thinking that's where any survivors will be. If you want, you could come, too."

Millie nodded slowly, contemplating. She loved her house and everything it stood for, but without her family it was just an empty shell. "Ok, I'll go."

"Cool. I figure we can leave in the morning." The room went silent, and he cleared his throat. "Could I-?"

"You can stay in the guest room. It's through there," she pointed to a door on the other side of the living room.

"Ok," Zach said with a smile, "Thanks."

"Let's go through the house for supplies tomorrow before we leave- it's getting too dark to really dig, now."

"Agreed."

"I know we have a lot of canned food; Nana always bought wholesale." Millie stood up, the wasp spray dangling by her side. "How do you feel about cold soup for supper?"

As the pair ate on opposite sides of the kitchen island, an uncomfortable silence hung in the room. Millie glanced around the kitchen, illuminated by the windup light's blinding bulb.

"So," she began slowly, shifting in her chair, "How have you been getting on?"

"Hmm?" Zach looked up from his bowl, cheeks chipmunked with soup.

"I mean, have you been just walking toward Tennessee?" Millie poked at the remaining alphabet noodles in her bowl.

Zach shook his head and swallowed. "Well, the big roads were too crammed with cars to drive and I wasn't too thrilled at the idea of what might happen if I crashed a motorcycle. So, I borrowed a bike originally, but the front tire busted a couple days ago and I haven't found a good replacement, yet." He raised the bowl to his lips and upended it, gulping the last of the soup down quickly.

"I have a bike in the garage, and I know the family...the *house* next door has a couple of them. Maybe one of them would work for you." Millie slid out of her chair and held out a hand for Zach's empty bowl.

He relinquished the bowl and sat fidgeting as she took it to the sink. "Thanks, I'll check it out tomorrow."

Millie rinsed the bowls and spoons, set them to the side, and turned around to face Zach across the island.

Millie opened a drawer behind her and rummaged around in it. She shut the drawer and turned back, flashlight in hand.

The silence returned.

"Well," Millie said, picking the wasp spray off the island, "It's late, so I'm going to turn in. The guest room is already made up, so you should be set." She clicked on the flashlight. "I'll see you in the morning."

"Goodnight," Zach said as she disappeared through the doorway.

Thump! "Gah!"

"Are you okay?" Zach jumped to his feet.

"Yeah," came the faltering reply, "Goodnight."

***

Louisiana

Gina carefully slid the pan out of the oven, wrinkling her nose at the foul smoke. Baking attempt number 4: failure. She dropped the pan on the stovetop and turned the oven off, discarding the oven mitts on the counter. She'd been squatting at the old-timey bed-and-breakfast since the owner died a couple of days after she got there. The owner's room was in the finished basement, so after the woman didn't come back upstairs a day after going to take a "quick nap," Gina wedged a chair under the door handle.

The gas stove was the only appliance that still worked, and Gina had been trying to make use of it. She grabbed a knife and sawed into the blackened casserole, smiling triumphantly at the un-scorched middle. She shaved the top off of the casserole and set it burnt-side-down on the counter, doubtful if even Hank would eat it. She spooned most of the middle in a bowl, put the top back into the pan, grabbed a fork, and took both containers into the dining room. Hank was lounging in the sun's last rays streaming in through one of the shuttered windows. As soon as he smelled the food he was on his feet, bounding toward Gina.

"Back off, Hank," Gina said, setting the bowl on one of the white-cloth-covered tables. She set the pan on the floor and slid into the chair. Hank sniffed the pan's contents once before tearing into it. "Don't act like I never feed you," she said, patting his side. She glanced out the window at the setting sun and picked up her fork.

After dinner, Gina let Hank outside one last time before locking the front door for the night. She had gotten into the habit of keeping the doors and windows locked after a close call with a half-naked delirious man while on a trip to the store. She'd come out empty-handed on her search for dog food when he stumbled by, babbling wildly to himself. He ran off, making a beeline for the city limits. Though he didn't look like he was planning to stop anytime soon, Gina preferred to be safe rather than sorry.

When the house was secured, Gina picked one of the flashlights off of the table at the bottom of the stairs and went up with Hank. The floorboards creaked as they made their way to the last door on the left, the only open one in the hall. Out of habit, she locked the door as soon as she shut it before changing into her sleep shirt and climbing into bed. Hank hopped up in the bed and curled up next to her, sighing contently.

Sometime during the night, Gina awoke to thunder. She got up to peek out the window, and sure enough, it was pouring rain. Lightning streaked across the sky, burning brilliant images into Gina's mind. "Some storm," she said absentmindedly.

Thud. She turned her head toward the door. Something hit against the outside of the house. *Thud.* She glanced at Hank, still snoring. *Thud.* No, she was definitely not imagining it. A chill ran up her spine. *Thud.* Hank lifted his head, ears twitching forward. He whined as the *thud* sounded again. "It's just a shutter or a branch or something," she told him, sitting back down on the bed and reaching over to scratch his ear. "Nothing to worry about." *THUD.* The house shuddered and Hank jumped to his feet and bounded to the door. *Thump, thump, thump.* Someone was inside. Gina's heart pounded as she felt around under her pillow. Where was it? She leapt off the bed and crouched next to her bag. She dumped the contents and fished around for the knife. *Thump, thump, thump.* The footsteps were getting louder. She threw the contents of her bag around, desperately looking for the blade. *Thump, thump, thump. Thump, thump, thump.* The steps were speeding up on the stairs. Gina shook a folded shirt desperately, flinging the knife across the room. It glinted in the lightning as it skittered on the floor, sliding deftly under the armoire in the corner of the room. Hank barked at the door as the footsteps echoed in the hallway. *Thump, thump, thump.*

Gina ran across the room, fell to the floor, and jammed her arm under the armoire. She felt blindly around for the knife, accidentally knocking it out of her reach. *Thump, thump, thump. Thump.* She looked over her shoulder at the gap at the bottom of the door. Lightning flashed for a moment, revealing the shadows of a pair of large shoes on the other side. Gina stretched for the knife, her eyes never leaving the door. The knob jiggled. *THUD.* The entire room shook at the force of the hit. *THUD.* The door groaned and creaked as if in pain. Gina reached desperately for the knife, shoving her arm as far as it would go under the wood armoire. Suddenly, she felt the smooth metal tip of the knife. She grasped it right as the door gave in. She wheeled around on the floor with the knife hidden behind her back, looking up at the towering intruder. Hank alternated between snarling and whimpering and backed into the corner. Lightning lit up the room. The intruder was dripping wet and reeked of tar; steam rose from his shoulders. The face was charred and partially melted, yet unmistakable. Dirk. She screamed.

Hank flew at the intruder just to be caught by the throat and thrown forcefully into the corner. The dog screeched once and didn't move again. Gina froze when Dirk turned toward her.

"So," he hissed, taking a clumsy step forward, "Looks like my dear stepdaughter has been an even worse girl than we thought." His bones cracked and groaned under the weight of his melted flesh. "Looks like we'll have to teach her a lesson." Gina lay with her back to the armoire, petrified. "Did you really think that fire would get rid of me? That by running away you'll be 'free' from me?" He stumbled closer, throwing his seared head back to laugh. "That's the secret, *dear*: I'll never be gone. You can never get away. I'll always be here, waiting, watching. I *own* you." He snarled and reached down for her. As soon as he got within reach, she slid the knife from behind her back and plunged it into his decomposing chest. He looked down at the knife and grinned wickedly through rotted teeth.

"You shouldn't have done that." The exposed bones of his fingers closed around her neck and ripped her off of the floor, slamming her head into the wall. She clutched at his wrist and kicked her feet as he squeezed tighter and tighter. He pulled the knife out of his chest with his free hand and gave another vicious smile.

Gina awoke with a scream. She bolted upright in bed and looked wildly around the room, startling Hank. Empty. There was no storm, only silence punctuated by wind, whipping outside the window. The dog sat up as well and Gina clutched him to her, heart pounding. *You can never get away...*

Chapter Thirteen

Isherwood, PA

"Do you have any allergies?" Millie asked her neighbors' broken garage window.

"Huh?" Zach called from somewhere inside. The sound of something metal sliding and bouncing off the concrete floor echoed from inside, and Zach swore.

"You okay?" Millie asked.

"Yeah, peachy."

"I mean, I just think it would be a good idea if we're going to travel together to know each other's limitations and such. It wouldn't do much good if I accidentally killed you with peanuts or something."

"Only way you could do that is if you fired them at me out of a cannon." Something in the garage clicked, and a bike wheel appeared in the window. Millie reached up and grabbed the wheel, guiding it carefully out so as to not catch it on any stray glass shards. There weren't any poking through the thick quilt that Zach draped over the sill after busting out the pane and clearing the debris, but Millie moved carefully nonetheless. She turned the wheel sideways to grab the seat and pulled it through the window. Zach appeared as the bike hit the ground, stepping up on something and adjusting the quilt on the sill. "What kind of people don't have a regular door leading out of their garage?" He muttered, swinging his leg carefully through the window. "And who chains their bike to the wall in an enclosed brick room?" He hopped down from the window, bypassing the crate he'd used to climb in the garage in the first place. "Someone was way too paranoid about their stuff getting stolen." He grabbed his backpack off the ground, took the black mountain bike from Millie, and began to wheel it around to the front of the garage toward the street. "I'm allergic to pollen. Or ragweed, or something. But no food allergies."

Millie picked up her purple backpack up off the ground, slipped it onto her shoulders, and followed. "Good, that makes it easier." When they reached her bike standing in the middle of the street, the pair mounted their bikes and kicked off down the street.

"How about you?" Zach asked, adjusting the speed setting of his bike.

"Strawberries make me break out in hives," she said, nodding down the road. "Highway is that way."

"That sucks, strawberries are awesome."

"They really are. It used to drive my Nana insane whenever I would get into the strawberry jam, because I'd always puff up just enough to swell my eyes shut, but it was worth it."

Zach chuckled. "Sounds like the time my neighbor Connie got stung by a bee. I thought they'd never get her head back to normal size."

They rode in silence for a while longer before Millie spoke up again. "So," she began slowly, shifting on her seat, "What's your story?"

"Huh?"

"Or like, are there any interesting or pertinent facts about you I should know?"

"Well..." Zach glanced at her, testing the waters. "Everything, obviously. I'm Captain Interesting. Women come from miles around to hear my tales of interest. I'm like the James Bond of interesting and pertinent stuff."

"Your sarcasm is enthralling."

"Who said I was being sarcastic?" Zach glanced at her again. "You first."

"Ok." Millie cleared her throat. "I'm half Filipino and I play the violin."

"Part Norwegian and I play the rock tambourine."

"Wait, really?"

"Nah, no ancestor I know of ever set foot in Norway. My people thrive where there's plenty of sunlight. Or, at least, we did until we all died out."

Millie's face fell slightly. "…how are you so…nonchalant about all this?"

Zach shrugged, turning onto an empty road that led up a large hill. "I don't know. I guess I got all my shock and horror out early. Plus, I saw it while it was happening, and figured how it was all going to go pretty early on."

Millie nodded, focusing on pedaling.

"My favorite color is blue," Zach offered after a moment.

"Mine's orange."

"I hate snakes."

"Me too." Millie switched gears on her bike to make it easier to go up the hill. "What do we do if we come across one?"

"Run away, I'd assume."

As they crested the hill, Millie stopped, looking out over the landscape. Cars lined the highway, crashed into one another and the ditch indiscriminately; thick smoke rose from somewhere in the distance, blurring the scene to the south. Millie realized she'd been holding her breath, and exhaled.

"Never ceases to amaze me," Zach said quietly, putting a foot on the ground.

"Yeah," Millie replied, "I can see why."

"…well, guess we'd better get to it," Zach said, easing his bike forward down the gradually sloped hill, heading for the highway's congested on-ramp.

*

"Sir?" Zach awoke to one of the nurses gently shaking his arm. At some point in the night he'd slumped over in the chair beside his mom's hospital

bed and must've dozed off. He glanced up at the nurse who gave him a look of pity. "I'm sorry, sir, but there aren't any available cots or I'd bring you one."

"It's okay." Zach rolled his neck slowly, grimacing. "Any news?"

The nurse gave a small smile, moving to check his mom's monitor. "The doctor will let you know as soon as he knows anything." She made a couple of notes on the chart and turned back to Zach, brushing a black strand of hair out of her face. "Would you like something to drink? Or a blanket maybe?"

Zach looked up at her again, meeting her yellowed eyes with dread. "Nah, I'm good for now."

"Ok. Just press the call button if you need anything."

As the nurse disappeared through the door, Zach turned back to his mother. Her normally medium skin was pale and clammy, and she hadn't woken since Zach had found the right hospital the previous day. His stomach growled angrily, sending hunger pangs shooting through his abdomen. He stood up and fished his wallet out of his pocket.

"I'll be right back, mom."

*

"Got any hobbies?"

Zach snapped back to the present. "Oh, yeah. A few."

"Like what?"

"I used to fish sometimes. And swim. I'm from Watertown, so I guess it makes sense."

"I used to spend almost every single day in the summertime at the pool when I was younger," Millie said. "I'm a little out of practice, but I always used to love it. Never been fishing, though."

"Fishing is fun enough," Zach replied. He sped up to get in front of Millie as they approached a narrow gap between some cars. "You have to be really, really quiet, though."

"Ah. I wouldn't have been very good at it." Millie mused.

Zach chuckled again. "How about you?"

"I read some, and watch old movies with my dad…" Millie trailed off. "That was kind of our ritual, just the two of us. Sometimes Nana would jump in, but more often than not it was just me and dad, making fun of old movies and eating pizza."

"That sounds like a lot of fun." Zach said sincerely, pedaling a little harder to get up another hill.

"It really was," Millie replied.

After almost a solid hour of biking, they came across a detour in the road. Police cars blocked all the lanes; some were crashed into by other vehicles. Further up ahead, two eighteen wheelers lay on their sides, the cabs burned out almost entirely and the cargo spilled across the highway.

"I'd sure hate to be the guy who'd've had to clean that up." Zach dismounted his bike, and began to walk it around to the blockades. Millie followed suit, avoiding eye contact with the corpses in the vehicles lining the road. Even with most of the vehicle doors closed tightly, the musty smell of death permeated the landscape. Zach suddenly paused, and put his bike kick stand up. Millie watched as he crossed to the corpse of a gray-haired police officer, and knelt down beside it.

"What are you doing?" She asked.

"Looting." Zach removed the belt from the corpse's waist with some difficulty and gingerly removed the revolver. He fiddled with it for a moment before hitting the latch that flipped the cylinder open. A bullet fell out, making a "plink" sound as it hit the asphalt. Zach grabbed it and put it back into the gun. "Five bullets. That'll do, I guess." He crossed the road to remove the belt of another policeman. He pulled the gun – a heavy semiautomatic pistol – out of the holster and checked the magazine. "Here," he held the belt out to Millie. "There's only a couple of bullets in this one but I don't know what we're going to come across, and you need to be able to defend yourself."

Millie eyed the gun with distrust. "That's okay," she said shaking her head. "I've got my bug spray, I think I'm good."

"Bug spray might work, but a gun is infinitely better." Zach raised an eyebrow and continued to hold the belt out to her.

The girl shook her head again. "Really, I'm okay. I'm… not comfortable with guns."

"Suit yourself." Zach tossed the second gun and belt into the tall grass on the side of the road with a loud *thud*. He knelt and opened his backpack on the ground; he pulled a funny-looking radio out of the bag and put the first belt in.

"What's that?"

"Hmm? Oh, uh," Zach picked up the radio and stood up, showing it to Millie. "It's a transmitter radio. It's broken, but I'm going to try and fix it." He set it back in his bag and swung the pack onto his shoulders.

"Do you know a lot about technology?" Millie asked as they re-mounted their bikes.

"Nah, not really. Just radios. I listened for broadcast signals for the first two weeks, but heard nothing, so I gave up." Zach stood on his pedals to get some momentum going up a small incline. "I think I'll try again sometime, though."

*

The all-but-empty vending machines spit out a coconut protein bar. Zach wrinkled his nose and unwrapped it. He gagged slightly at the taste, but choked it down anyway on the way back to his mom's room. As he rounded the doorway, his stomach dropped. The monitors his mom was hooked up to were beeping wildly and doctor stood next to her bed; nurses moved quickly and passed each other and the doctor instruments.

"Mom!" Zach called, the protein bar falling from his hand.

"Sir please stand back," a nurse said, turning and trying to block Zach's view.

"What's going on, what are you doing?" Zach cried, pushing past the smaller woman. A male nurse that stood a good foot taller than Zach turned from the bed and tried to usher him outside. "No," Zach said, trying to get back into the room. "Tell me what's going on! Mom!"

"Sir, you need to calm down," the nurse said gruffly.

"No! Let me in there NOW!" An orderly appeared from somewhere behind him and grabbed Zach's arm. "Let go of me!" Zach spun on the orderly, shoving him back.

"Sir if you don't cooperate we'll be forced to call security," the nurse said, blocking the doorway. Zach strained to see around the nurse's shoulder. Suddenly, the beeping from inside the room stopped, and a singular long beep replaced it.

"Mom!" Zach yelled, barreling past the nurse and knocking his shoulder against the door frame. The doctor and nurses stepped back as he approached the bed. "No…" he whispered, not daring to touch her still form. She was gone.

"I'm so sorry, son," the doctor said quietly after a moment. Zach staggered back, bumping into the male nurse he'd just pushed past. He turned around and left the room, making a beeline for the hospital's exit.

*

Zach glanced over his shoulder out of habit as he and Millie combed the aisles of the ransacked grocery store. The light streaming through the windows up front barely reached the back of the building where Zach searched through a collapsed display, so he held a flashlight tightly in his teeth as he rummaged. The smell of the rotting dairy section at his back was nauseating, but he breathed through his teeth and kept digging.

Finding nothing of use, he took the flashlight out of his mouth and stepped back, accidentally kicking a tin of cat food loudly across the floor.

"Zach?" Millie called from across the store.

"Just me," he replied.

"Okay. Just checking."

Zach went back to scanning the all-but-bare aisles. The girl seemed sane enough, albeit a bit paranoid. But then again, who wouldn't be in her shoes? He reached the end of the last aisle and turned the corner. He saw a pair of doors leading to the back room and wheeled his mostly-empty buggy over to it. He parked the buggy and stepped in to see if there was anything worth keeping stashed away. The batteries in the flashlight he carried were starting to give out, so he hit it a few times to stop it from flickering so much. The back room was dark, the only light coming in from a row of small windows at the top of the tall, far wall. Zach waded through a fallen stack of empty crates and boxes until he found a half-empty box of cans. Most had messed-up labels and some only had label remnants, but none of the expiration dates printed on the cans were past. He put the flashlight between his teeth again, picked up the box, and kicked his way through the debris. Suddenly, he tripped. His teeth clenched painfully as he caught himself with the box, one of the handles breaking as he hit the ground. The flashlight flickered as he turned back to see what he'd tripped over. Staring back at him was the shriveled, bug-eaten face of a bagboy. The corpse's mouth was open, shrieking silently at Zach. The flashlight fell into the box and shut off. Horrified, he got to his feet and fled with the box back to the main room.

"What'd you find?" Millie sat on the motionless conveyor belt of checkout stand 9, munching on a granola bar. Zach set the box on the counter next to her.

"Everything that nobody else wanted," he held a can of spinach aloft, "And some mystery munchies." Millie picked up one of the unlabeled cans and shook it. "Best guess?"

"Soup," she stated. "Or beans of some sort."

"Good enough for me." Zach opened his backpack and shoved the cans in.

The pair squinted into the lowering sun as they exited the store.

"We need to find somewhere to sleep," Millie said, grabbing her bike from the wall she'd leaned it on. She swung a leg over it and sat, pushing off of the ground as Zach climbed onto his bike.

"There's gotta be a neighborhood down one of these roads," Zach replied, standing up slightly on the pedals to get the bike moving faster. "We could find a house and break a window, we're pretty good at that."

"Eh…" Millie wrinkled her nose at the thought of sleeping in a dead person's bed. She glanced to her right across the parking lot and stopped. "What about that mattress store over there?"

Zach put a foot on the ground and followed her gaze. Sure enough, there was a giant sign outside of one of the doors in the strip mall that proclaimed "Select mattresses half off this Labor Day!"

"They're a bit off season, but I can't argue with a conveniently-placed sale." He shrugged.

Millie rolled her eyes and pushed off from the ground again. "C'mon, let's go see what we can find."

Chapter Fourteen

Louisiana

The only things left in Gina's duffel were a jar of peanut butter, ten protein bars, powdered Gatorade, a map, and the two envelopes. Hank walked just ahead of her as they meandered down the road, stepping over fallen branches as a car alarm sounded weakly in the distance. The map said to stay on this road for another ten miles until she hit the interstate, where she would hang a right. From there, it was almost a straight shot to Greenville.

She couldn't have stayed in the B&B after the nightmare even if she'd wanted to; the windstorm sent half a tree through the roof the previous night, taking out a wall and destroying the structural integrity of the old house. Besides, she reasoned, what could it hurt to find out if any of her relatives were alive?

The Louisiana sun beat down harshly, as if its sole purpose was to burn any redheads who happened to be passing through. Gina shifted the LSU umbrella she'd lifted from the B&B and wiped her forehead on her arm; the tradeoff of wearing a short-sleeved shirt instead of a longer one that would keep her skin from blistering was that she had to find a more creative way to outsmart the sun. She smiled to herself, remembering the old movies she used to watch on late-night TV. She was no Audrey Hepburn, and the purple-and-gold umbrella with snarling tigers on it was no white parasol, but she held her head a little higher as she walked just the same.

Suddenly, Hank stopped moving, giving Gina pause. She followed the dog's eyeline and looked down the road to try and figure out what had caught his attention. There, fifty or so yards away, was a figure bending down next to a red pickup truck on the side of the road. Gina's pulse quickened and she stepped slowly off the road, dropping the umbrella and duffel and crouching behind an abandoned car. The figure had its back to her, and had a messenger bag slung across its back. Gina looked to Hank, who wasn't where she left him; the mutt bounded quickly toward the unsuspecting person, giving Gina no time to call him back. The person – a boy – suddenly turned around and shrieked, jumping up.

"Hank!" Gina called, running toward the truck as the boy scrambled into the bed of the pickup truck to get away from him, losing a shoe and falling into the back in the process. Hank leapt against the side of the truck, barking. Gina could tell by the pitch of his bark that Hank just wanted to play, but obviously the boy couldn't. "Hank, c'mere, boy!" Gina called again as she approached the dog. He turned and loped back to her, tongue out and tail wagging furiously.

The boy – looking to be a little younger than Gina – slowly raised his head up, eyes wide. Gina grabbed Hank's collar and held him at her side awkwardly.

"…sorry," she offered, adjusting her grip on the collar.

"Does he bite?" The boy asked, sitting up fully and scooting to where his back rested against the truck's cab. His gaze fixed warily on Hank as he reached behind him to pull his bag into his lap.

Gina hesitated, choosing her words carefully. "Only if I tell him to."

The boy's lifted his brown eyes to hers. "Please don't tell him to bite me."

"Okay." Gina shifted on her feet, wiping her forehead again. She didn't realize how useful the umbrella really was until it was gone.

The boy's watch started beeping, and he switched it off. "Just a minute." Looking back at Hank, the boy started to open his bag, and Gina tensed. Hank closed his mouth and looked up at her as the boy pulled a smaller bag out of the bigger bag. He pulled a small pen-like device out of the bag along with something that resembled a small calculator, and plugged a tiny plastic strip into the calculator. Gina suddenly noticed that his right pinky was gone entirely, and the ring and middle finger on that hand were only stubs. She watched, fascinated, as he pressed the pen to his left ring finger and there was a small pop; he put the pen in his lap and squeezed the finger until a drop of blood appeared. He wiped the blood onto the plastic strip and pressed a button on the calculator-thing, and after a moment it beeped loudly. He reached into the bag again, pulling out a package of slightly-melted gummy bears. He opened them and popped one into his mouth, holding the package out toward Gina. "Want one?" She shook her head. He pulled out a couple more and ate them slowly one after another, eyes fixed once more on Hank. "Type one diabetes, diagnosed when I was eleven because God hates me."

"Is that what happened to your fingers?" Gina heard herself say. Mrs. Winston, a lady back in Sparta that she had cleaned the house of a few times, lost her entire hand to diabetes.

"Nah," he replied, eyes not leaving Hank as he put everything neatly back into his bag, "That was my uncle's dog."

Gina glanced first at Hank then to the boy's shoe on the ground. A series of straps stuck out of the tennis shoe, and she squinted at it, confused.

The boy leaned over the side of the truck and followed her gaze. "Ah. Yeah, *that* was diabetes." He lifted his leg, showing off a socked nub that ended right above where his toes should have been. "If I get sick, I don't always heal as well as I should. I got a bad infection and the piggies had to go. Sometimes my prosthetics don't fit right." Gina looked back at the shoe, then to the gas can and hose beside it. "I'm siphoning gasoline for my generator back home," the boy said, as if reading Gina's mind.

Gina was suddenly pulled toward the ground as Hank decided to lie down. She let go of his collar and stood up, registering the sudden panic on the boy's face. "It's okay, Hank's not mean." Regardless, the boy's brown eyes were wide with fear. Gina crouched back down and grabbed ahold of Hank's collar, attempting to coax the dog into a sitting position so she could maintain her grip on him. He didn't budge, so she took off her belt and looped it around his collar as a makeshift leash.

The boy sat up straighter, adjusting his bag on his shoulder. "Can you hand me my shoe?"

When the boy had strapped his shoe back on, he stood up in the bed of the truck. "I'm Eric. Eric Perez."

"Gina."

"You're sure he doesn't bite?" Eric ran his fingers over the brown canvas bag at his side absentmindedly.

"Yeah."

Eric hopped down from the bed of the truck. Even standing a good ten feet away, Gina could tell that he was a lot smaller than she was – quite an accomplishment. Eric wheeled a previously unseen wagon of gas cans out from in front of the truck.

"I still have a few more cans to try and fill up before I head home. If you want, you can come with me." Gina hesitated. She couldn't help but feel a little guilty for feeling more secure in the fact that Eric was afraid of Hank. But at least if something went wrong, she would have protection.

"Okay."

Two hours and two stops to check blood sugar later, the sun was fading in the distance. Eric walked ahead of Gina and Hank, pulling the wagon.

"My house is up this way," Eric called over his shoulder, glancing at Hank for the thousandth time. "The driveway is no good, so be sure and watch your step." Eric's house sat back about 20 yards from the road; it was a small, one-story paneled house, with what appeared to be a detached garage and breezeway. Its paved, half-circle driveway didn't quite reach the road, so there was a small gap between the asphalt and concrete. Eric jerked the wagon over the gap, and marched ahead toward the breezeway, leaving Gina unsure as to if she should follow. As if reading her mind, Eric looked over his shoulder again and said, "If you want, you can go into the house. The key is under the mat."

The front door opened up into Eric's living room, a modestly furnished home that obviously had been decorated by an older woman. Hank tried to climb onto the pastel plaid couch, but Gina held him fast by the makeshift leash. The dog whined, and Gina crouched to his level. He licked Gina's face mercilessly and she pushed him away, laughing.

"Calm down," she said, putting her duffel on the floor. She unzipped it and pulled out Hank's leash, clipping it to his leather collar. "You can't go loose because he's afraid of you." *Which may actually be to my advantage.* Gina slipped her belt back on and looked out the front window, checking for any sign of Eric. Seeing none, she took Hank and went to find the kitchen. She was greeted with walls lined with shelves; on those shelves sat hundreds of jars of canned food. She marveled at the sheer volume of food being stored in such a small space, and wondered to what degree Eric's family had prepared. She went to the fridge and opened the cabinet above it. More cans. She shut that cabinet and quickly look through all the remaining cabinets in the kitchen, finding more and more non-perishable food items.

"What are you looking for?" Gina spun around and saw Eric standing in the doorway, eyebrow raised.

"I was checking to make sure that you aren't an alcoholic," Gina stated bluntly.

"Oh," Eric said quietly. "Well, my grandfather was a Baptist who believed alcohol's sinful, so you won't find any here." Eric glanced at Hank. "Is there a specific kind of dog food that he has to eat?"

Gina shook her head. "He eats what I eat mostly." Eric crossed to the refrigerator and pulled it open. It was full to the brim with vacuum-sealed meats.

"Do you eat meat or are you a vegetarian?"

"Not a vegetarian."

"Cool. I'm glad I started up the grill, then." Eric grabbed a package of sausage links and skirted around Hank to grab a jug of water and two plastic cups. He opened one of the lower cabinets and pulled out four plates, balancing it all clumsily. "Could you help me carry some things outside?" Gina nodded, following Eric to the hallway. Eric opened the hall closet, revealing that it was full almost to the brim with fireworks. "My family really liked fireworks," Eric said with a small smile. Gina had a sudden flashback to Sparta. *Sparta, the house. Dirk.*

"Do you like fireworks?" Eric asked. Gina squeezed her eyes shut a moment before looking back at him.

"I don't know," She shrugged. "I've never really seen them. Not up close, I mean."

"What?" Eric's jaw dropped. "How on earth have you not seen them up close?"

Gina shrugged again. "I just... never got around to it, I guess." Eric gathered up an armful of fireworks and handed them to Gina, stepping back and away from Hank immediately.

"Where are you from, anyway?"

Gina cradled the fireworks in her free arm like a baby. "West Texas."

"What are you doing all the way out here, if you don't mind me asking?" Eric loaded up his arms with fireworks as well and nodded for Gina to go back down the hall.

"I think I've got family out here." She opened the back door and stepped out.

"You think?" Eric gestured with his head toward a picnic table under a small tree. "Over there."

"What are the fireworks for?" Gina asked, dodging the question. She dropped the fireworks onto the picnic table and surveyed the huge yard.

"…well," Eric replied, placing his load of fireworks next to hers. "In my family, we always believed that every day is a day for celebration; that every day is worth throwing a party for. When you've got two kids with health problems that may or may not make it to adulthood, you learn to appreciate the little things." He opened the package of sausages and started putting some on the grill. "Besides," he added, "Fireworks are really fun, and it gave us an excuse to annoy our neighbors."

"Aren't you worried that the fireworks might draw attention to you and your house and all the things that you've got here?"

Eric rolled the sausages on the grill, jumping back as one popped and shot juice at him. "I hate being by myself…I've never liked being completely alone. So, if my fireworks bring people to me, then I'm okay with that."

"Has it brought you people before?"

"Not exactly," Eric poked one of the sausages and jerked his hand back. He grabbed one of the plates and transferred the meat to it. "A couple of kids came through, but they were in a hurry and didn't much care to stay. They wouldn't say where they were going, they just said something about preparing for the zombies and took off. They seemed a little… off their rockers, if I'm being completely honest." Gina sat down at the picnic table as Eric set the plate down in the middle. She slid some onto her plate, and some onto the third plate for Hank. She walked him over to the tree with the rope around it and tied his collar to the end.

By the time they finished eating, the sun had set and dusk began to creep in.

"Now, for your firework education," Eric said with a smile. He grabbed a handful of what looked like very long and colorfully wrapped cigarettes on sticks from the pile of fireworks. "Uh," he looked at Hank, you probably don't want to get him too close to these."

Gina tied Hank's leash to the picnic table and stepped back.

Eric pulled a lighter out of his pocket and flipped it on, lighting all six of the sticks' ends. They sparked suddenly, and Eric put the lighter back into his pocket.

"Here," Eric held out one of the sticks to Gina as it began to sparkle and pop. She stood and crossed to him, eyes never leaving the sparklers. Eric separated his handful of sparklers into two bunches, handing three to Gina and keeping three for himself.

"What do I do now?" Gina held the sparklers at arm's length.

"Wave them around!"

She moved slowly at first, before waving them around faster, mesmerized by the smoke trail and sparks that hung in the air.

Eric watched her curiously. "You really haven't ever played with any fireworks, have you?"

"No. I like them," Gina said, eyes never leaving the sparklers. Suddenly, they sputtered and went out. "Aw."

"Want more?"

Gina looked back at the picnic table and pointed to a package of colorful tubes. "What do those do?"

"Those are Roman candles," Eric went back to the table and opened the package, removing two of them. "You're technically supposed to put them in the ground, but…"

"What?"

"Well, I'll just show you." Eric handed a candle to Gina and told her to hold it away from her body. "Don't freak out, it's going to shoot things."

"Shoot… things?" Gina raised an eyebrow. Eric moved closer, putting his hand on the Roman candle above Gina's.

"There will be eight of them, so be sure and count," Eric pulled out the lighter and flicked it on. Gina resisted her natural instinct to move away from him as he held the lighter to the candle. It sparked, and Eric stepped away. "Point it out!" Gina did, and was amazed when a blue ball of light shot from the end. A second ball of light, a red one, followed the blue one, and arced higher than the first.

"Two," Gina murmured, watching as the ball of light faded into nothingness. Another soon followed, only this time it crackled loudly as it streaked across the sky. As soon as that one began to fade, two more shot out in rapid succession; one sizzler and one green ball. She tilted the Roman candle up more, still pointing it forward but at a much sharper angle. The next stream of light went higher than any of the others, disappearing a lot sooner. The final two were both sizzlers that shot out one right after another.

"Ta-dah!" Eric proclaimed, smiling. "And that, my friend, is a Roman candle." Gina returned the smile, and glanced back at the Roman candle that she still held away from her body pointed skyward. "Here," Eric held his hand out, "I'll take that." He took it to a patch of dirt and rubbed the tube into the ground.

They quickly exhausted the supply of Roman candles and sparklers they'd brought out. Gina was just as mesmerized when Eric fired off a few bottle rockets.

"These are technically illegal," he told her, wedging one into the ground. "But I don't know if laws really apply here anymore." He lit the fuse and ran back toward Gina.

"I wonder what's going to happen now."

"What do you mean?" Gina squinted toward Eric in the ever-dimming light. It was at a point where she could only make out the big shape of his head.

"I mean…what happens to people in general." Eric picked up the last firework from the table, a fountain sparkler, and walked it out to where he fired off the bottle rockets.

"I don't know." He crouched down and lit the fountain, returning to where he originally stood as the sparks began to shower down. "I guess," He continued, "I guess that it will kinda be like it was in the pioneer days. When the generators break down and we run out of gasoline, I mean. There's only so much that we can take and not remake."

The fountain ended and the yard became eerily dark.

"Let's go back inside," Gina said, unnerved by how dark it had suddenly become.

As she walked Hank through the door of the house behind Eric, she suddenly realized that she didn't have a plan from here.

"It's dark outside," Eric stated awkwardly, picking up his diabetic kit off of the kitchen table.

"Yes."

Hank panted contentedly at Gina's side. Eric sat down at the end of the table and opened the kit, removing the smaller bag from the larger bag.

"Do you," he began, halting as the pen punctured his finger, "Do you want to stay here? You don't know this town and it's dark…" he trailed off. "We don't have a guest room, but…you can take my sister Trinity's room, if you want. It has a lock on the door," he added, sensing the awkwardness in the room.

"Thank you," Gina replied quickly. "Hank and I will be fine in there." Eric's meter beeped three times in rapid succession. He sighed.

"I'm going to have to be here for a while," he pressed a button on the meter. "The bathroom is down the hall across from her room, just so you know. We've still got water for a little while at least."

"Okay," Gina said, picking up her duffel from the floor by the door. She and Hank quickly went down the hall into the bathroom, where she habitually locked the door behind her.

When she was done showering, Gina returned to the kitchen to find Eric not there. "Eric?" The hair on the back of her neck stood up.

"In here," came the feeble reply from beyond the kitchen. Gina carefully looked around the corner to find Eric sprawled out on the couch panting. Next to him on the coffee table lay his kit. "Sorry," he almost whispered, "This happens sometimes when I'm waiting for the insulin to kick in." Gina watched, wide-eyed, not saying anything. Eric rolled his head toward her, his pupils dilated so much that his light brown eyes were black. "I'll be okay." He said weakly, giving a small smile.

"Okay," Gina replied, unsure of what to do.

"This happens a lot actually," Eric said, almost laughing. "I called them the sugar shakes." Eric once again looked warily at Hank, who was focused intently on him. "I'm fine, really. You don't have to worry about me."

Gina shifted on her feet in the doorway. "How does that work?"

"What?"

"Diabetes."

"Well, most people's pancreases make insulin to keep their blood sugar in check, but mine doesn't. It did a little when I was younger, but it stopped making any at all somewhere along the line." Eric looked up at Gina. "I'm totally dependent on insulin to keep me functioning. I have to check my blood sugar a lot and keep my kit with me or I could be in a lot of trouble."

"So if you don't have insulin, you'll die."

"Yes." Eric looked up at the ceiling. "If I eat something sweet, insulin. If I have too much insulin, I have to eat something sweet."

"How do you know how much insulin or sugar you need?"

Hank lay down on the hardwood floor, heaving a sigh.

"Trial and error, mostly." Eric let out a long breath, his voice steadying. "Luckily it kicks in pretty quick for me so I can see results fast." He raised his hand above him, noting that the shakiness was diminishing. "Insulin lasts longest when it's refrigerated, and I've got a couple fridges full. One in the garage, one in my room."

"That's a lot."

"Yeah. My grandpa was one of those preppers, always ready for the end of the world." He went quiet a moment, lost in thought. "It was supposed to be one fridge for me, and one for Trinity. My sister. But she…" he trailed off. "We lost her right when all this went down."

"I'm sorry." Gina said after a moment.

"It's okay." Eric rolled onto his side. "I miss her, but I'm glad she didn't have to see Granny and Grandpa go."

Gina looked around the room. "What'll you do when you run out of insulin?"

"I don't know." The boy said quietly. "I'll have to figure out how to make it, I guess." He glanced at his watch and rolled back onto his back. "What do you think is going to happen now that so many people are gone?" He sat up slowly.

Gina shifted on her feet. "I think anybody left will try to find other people, maybe."

"Nobody likes to be alone," Eric said with a yawn.

"Yeah. Nobody likes to be alone."

Chapter Fifteen

After

Sacramento, CA

The girl circled her mouth slowly with the lipstick. She adjusted the leotard straps and spritzed her braided blonde bun with extra hairspray before placing the dainty rose coronet on top of her head. She smoothed the pale lavender tutu and took a final look in the dim dressing room mirror before stepping out into the wing. Fourteen years of dedicated training, months of grueling rehearsal; she beat out hundreds of other candidates for the coveted title role in *Sleeping Beauty*. Her entire life had been working for tonight, opening night. She took a deep breath and stepped out onto the stage, a smile illuminating her face. She looked out at the dark, empty seats and saw her parents sitting center on the first row beyond the orchestra pit. Her mother wore her best dress and her father held a bouquet of browned flowers in his lap. Their eyes were closed but she knew they were smiling. She hummed the waltz and pirouetted into the dance. As she moved, music seemed to float from the orchestra pit to join her humming. The performance was spectacular, every hour of rehearsal paying off in the role of her lifetime. She jetéd and adagéd with confidence and poise. Suddenly, the music dropped off. This was it; the grande finale. The music began its final build; the girl preparing for the vault into the prince's arms. As the music intensified, she ran toward the front of the stage, closed her eyes, and leapt.

***

Murfreesboro, TN

The juvenile detention center's cells were designed so that if someone tried to escape, an alarm would sound and send guards to check the detainee and turn off the alarm. At least, that's what would happen under normal circumstances. After two straight days of trying every way the boy could think of to break out, the alarm seemed to be getting louder. If he didn't get out of there soon, he knew he would go mad from it. He'd turned the cell cot on its end beneath the window and was teetering atop it, the sheet tucked into his waistband. For hours, he patiently hit the window with his metal food tray again and again until finally the cracked glass broke. *Sweet fresh air.* Tying the sheet to the light hanging above the window, he quickly climbed through the window and rappelled to the ground. As he strolled across the lawn, he made a mental checklist of what he'd need to do. Firstly, find different clothes. If there were any other people out there, they didn't need to know where he'd been or why. Secondly, eat something. Thirdly, arm himself. He who has the gun controls the transaction. The front gate guard's body lay slumped against the fence. He took the key from the belt, unlocked the gate, and kicked the guard's wrinkled face until it caved.

***

Eureka, NV

The humans had been gone for five days, and the calico's bowl had been empty for four. Though the open window in the kitchen was just big enough for her to leave through, she had to stay and protect her domain until the humans returned and filled her bowl. When the humans left, they forgot to turn off the noisemaker. It played noise after noise, and the cat had begun to grow weary of it. She had tried laying on the noisemaker to make it stop, but it just tickled her stomach. She tried scratching it, but her claws got caught in the front of it. It was too hard to bite, and too big to intimidate. She soon discovered that by butting it with her head, she could move it a bit. She did this for a while before she got bored and went to fish the remaining tasty swims out of the water box in the other room. Returning to the noisemaker, she eventually succeeded in pushing it off of the surface. It fell to the carpet and broke, the sounds becoming garbled static. Suddenly, there was a spark.

***

Plain Dealing, LA

"Now you listen here," the old woman tutted, pulling on the rope leading to the pony's halter. The palomino stamped its foot, snorting at the old woman defiantly. The woman flipped a long white braid over her shoulder and dug her heels into the soft garden soil, leaning on the gatepost for support. "You are gonna come out of there if I have to spank you." The pony shook its head, stepping backwards onto a tomato plant. "Now look what you've done!" She exclaimed, dropping the rope and rushing past the pony. She knelt down next to the squashed tomatoes, smacking the pony's hind leg to try and get it to move off of the plant. The pony lowered its head toward a head of lettuce sticking out of the ground, and the woman shouted. "Don't you even think about it, mister," she clambered to her feet and grabbed ahold of the pony's rainbow halter, trying to keep it from destroying any more of her produce. The pony suddenly lifted its head, sniffing at her apron pocket. The woman stepped backwards through the gate, reaching into her pocket. She pulled out a carrot, and the pony started after her. "That's all it took, huh? Good grief, Sunshine, you're going to make me bald from stress." She lured the pony out of the gate and quickly slammed it behind them, chortling to herself as she started across the yard.

***

Rock Springs, WY

There would be no Mathletes practice that day. The boy sat in the tree house, staring at the picture he kept in his folder. Thirty-two smiling faces looked up at him. Thirty-two. Out of the thirty-two people who lived on the eight-hundred-acre ranch, there was one left. Eight-hundred divided by thirty-two equals twenty-five, the number of people in the picture who were older than him. Thirty-two minus twenty-five equals seven, the number of foster siblings he had before the sickness. Thirty-two plus twenty-five plus seven equals sixty-four; divide that by thirty-two and you get two, the number of graves the boy had dug by himself. Eight-hundred plus sixty-four plus twenty-five plus seven divided by thirty-two divided by two equals fourteen, the number of days it took to wipe out the entire town. Thirty-two adopted family members divided by one lethal virus equals one lonely twelve-year-old.

Math never was his favorite subject.

***

Portland, ME

Her breathing was labored and shallow, chest burning with every breathe she drew. She'd woken from her sleep with a cough that morphed into pneumonia after she spent an entire lethargic day sitting in cold bathwater. She now lay on her side in the bottom bunk of the bed she shared with her sister whose corpse slept peacefully in the bunk above her. Her stomach ached, groaning in emptiness. She licked her cracked lips and thought briefly about trying to crawl to the kitchen for food. *Why bother?* A wheezing breath caught in her chest, sending her into a nasty coughing fit. She gasped for air, lungs refusing to cooperate. She struggled against the weight of her limbs, trying to sit up for some sort of relief. She tried to cry out, but her chest was too heavy to move. Tears blurred her vision as the world went dark.

***

Simms, LA

The hiker was walking up a steep dirt path in Kisatchie National Forest when it hit him. He passed out and toppled backwards down the hill, his backpack spilling open and scattering the contents about the road. His glass water bottle rolled off the path and down a steep drop-off, shattering in a patch of dried grass. The ground absorbed the water thirstily. The sun caught up with the bottle a few days later and tried to make friends with it; the resulting heat set the parched grass and surrounding plants aflame.

Chapter Sixteen

Lexington, KY

"Welcome to Lexington," Millie read the sign aloud. "Population: dead." She stared at the red paint sprayed over the original number.

"Well that's nice and cheery," Zach said, readjusting his backpack.

Millie started forward, walking on the left side of her bike. "We'd better get a move on. The sun will be setting soon." Millie glanced behind her. "We need to find a place to stay for the night. I don't want to get caught in the dark in a city full of who knows what."

"What, you don't think I can take on whatever murderous boogiemen are out there?"

"No," Millie replied flatly.

"...I didn't hear that." Zach jogged a little to catch up with her. "If I remember right, there's a bank near the store that we could bunk at. It's convenient, and defendable should there be any creepy things lurking in the dark."

"Please stop talking about that." Millie looked quickly over her shoulder.

"What, watched too many zombie movies?" Zach stuck his free arm straight out in front of him and reached for Millie's head. "Braaaaaaains," he hissed, making the hair on her neck stand on end.

"Stop it!" She snapped, face reddening in embarrassment.

"I was just picking at you...you don't have to be so wound up all the time."

"Zombies don't exist and they *can't* exist. Once someone's dead, they stay that way. Reanimation isn't possible for a multitude of reasons." Millie stated clinically. She grimaced as a chill shot down her back and made her shiver.

"Well sorry," Zach muttered as they turned onto the next street. "Didn't mean to scare you."

"I'm not scared; I'd just rather be factual than believe nonsense," she said, following him around the next street curve.

"M'kay, no zombie jokes anymore," he sighed, rolling his eyes at the sky as he rounded the corner ahead of them. "I w-" he stopped short, feet freezing in place.

Millie almost bumped into him. "You what?"

"I think I'm hallucinating." She followed his line of sight. There, lounging on the lawn of a convenience store, was a tiger. It leered at them, looking none too pleased that its nap had been interrupted.

"Oh my God... Is that-?" Millie's mouth fell open slightly as her eyes widened. Zach quickly looked around. Over his left shoulder just past a tire shop was an old antiques store; a brick propped one of the doors open.

"Ok, there's an open door behind us about twenty yards away. Let's just back toward it slowly," Zach whispered to Millie, taking a few steps back. "And maybe it won't-" The tiger stood up. It locked eyes with Zach and let out a low, rumbling growl. It lowered its head, lip lifting in a snarl. "New plan. Run," Zach said. Millie was frozen, eyes locked on the cat. "RUN!" Zach grabbed her wrist and took off, knocking her bike over and pulling her toward the wooden door. The tiger let out a roar and exploded from the ground, each powerful stride bringing him closer to the two. Zach reached the door and threw Millie and himself inside. He knocked the brick out of the way and slammed the door shut just as the tiger propelled off the ground. It smashed the door's small window, showering Zach with glass and eliciting a scream from Millie. The door began to groan inward under the tiger's weight as it clawed at the air through the window.

Millie clambered to her feet and pulled a dazed Zach from the floor toward the back of the shop. "That door isn't going to hold forever."

"I… I don't…" Suddenly, Zach dropped to the ground, fished to the bottom of his backpack, and gingerly pulled out the revolver he'd stashed. The tiger lunged again at the door, the force knocking a rack of tin signs from their wall display. Zach stood and scanned the shop quickly. An "Employees Only" sign hung above the door behind the counter. "Go in there and lock the door," he told Millie, pointing at the door. The tiger let out another frustrated roar and pounded against the door.

"What are you…?" Millie looked from Zach to the gun.

"What do you think?" The sound of splintering wood echoed in the shop. "Go!" He shoved Millie toward the door and waited until she was inside before picking up the revolver and cocking it. The tiger had framed his head and left front leg where the window used to be, growling and clawing at Zach. The door wasn't going to hold much longer. *Five bullets. One tiger. Bad aim.* Zach took a deep breath and eased toward the snarling beast, gun pointed at it. *Gotta get close enough not to miss.* His hands shook as he squeezed the trigger.

Zach reeled from the deafening echo of the shot. His ears rang and his vision was momentarily splattered with tiny black dots. He shook himself out of it as the tiger roared angrily and backed off. It lunged again, knocking the door down. As it leapt toward him, Zach heard himself scream. He squeezed the trigger four times in rapid succession. Wall, wall, shoulder, head. The tiger fell, knocking Zach's feet out from under him as it slid. Zach yelled and kicked away from the animal, scrambling to his feet. He stumbled backwards and fell over a footstool, landing on the floor against the wall. He fumbled with the revolver, but the tiger didn't move. The gun clattered to the floor.

"Zach? Zach!" Millie called from the other side of the door.

"It's dead," Zach managed, voice cracking.

The door flew open and Millie stood in the doorway for a moment, shocked. Her eyes scanned the scene before her, from the destroyed door to the tiger sprawled on the floor. "Oh my God…" She glanced to her left and saw Zach shaking uncontrollably beside the dead tiger's outstretched paws, arm tucked awkwardly under him and head leaned against the wall.

"Zach!" She dropped to her knees and grabbed his shoulders, looking him over for signs of injury. "Are you hurt?" She reached behind his head to feel if any of the bones in his neck were broken. "I thought..." She trailed off as she glanced at the tiger. She suddenly realized that her hand was still firmly planted behind his neck and looked back at him. She dropped her hands and stood awkwardly.

"A tiger!" Zach exclaimed, stunned. "I just killed a tiger. In Kentucky. In an antique store." He slid up the wall to his feet, reaching back to push himself off the wall. "Bull in a china shop, my a-" A sudden burning sensation in his left palm turned the last word into a hiss. He jerked his hand away from the wall, smearing blood on the wood paneling. There, embedded in his palm, was a fairly large shard of glass. "How'd that get there?" Zach shakily grasped the glass to pull it out.

"Stop!" Millie cried. "Don't take that out."

"What? Why not?" He suddenly winced as the pain deepened.

"If you do, it'll bleed a LOT more." Millie carefully took his wrist to examine the cut more closely. "You're going to need stitches."

"Let's just duct tape it," he pointed to a roll sitting on the counter next to a rusted can of oil, shifting the glass in his palm. "Ouch. Or just dump some superglue on it and call it a day."

"If it's as deep as it looks, superglue won't cut it." She hesitated. "I can suture it."

Zach chuckled and shook his head. "No thanks, Doc. I don't wanna play 'wounded warrior' right now."

Millie's eyes darkened. She pursed her lips, releasing his wrist. "I'm just going to fix your hand, not sleep with you."

"Whoa, whoa," Zach said, wide-eyed. "I wasn't...that's not at all where I meant that to go."

"Good," Millie said deliberately. "Because we really don't know each other, and I'm not looking for anything except a traveling partner to get to Tennessee."

Zach nodded slowly as his face reddened in embarrassment. "Same."

"Ok, then," Millie said, demeanor softening. "I just wanted to make sure that was clear."

"It's as clear as the glass in my hand," Zach said with a grimace.

Millie looked at his hand again, mentally switching gears. "Right. Let's find a first-aid kit before you bleed out on the floor."

Zach swore and jumped in his chair as Millie dripped the diluted iodine into his palm. "Geez! What the hell?" He jerked his hand away and frowned at Millie. "What happened to 'on the count of three?'"

"If I would have waited until three, you would have tensed up and it would have hurt more," Millie replied, removing the thread and needle from the bowl of iodine and laying it on the paper towels to dry. "It's literally *the* oldest trick in the book for nervous patients." She patted the tiny table. "Hand, please."

Zach muttered an "I'm not nervous" under his breath as he laid his throbbing hand where she indicated.

After checking the antiques shop to make sure there weren't any more animals lurking about, Millie found a first-aid kit in the back room kitchen. She set out the wind-up light, sanitized the tiny kitchen's counter, and got to work.

"You're lucky that the glass didn't sever any muscles that lead to your fingers," she'd told him after removing the glass, "I couldn't do anything about it if you had."

Millie dabbed away some of the pooling blood with the iodine-soaked tissues, eliciting another yelp from Zach. "Put pressure on this." She pressed a tissue into his palm. She turned to the topical painkiller and cotton swabs. "This won't hurt a bit."

"That's what you said last time," Zach leaned away as she turned back to him.

"It would be a lot worse if I had to stitch you up without anesthetic." She said, reaching for his hand. Zach raised an eyebrow and removed the tissue.

"So, Doogie," Zach tried to make conversation as Millie swabbed the cut. "What was it like, being the only twelve-year-old at med school?"

Millie stuck the swab deep inside the cut, causing Zach to grunt. "Funny."

"Well?" He looked at her expectantly.

"Well what?"

"How do you know so much about doctoring?"

"Well, my dad was an ER doc before becoming Dean of Medicine at the hospital."

"That explains the house."

"Dad brought me to work with him pretty much every day during the summer, so I spent most of my afternoons at the nurses' station or following interns around or in Dad's office reading medical books." Millie dabbed blood away from the edge of the cut. "The staff became this weird extended family to me. Nobody really questioned it, and as long as I didn't go into any patient rooms or the ER unaccompanied, it was fine. It's funny," she mused, removing the swab and dropping it into the trashcan beside the door. "I spent more time as a kid at the hospital than the park."

"Sounds like fun." Zach listened intently, his head tilted to one side. Millie had obviously told this story many times, but she didn't seem to mind.

Millie turned to the sink, flipped the tap on, and washed her hands for the third time. "It was, actually."

"So you want to be a doctor?"

Millie elbowed the tap, turning it off. "I have for as long as I can remember. There's been at least one Dr. Macaraeg for the last five generations."

"Wow."

"Yeah. I guess it's just in my genes." She smiled and looked at him. "Why all the questions?"

"Just curious." Zach shrugged. "We didn't get much past the surface when we played Twenty Questions last time."

"Hmm." Millie picked the needle and thread up. "Numb yet?"

"Yup. That stuff works fast."

Millie dabbed a bit of remaining blood from the gash before poising the needle on one side of it, nodding to the other side of Zach. "Hey, look over there and talk to me."

"What?"

"I don't want you passing out."

"I won't!" He scoffed. "I can handle it."

"It doesn't matter how strong you might be, the sight of a needle going completely through your flesh is unsettling, period. And with as much blood as you've lost, I don't want you to pass out." Millie blinked. "Please?"

Zach rolled his eyes and turned his head to the corner with a sigh. "Fine."

"Thank you much." Millie worked carefully, making sure the edges of the wound lined up. "So now that you know more of my life story, tell me yours."

"There's not really much to tell. We lived in Erie until my dad died in a car wreck when I was three."

"I'm so sorry…"

"It's okay," Zach shrugged. "I mean, sure it sucks, but it's hard to miss what you can't remember."

"I understand that. My mom died when I was eight. Breast cancer."

"Sorry to hear that." Zach glanced at Millie out of the corner of his eye. "We should start a club for people with dead parents."

"We'd have to include the entire remaining population of the world."

"Look who's making dark jokes, now!" His smirk disappeared and he inhaled sharply as the needle went through a spot that the numbing gel hadn't reached.

"Sorry," Millie grimaced. "You were saying?"

"A couple years later, my mom met a guy and followed him to Watertown where we lived for a while until they split. After that, we moved to a trailer park. Mom took on two jobs, so I pretty much hung out with Oleson all the time."

"Oleson?"

"Yeah, he was this retired engineer that had an obsession with radios." Zach chuckled. "I remember this one time, he met me at the gate when I got home from school and was just about to jump out of his shoes because he had just talked to the crew of the last space launch. Apparently, he'd fiddled with his radio so much that the signal was boosted into space. A few days later, he tried to teach me how to rewire a speaker. He was a good teacher, I was just too ADD to hang on to the information." Zach's grin fell slightly. "He was a hell of a guy." The room fell silent a moment. "So yeah. It's not exactly *Forrest Gump*, but there it is."

"Done," Millie said, stepping back from the table, dropping the needle in the trashcan.

Zach looked back to his hand. Three stitches lay evenly spaced in a row where the glass shard used to be. "Three?"

"Three was all it took," Millie replied, dumping the iodine down the sink.

"I feel vaguely cheated of my bragging rights." Millie gave a bemused smile and threw the bloodied tissues in the trash. Zach studied the stitches closely. "Ever considered taking up knitting?"

She gave him a sideways glance. "Knitting?"

"Or something like that. Somewhere a sewing circle is missing their prime stitcher." Zach poked at the threads with his fingernail, strumming them like guitar strings.

"Nah-ah! Don't do that." Millie reached into the first-aid kit and pulled out a large bandage.

"Why not?"

"First of all," she frowned, "It's weird." Zach smirked. "Second, you'll pull it wrong and start the bleeding all over again." She picked up the antibiotic cream and dabbed a copious amount on top of the closed wound. She unwrapped the bandage, stuck it over the stitched area, and turned to wash her hands again.

"Cool." Zach stood, grabbing his bag off of the floor with his good hand. He awkwardly slipped it onto his shoulders. "Oh, and thanks, by the way."

"Of course," Millie nodded and elbowed the tap, shaking her hands dry toward the wall. She closed the first-aid kit up and shoved it into her backpack on the floor.

"Well, guess we'd better get a move on," Zach picked the lamp up by its handle and stepped out into the hallway. He pulled the door leading to the front room open, and was greeted with a large expanse of blackness. "Er... maybe we should camp here tonight."

Millie zipped her bag shut. "Why?"

"No reason. Just that the moon is gone."

Millie peeked out of the room. "Oh."

Suddenly, a shuffling noise echoed in the shop, followed by a throaty hiss. The pair exchanged a terrified look and slammed the door.

Chapter Seventeen

Winnfield, LA

Hank bit Gina's hand.

"Ow!" She woke from a dead sleep and jerked away from the edge of the bed. "What a-?" Suddenly, the hair on the back of her neck stood up.

Smoke. She smelled smoke. She threw off the blanket and stumbled across the dark bedroom to the window, pulling back the curtain. To her horror, the trees just beyond the edge of the property glowed orange as a wall of fire steadily made its way toward the house. She jerked the door open and bolted down the hallway, turning on the lights as she ran.

"Wake up!" Gina pounded on Eric's door as Hank barked wildly. "We have to get out of here!"

After a minute, Eric's door opened and he appeared in a t-shirt and sleep shorts, a dazed look on his face. "What's going o-"

"Fire," Gina stated, shaking. "Outside, coming this way."

"Oh, God."

"We have to go," Gina said, pulling the boy into the hallway toward the living room.

"Wait!" He broke free of her grip, turning back to hop back into his room.

"There's no time!"

"I need my kit; wet some towels!"

Hank spun in circles and continued to bark, nudging Gina with his nose. "It's okay, good boy," Gina told the frantic dog as she ducked into the bathroom, yanking towels out of the cabinet under the sink. She threw them under the tap and flipped it on, spinning back around. She jumped back into the bedroom and dove for her boots, pulling them on with some difficulty.

Eric suddenly reappeared in the doorway, wearing jeans and carrying the towels from the bathroom. His prosthetic shoe was attached and a much bigger bag than before was slung across his chest; he tossed a towel to Gina. It hit her in the shoulder and stuck, the water seeping quickly through her baggy t-shirt.

"Put that over your face when we get outside," he said, turning for the hall.

When they made it out the back door, Gina was horrified to find that the fire had almost surrounded the house. She stared wide-eyed at the flames, paralyzed. *You can never get away...*

"Gina!" Eric called from halfway to the go-cart, snapping her out of the trance. "We're gonna barbecue if we don't get out of here *right now*, come on!"

Gina took the passenger seat and threw on the seatbelt, clutching the wet towel to her face. Eric jumped behind the wheel and snapped his goggles on in one fluid motion. The bag swung around so that it nestled between him and Gina, and he tied the towel around his face so that it covered his nose and mouth. Hank barked at the cart, alternating between whimpering and whining.

"Hank, get in," Gina told the dog. He spun in circles, backing away from the cart. "Hank!"

"We have to go," Eric said, voice muffled. He cranked the engine and it sputtered.

"Not without my dog!"

"We *have to go*," Eric said louder, looking Gina directly in the eye as he tried again to start the engine. "He'll follow us." The go-cart roared to life. Gina clutched the worn cloth strap hanging from the ceiling with one hand and held the towel to her face with the other. Eric floored it, and they were off.

"Come on, Hank!" Gina yelled over the sound of the engine as they rumbled down the driveway. The dog took off after them, barking and weaving to each side of the cart. The smoke seemed to seep in from everywhere, stinging Gina's eyes and making her squint. It would've been near impossible to see were it not for the constant backlit glow of the trees.

Eric veered left onto the main road, heading toward town. As they rounded the first corner he threw on the brakes, stopping short of an ablaze fallen tree that blocked the road.

Gina dug her bitten nails into the ceiling strap as the boy skillfully threw the cart into reverse, spinning them the opposite direction with a jolt. He slammed the gas pedal down, and they shot down the road in the opposite direction. Gina squeezed her eyes tight, wanting desperately to wake up from this nightmare. Even through the towel, the smoke began to claw at her nose and throat. The heat from the surrounding flames dug into her like knives. *You can never get away...*

The cart zoomed around a curve in the road and Eric swerved to avoid a pothole, slinging Gina against her seatbelt. She looked back to make sure Hank was still following, but couldn't see very far through the rapidly thickening smoke.

"Hank!" Gina called frantically, removing the towel from her face to better call the dog. "Hank!"

"He'll be okay," Eric yelled, swerving again, "Animals know their way out better than people!"

A cracking sound exploded in front of them, and a smoldering limb fell directly into their path. The cart jerked to the right and the front wheel went over the limb, sending a shower of sparks into the air and onto Eric. He cried out and slapped at his shoulder as the cart veered off into the ditch. Gina flung the end of her towel across him to where the embers latched on, extinguishing them.

"Thanks," Eric choked out. Gina just nodded and coughed, pressing the towel back to her face. Eric threw the cart into reverse, but the wheels only spun. Eric swore and pulled himself up and out of the cart, stumbling slightly. "It's stuck, help me push!" Gina leapt from the cart and got in front of it, shoving it with all of her might. It wouldn't budge.

"It's too steep!" Gina stepped back, coughing.

"We'll have to go on foot," Eric said, grabbing his bag and Gina's towel out of the cart. He slung the bag's strap across his body and tossed the towel to Gina. "There's a river that way," Eric pointed as they scrambled up the embankment, "If we can get to it we'll be okay." Gina scanned the road in vain as they ran down it, desperately hoping to see Hank appear through the haze. The smoke burned her eyes, forcing her to close them almost completely as they turned a corner. She pulled ahead of Eric on the suddenly straight stretch of road, pumping her legs as if her life depended on it. She stopped at a fork in the road to allow Eric to catch up, breathing heavily through the towel.

"Which way?" She removed the towel from her face so he could better hear her as he awkwardly jogged toward her.

"That w-" A loud cracking sound cut Eric off, and Gina looked up just in time for a smoldering branch to smash into her face. She screamed and staggered back, hands and towel flying to her right eye. The pain almost brought her to her knees as she coughed and sobbed. Eric was at her side in what felt like minutes.

"Oh, no, no, no," Eric uttered over and over again, frozen.

"Which…way?" Gina sobbed, squinting at him with her remaining eye. The pain was excruciating, but they couldn't stop moving.

Eric grabbed her hand and pulled her after him. "The river," he said, "We have to get to the river."

Gina fought to stay awake as he all but drug her down the road. Everything was so smoky, each breath felt like she was inhaling embers. She alternated between holding the towel to her burn and covering her nose and mouth with it, trying to keep both covered as they ran. The grass on either side of the narrow road was on fire, and they dodged many fell trees and branches as they ran. The trees were more burned out, here; fewer and fewer were still aflame the further they went. Eric suddenly veered to the left, jerking Gina down a dirt path.

"We made it," he wheezed. Gina opened her eye wider to see another embankment, this one leading down into a small stream.

As they descended to the stream, Gina suddenly realized that Eric was shaking. Badly.

"Eric," she began. Suddenly, his hand slipped from hers and he pitched face-first down the embankment. "Eric!" He rolled to the water, head stopping right before it went under. His body went limp, and Gina rushed down to him.

"What do I do?" Gina asked, dropping to her knees beside him. "Eric tell me what to do!"

"Mm..." Eric tried to say something, but couldn't form the words.

Gina opened his bag and pulled out a juice box and an insulin pen. "Which one? Which one do you need?" She held them in front of Eric's face, and he jerked his head toward the juice box. Gina stabbed the straw into the foil opening and put it in Eric's mouth. Silence fell as his shakes became less and less. Gina's head swam all of a sudden, and her chest constricted.

"I," she wheezed, catching herself with one hand as she fell to the side, "I can't-"

Eric struggled to sit up as Gina's vision went dark and spotty. "Gina?"

"I..." Gina gasped in a panic, the darkness overtaking her

Chapter Eighteen

Tennessee

"Hey look, another farm." Zach said dryly. He and Millie had been biking the same road for a day, and the scenery was becoming increasingly repetitive.

"That's what, sixty now?" Millie remarked, panting slightly. The heat seemed to double when they'd crossed the border into Tennessee, and the sky lacked any clouds to soften the late afternoon sun.

"Mmhmm." He wiped his forehead on his shoulder and resumed steering with his forearms. It hurt his back after a while, but it was better than pressing on his palm. "You'd think the weather would at least *try* to act like fall."

"Be careful what you wish for," Millie said as a sudden gust of wind blew around the bend in the road in front of them. "It may skip fall altogether and go straight to winter."

"I'd be okay with that." Zach mused as they pedaled through a rare patch of trees. "Give me cold over heat any day!"

"Except that freezing to death is a much bigger problem than a bit too much sun."

"Welcome to life after the apocalypse."

When the trees cleared around the bend, the pair simultaneously came to a halt. A green sign reading "Fly City Limits" greeted them; beyond it lay another stretch of road. In the distance, three tanks and five smaller, tracked vehicles were parked in an empty lot across from a small park. Scrawled in electric blue paint on the side of the tank nearest the street was the word "hope." Painted on the road next to the building was a large arrow, also in blue, with "follow me" sprayed over it in white.

"About freaking time," Zach said. He whipped his head toward Millie, a grin sneaking across his face. He sat up quickly and grabbed the handlebar with his good hand and bad fingers. "Race you."

"You're on, Radio Boy!"

They kicked off hard from the ground, speeding toward the arrow. Zach pulled ahead, laughing heartily at Millie's protesting, "Hey!" They reached the arrow fast, zipping ahead to the next one in the middle of a road intersection that pointed down the road. The one after that took them right, past a small library. Zach slowed slightly on the turn, allowing Millie to catch up with him. The pair were neck-in-neck as they breezed by a church; tire-to-tire when they passed a row of tiny shops. The farther they went into the town, the more signs of civilization they saw. A couple of the streets they whizzed past were lined with abandoned cars, but most were vehicle-free.

Suddenly, a shopping cart rolled into the road in front of them, forcing the pair to slam on their brakes to avoid colliding with it. They looked where the cart had come from just in time to see a young boy with long black hair appear in the doorway of a small store. His light brown eyes grew large as he stared at them.

"Wyatt!" The boy called. A tall, serious-faced boy looking to be closer to Zach and Millie's age appeared in the doorway behind him. He pulled a handheld radio from his belt loop and raised it to his mouth.

"This is Team 3, we have company. Party of two at Helsing's."

"Copy that," came the radioed response, *"See you at Town Hall."*

He moved through the doorway toward the pair. "I'm Wyatt Kemp. Welcome to Fly." He adjusted the cap on his head that held down dark blonde curls as the pair introduced themselves. "Xavier and me-" he nodded his head at the younger boy who retrieved the shopping cart, "-Were just about to head back to base. Why don't y'all come with us and meet everybody?" He turned away from them without waiting for a response. Zach and Millie exchanged a glace and dismounted their bikes to follow.

"So," Millie began, "What is this place?"

"'Humanity's Last Best Hope' is what some of us call it," Wyatt said. They turned down a street next to a building with a blue arrow.

A bit dramatic. Zach held back a smirk. "How many of you are there?" He glanced into Xavier's cart, full to the brim with miscellaneous boxes.

"Seven so far."

"Only seven?"

"So far," Wyatt corrected. "Drake was the first. He grew up here and was the one who started everything up after The Sleep hit. He can answer any other questions you have when we meet up with the others."

As they crossed the next street intersection, they came upon a large red brick building with white columns. On the steps stood three teens: two girls –

one tall and muscular, the other short and scrawny – and a boy with neat chestnut hair and a deep tan, who looked to be a bit older than Zach. The boy smiled broadly and walked down the steps as they approached.

"Welcome, welcome! We're so glad to see new faces." He briskly walked up to Zach and shook his hand. "My name is Drake Doyle."

"Zach Carter."

"Great to meet you, Zach." Drake took Millie's hand next and she introduced herself. "Millie, what a lovely name! I see you both have already met Wyatt and Xavier. This is Cleo," he looked to the tall girl with dark eyes and curly black hair pulled back in a low ponytail. She gave an almost regal smile and a small nod to the newcomers. "And Caprie," Drake continued. The shorter girl with the stringy red hair swatted at a mosquito. "The rest of our group is prepping dinner at the diner. Are you two hungry at all?"

"A bit," Millie said.

"Why don't we go see how they're coming along with dinner and get to know one another better!"

When the group reached The Corner Diner – part of a small shopping strip lined with large windows – Wyatt and Xavier took off down the street with the buggy. "They'll deliver the last of today's haul to the Warehouse for sorting tomorrow," Drake explained, pulling on the glass door. "It's one of the many efficient ways our little town works." A bell on the door jingled as the four stepped inside. "Smells like supper is almost done," Drake said merrily as they filed into the room. "Roseline, Kathryn," he called to the back of the diner, "We have guests!"

A door that presumably led to the kitchen opened, and a short blonde girl with darker roots and bright blue eyeshadow stuck her head out. She looked to Millie and Zach. "Well hi!" She pushed past the door and walked briskly up to them, dusting off her short black cutoffs as she moved.

Drake gestured to the girl. "Zach, Millie, this is-"

"Kathryn Pemberley-Deburghe," the girl interjected, waving her fingers at Millie. She put a hand on her hip and gave Zach a smile. "Pleasure to meet you."

The door opened again and a girl with a light brown braid and long denim jumper dress stepped out and walked toward the newcomers.

132

"Ah, Roseline!" Drake beamed, holding out his hand, "Come meet our new friends."

The girl moved closer, eventually stopping next to Drake. "Rosie, here, is our lead cook," Drake explained, putting a hand on the girl's shoulder, "You two have come on a good night; she's making her fantastic, famous chili!"

Roseline's cheeks went pink and she gave a small smile. "It's an old family recipe; I really just follow the directions."

"Nonetheless, it's out of this world."

"Is it ready yet?" Caprie asked, scratching her head.

Roseline nodded and turned to the kitchen. Kathryn and the other girls minus Millie followed her through the door.

Drake gestured to the long table in the middle of the room. "Please, everyone, sit!"

Soon, Cleo and Roseline carried the large pot of chili out and set it in the middle of the long table. Caprie passed out paper bowls just as Wyatt and Xavier returned and took their seats. Drake, at the head of the table, ladled some chili into his bowl. "I guess I'll start with a bit of Fly's history: After some website's claim that a vaccine was found at the research center here spread, it turned into complete chaos," Drake said, passing the ladle to Wyatt on his right. "Military vehicles and soldiers appeared within hours, and they put up blockades at all the roads leading into town in an attempt to keep people from storming the city."

"Was it true? Did they actually find a vaccine?" Millie asked, taking the ladle from Wyatt.

"No," Drake said after a moment. "We don't know why those of us who survived did, but we did without the help of any vaccine."

"So," Zach began, "How does this place work?"

Caprie piped up. "Oh, it's really cool. Drake set it all up and had it running weeks before any of us showed up. Tell 'em, Drake!"

Drake smiled serenely. "It's simple, really. I knew right away that I wanted to establish Fly as a haven for anyone who wanted to join. Basically, we all pitch in and do our share to make the community run, and use everyone's strengths to our advantage. For example, Caprie can memorize and compute numbers very quickly, so she's our lead at the Warehouse; Wyatt is very strong, so he's our heavy lifter; and Cleo is incredibly diplomatic and objective, so she helps with the creation and encouragement of our rules. Our rules are ones that we all abide by, and infractions are noted on

Cleo's clipboard. Any intentionally broken rules will be dealt with by the rules committee, and if the crime is severe enough, the offender will have to be exiled." Drake's face was solemn. "But," he added, "We haven't had any problems with that so far!"

"What are the rules, exactly?" Millie asked, glancing at Zach.

"Most are based on basic human decency and common sense," Drake explained, "For example: respect your neighbors and their property, help one another as much as you can, and make smart, safe choices. All others are for everyone's own safety; keep your radio with you at all times, use the buddy system, and don't roam around by yourself after dark."

Cleo spoke up from across the table next to Wyatt. "Most of us have the rules memorized, but the full list is posted at the entrance of every building we use, right next to the schedules."

"Ah, yes. Thank you for reminding me," Drake said, "Shortly after Cleo and Wyatt arrived, we sat down to create a schedule that makes the most out of every day available. Monday through Friday, minus Wednesday, we scavenge for supplies and sort them in the warehouse. Wednesday and Saturday are maintenance, cleaning, and sign-posting days, where we leave messages in the surrounding towns beckoning people toward Fly. Sunday is a free day to do with what you please. Anyone is free to leave whenever they want, but if they leave the community, there is a chance that they may not be welcomed back, unfortunately."

"But you'd pretty much have to be crazy to want to leave this place," Kathryn said with a sniff. "Nobody wants to be all alone out there."

Xavier and Roseline nodded in agreement.

"That old saying 'there's safety in numbers' is very true," Cleo said, sitting up straighter. "We don't know what all is lurking out there. In here we have a much better chance of survival."

Caprie piped up, scratching her face. "We're sorta like one giant family. We've had some problems, but, y'know, everyone always works it out in the end."

The sun had just begun to disappear behind the row of shops across the street when the group emerged from the diner.

"We're so glad that you both are here," Drake said, smiling at Zach and Millie. "Our little town isn't much, but we'd love for you to give us a try if you'd like." The newcomers exchanged a glance. Drake turned to the rest of the group and gestured down the road. "Why don't we all go start on the campfire, and Zach and Millie can join us when they're ready."

As the group walked away, Zach turned to Millie. "What do you think?"

"I think they're a little overly enthusiastic, to be honest, but they seem okay otherwise. Maybe we should stick around for a while," she said decidedly. "I'd like to see how everything works around here."

Zach nodded. "Same. I like the idea of being around live people again."

"First impressions?" Drake asked when the town residents reached the motel parking lot. To one side of the lot sat a fire pit they'd built around an existing pothole, surrounded by lawn chairs and benches. Drake nodded at Xavier, who nodded back and headed for his room.

"They seem a little quiet," Kathryn said, flipping her hair out of her face.

"They were probably just soaking everything in," Wyatt replied. He struck a match and set it to the kindling.

"They could be nice additions," mused Cleo, "Millie seems a bit type-A, like she'd do well with organization."

"Zach looks like he could carry his weight for sure," Kathryn added with a smirk.

"If they want to stay, we can see how they work and assess their skills better tomorrow," Wyatt said.

"Good thoughts," Drake said. "And just in time!" He gestured up the street at the newcomers as they approached.

"What's the verdict?" Kathryn asked as Zach and Millie took seats by the fire.

"I think we're going to stay a while," Zach said.

"Fantastic," Drake beamed. "You'll both fit in perfectly. We'll get you both set up at the motel after this." He reached into his pocket and pulled out a large key ring. "Many of the rooms have been modified to use regular locks and keys instead of the electronic ones that were originally installed there. The ones that had occupants in them at the time of the Great Disaster are just storage now."

"We had to go clean the dead bodies out," Caprie said, watery eyes growing large. "They looked like mummies, and some got stuck how they were when they died, like with a phone in hand. It was so cool."

Drake grimaced slightly. "I wouldn't say cool, but it was definitely…an experience. We were very fortunate that all of the ground floor rooms that don't have rooms above them, as well as the second-story rooms, have skylights. It keeps things from being too dark all the time, though there are blinds that fold over the skylights to block the sun if you prefer."

"This place must've been built in the 60's or something," Millie mused. "My best friend's house was a 60's house and it has five skylights."

"They aren't very aesthetically pleasing," Drake said, smiling at Millie. "But they do serve a good purpose."

Xavier appeared almost magically in the darkness, cradling an acoustic guitar. "I had to tune it," he explained, taking a seat on a bench.

"Everyone's talents are useful here," Cleo told Millie, who studied the guitar with fascination. "And Xavier is the best guitarist around."

Xavier smiled shyly, glancing at the newcomers. He looked back at Cleo, who gave him a motherly "go on" nod. The boy immediately began to pick at the strings, filling the air with a beautiful melody that neither Zach nor Millie had ever heard before. They all sat in silence as Xavier strummed, letting the sounds of the crackling fire and the guitar take them away.

Zach glanced at Millie, who stared, mesmerized, into the fire. Her eyelids drooped, and Zach felt a yawn coming on just watching her. As Xavier finished the song and the light began to fade entirely, Zach spoke up.

"Not to interrupt this amazing music," Zach started, stifling a yawn. "But we've come quite a ways today, and I'm exhausted. Howsabout you show us where those rooms are?"

"Of course," Drake said, standing and reaching behind his chair. He brought out a previously-unseen oil lamp, and pulled a lighter from his pocket. "I'll show you to them."

Drake led them by lamplight to a single-story row of rooms on the left side of the parking lot first. He pulled the keys from his pocket, and thumbed through them. "Ah, here it is." He flipped to one of the keys and pulled it off of the ring. He held it out, and Millie took it. "Room 126 is all yours."

"Thank you," Millie said with a smile. She adjusted her backpack and slid the key into the knob.

"There's candles, a lighter, and a battery-operated clock with an alarm in every room. Please do remember to put out the candles before you go to sleep and when you leave," Drake added as Millie stepped through the door. "Breakfast is at nine."

"Then I'll see you both then. Goodnight."

The room that Drake assigned Zach was at the end of a long hallway in the two-story part of the complex. "I hope you don't mind, this one doesn't have a skylight. But it does have a few extra candles and a lamp for your use."

"I'm not picky," Zach said, taking the key from Drake. He swung the backpack from his shoulder and unlocked the door.

"We're so glad to have you both here. It's nice to know that our efforts are not in vain."

Zach dropped his bag inside the door and looked back at Drake, who stood there smiling, almost expectantly. "Yeah...thanks for putting us up."

Drake beamed. "Glad to do it. See you in the morning!"

Zach closed the door, locked it, and shook his head at the darkness.

Chapter Nineteen

Somewhere in Louisiana

The sun was unforgiving. The sweltering heat, coupled with the lack of shade on the uphill stretch of road, made the biker want to just lie down on the pavement and melt into a puddle. He hadn't been an athletic person by any stretch before, but he had found the bike on the side of the road and figured it would be faster than walking. After two weeks of biking up to 12 hours a day, he'd built up enough muscle and stamina to not have to get off and walk the bike up hills like this one. On either side of the road the grass and trees had been burned to a crisp. The lingering smell of smoke made the biker feel almost like he was in an ad for preventing wildfires.

He topped the hill and gazed around, taking in the sobering scene. The blackened landscape stretched for as far as he could see, with the occasional greenish swamp breaking the monotony. He took a second to catch his breath and adjust his backpack, then pushed off hard on the pedals. The wind was an amazing relief from the heat as he coasted down the hill. As the road leveled out, he passed a wide dirt path leading off of the main road and out of habit glanced down it. He did a double take and slammed the brakes. He stopped and stared for a minute, taking off and wiping his glasses to make sure his eyes weren't playing tricks on him. The dog was sprawled out in the path, panting heavily. His ears perked up and his tail wagged as the biker dismounted, put the kickstand down, and approached. The dog struggled to his feet and limped over to the biker with a wagging tail. His fur was singed almost completely off in some patches, and his paws were red and swollen.

The boy knelt down to pet the dog's head. "Hank! Where's Gina, boy?"

***

Nowhere, OK

Ira hunched over and grabbed the microphone from the back of the desk. A slight twinge in his lower back made him wince slightly, then smile ruefully. *You're not as young as you once were, old man,* he thought, switching the microphone on.

"Friends, this is Radio Nowhere calling to you once again from Nowhere, Oklahoma. As always, I'll be transmitting every night from 8 pm Central time to 10 pm Central time. I know things are bad…real bad for many of you. But G…" He swallowed hard and looked away from the microphone, taking a deep breath before continuing. "What I was gonna say is that…God is with you. That He will watch over you. And that you can…should have faith in Him. But friends…" His voice cracked. *Can I really do this?* Abigail's beautiful face stared at him from the photo he kept at the desk, a bouquet of lilies clasped in her small hands. Tucked into the corners of the frame were a picture from Marianne and Adam's wedding, and a picture of Marcus and Marianne as children. *Abigail always did favor her mother.* Ira sighed deeply, gray eyebrows knitting together. "I was gonna say that, but I have to tell you…I'm just not so sure any more. I know that loss is part of life. That without pain there's no joy. I know it here," he tapped his head audibly, "but not here," he said savagely as he thumped his chest. "We've lost so many…so many. It's hard for me to square that with my belief in a loving God. So I don't think I'll talk about the Lord until I'm no longer angry with Him."

He grabbed a book off the cluttered desk, flipping it open. "So tonight, let's talk about danger. Friends, there are no doctors left…that is, unless we're very lucky. And I sure don't feel lucky. So be careful."

Ira cleared his throat and took a swig from his water canteen. "Firstly, do not do anything needlessly dangerous or that might put you in harm's way. If you're driving a motorcycle and have a wreck, even with the proper safety equipment you may die. Remember…it's a lot riskier to take chances now. There are no more ambulance teams and staffed hospitals to come to your aid if you get injured. Whatever you do, take it slow and easy. There's no rush. Secondly, if you cut or scratch yourself, stop immediately and clean the wound out. Carry iodine and a decent first aid kit with you. Stop in a book store, get a good first aid book, and read it...

Chapter Twenty

Fly, TN

Zach never liked oatmeal, but he ate it without complaint at breakfast. He glanced at Millie sitting caddy-corner opposite him at the table. She listened vaguely to Kathryn, who chattered on with the occasional glance around to make sure people were paying attention. Millie caught Zach's gaze and gave a look that said, "Help me."

"Hey, Mil," he began, scrambling to think of a topic to change to. "What ever happened to that flashlight I gave you?"

"Oh that one," Millie replied enthusiastically. "I think it's somewhere in my backpack, I'll look for it later. Why, did you need it?"

"Yeah, it's…bright enough to act as a night-light for reading."

"Oh, you read?" Kathryn butted in, swiveling to face Zach. She sat next to him, and seemed to move closer on the bench.

"Er, yeah," Zach replied, "Got a real nice…repair manual that I've been digging into," he offered, eliciting an amused eyebrow raise from Millie.

"Oh. Well, that's actually kinda-" Kathryn was suddenly cut off by Cleo leaning over the table.

"Here are your schedules, and your walkie-talkies." Cleo handed the aforementioned to Zach and Millie, respectively. Zach glanced at his walkie-talkie, labelled with his name. "The walkie-talkies have fresh batteries in them, and if you turn them off at night they should last around two weeks before you need to replace them. Today's Tuesday," Cleo continued, "So the usual schedule applies. You don't have to worry about changes until tomorrow, that's maintenance day."

"Thanks," Millie said, looking over the schedule. It was hand-copied, and covered in clear packing tape as a crude form of lamination.

"Good morning, everyone," Drake's voice boomed through the room, silencing the residents quickly. He stood at the head of the table, smiling. "I hope you've all enjoyed breakfast; let's give the kitchen crew a round of applause." Everyone clapped heartily, and Roseline smiled at the ground. "Now, on to today's assignments. Some of you may already know that there's a medical supply store on the edge of town," Drake pointed to his right, "And for those who didn't, you do now." Wyatt chuckled slightly. "The scavenging team will be going to see what we can salvage from there while the warehouse team sorts and organizes again today. Cleo will tell you all more about that once you get there. Now," Drake looked to Roseline, "Unless there are any other announcements, let's get this day going!"

"I'll be right back," Millie said, standing and heading for the restroom.

Roseline disappeared into the kitchen, returning almost immediately with a large basket full of brown paper bags.

"It's peanut butter and jam day," Caprie announced. "There's other things too, obviously, but you know." She trailed off as a fly buzzed by her face.

"It's not strawberry jam, is it?" Zach asked, looking into the bag. "Millie's allergic."

"No," Roseline said, "Grape."

Millie reemerged as the group made their way outside.

"Alright everyone," Drake said, "We'll see you back here at supper time!" Drake set off down the road with Wyatt and Xavier in tow. Zach saluted Millie dramatically and spun on his heel, marching off to follow Drake.

"How far out is that supply store?" Zach asked.

"Five miles at least," Drake replied, "But there's no way we're walking in this heat." They rounded the corner of the building and Zach stopped in his tracks. There in front of him was a brand-new four-door black truck. He let out a low whistle.

"Since gasoline is so scarce," Drake continued, "We don't use vehicles very often. But for anything out of town, we do."

"How do you handle blocked roads?"

"There's a problem sometimes, but we've mapped and utilize most of the clear roads around town. It takes longer to get to places, but it's safer that way." Drake climbed into the front seat as Wyatt took the passenger's seat. "The goal is to eventually clear out all the roads in Fly."

"How are you going to do that?" Zach asked, climbing into the back seat.

"A bulldozer," Drake said simply.

"You've got a dozer?" Zach asked.

"Yes, we do," Drake replied, slamming his door.

Wyatt spoke up. "I've driven tractors all my life. A bulldozer is basically the same thing."

"Eh, you'd think that they'd be similar, but they're actually pretty different," Zach said, clicking his seatbelt. Xavier gave Zach a quizzical look. "I worked a few dodgy construction jobs back home," Zach explained. "They didn't ask my age, I didn't offer it up."

"You're just full of surprises!" Drake laughed, cranking the engine. "We are glad that you and Millie joined the family."

"I wanted to ask this earlier but didn't know if it was okay or not," Xavier said. "What happened to your hand?"

Zach glanced at the freshly rewrapped bandage. "You wouldn't believe me if I told you."

Wyatt turned around to look at Zach. "Try us."

"Okay," Zach cleared his throat. "We got attacked by a tiger."

Wyatt snorted and turned back to face the front. "You're right," he sneered, "I don't believe you."

The warehouse was very well lit, thanks to the row of windows surrounding the top of the building. Unfortunately, the sun streaming through those windows heated the air inside until it was quite warm. Millie sorted a cart of canned food, stacking the shelves neatly to maximize the room for more food.

"You know what I don't get?" Kathryn asked Millie, leaning against the shelves.

"Hmm."

"I don't get why Caprie hasn't tried to go after Wyatt yet. He's really fit, I'd break a piece of that off any day. Maybe she's a lesbian or something." Millie paused for a moment and raised an eyebrow at Kathryn. "Not that there's anything wrong with that!" The girl clarified, holding up a manicured hand. "It just doesn't make sense to me why she hasn't even given him a second glance. I mean have you seen his muscles?" Millie didn't reply. "Not that I really mind or anything," Kathryn glanced at her nails as Millie moved the cart farther down the aisle. "If I keep working on him, he'll crack one of these days. That's the great thing about there being only a few people left: the dating pool is much smaller, so people basically always have to settle."

Millie rolled to the cart a little way down the aisle and scooped up a few more cans to put away.

"Maybe Caprie is going to go after Drake," Kathryn continued. "Though I can't really see that happening because it's basically common knowledge that Drake and Cleo are together. Not officially or anything, but they're both in charge and have to have a lot of meetings about things so I can only imagine that there's something there. But then again Drake is also pretty cozy toward Roseline so maybe that's a thing and nobody knows yet." Millie remained silent, letting Kathryn babble on. "I mean he's hot in that 'camp counselor' sorta way, so I could see how Roseline could fancy him too. Though I think she's one of those weird fundamentalist chicks, so she probably wouldn't respond even if he did make a move openly instead of just watching her from afar."

Millie hummed in response and wheeled the cart further down the aisle, trying to hide her aggravation that Kathryn was not actually doing any work. She wiped her forehead on her sleeve.

Kathryn stepped closer to Millie's cart. "So what's the deal with you and Zach?"

Millie stopped and looked at her. "What?"

Kathryn rolled her eyes. "You heard me. Are y'all like, together or…?"

"No." Millie resumed putting the cans on the shelves. "Can you go get another cart?" She asked, giving Kathryn a pointed stare.

"Yeah," Kathryn said with a sigh, walking back down the aisle to the front of the warehouse. She stopped suddenly and spun on her heel. "Well, if you're not going to go for him, I think I will. You can't let that physique go to waste."

Millie cringed after Kathryn spun back around and flounced off down the aisle. *Well,* she thought, *this one will be interesting to watch.* She let out a huff of air, shook her head hard, and continued stocking.

Across town, Zach knelt on the cold tile floor, carefully packing the last of the cardboard boxes they'd found in the back.

"Here, hold this," Zach told Xavier, handing him a box of Band-Aids. Xavier watched, fascinated, as Zach reorganized the box to make room for the bandages. "Don't let anyone tell you that Tetris isn't a life skill."

Wyatt brushed past them, carrying three boxes stacked on top of one another. "Are y'all going to sit around giggling like girls or are you going to help load up the truck?" Wyatt asked sarcastically.

Zach bent the box flaps in on themselves securing the box closed. Xavier picked up the box with a grunt and followed Wyatt out the door. Zach used his good hand to push himself off the floor and stand. He took one final glance around the ransacked pharmacy portion of the medical supply store, and spotted a small box labeled medical sutures laying on the counter in the corner. He glanced at his hand and smiled to himself, grabbing the box and slipping it into his pocket.

Outside, Wyatt stacked the last of the boxes into the bed of the truck. He slammed the tailgate shut and stepped back triumphantly.

"Wonderful job today, Gents!" Drake said with a smile. "I'd say it's about time we head back to check in on the girls." Zach went to open the back seat, but Drake stopped him. "Would you mind riding up front this time? I want to talk more about your construction experience, and I can't hear you talking over the air conditioner." Zach glanced at Wyatt, who stood frozen, watching. Drake turned to Wyatt. "You don't mind, do you, Wyatt?" He asked coolly.

"No, I guess not," Wyatt grumbled. He climbed into the backseat after Xavier, shooting the back of Zach's head a glare.

The Diner's one gas lamp was lit and sitting in the middle of the long table as the sun hid behind the buildings.

"Phenomenal job today, everyone," Drake said lifting his cup of root beer into the air. Roseline snatched Zach's bowl immediately after he finished his soup, making him jump. "I would especially like to recognize the work of our newest community members and thank them for all of their help today." Everyone clapped, and Zach grinned cheekily while Millie gave a small nod. "Cleo and I talked a little while ago-" Drake continued, and Kathryn shot Millie a smirk, "-and we've decided that because of the large volume of supplies that we have gathered over the past week and accumulated in the warehouse, we think it would be a good idea to move maintenance day to Thursday and spend tomorrow sorting and putting away the remaining supplies. Is everyone alright with that?" Everyone looked around at one another. Satisfied that nobody had a problem, Drake continued. "I think after the past few days we could all use a bit of a break, so as soon as the supplies are all taken care tomorrow, we will call it a day."

"Booyah," Xavier said quietly, raising his fist level with his ear.

Drake smiled broadly. "Booyah indeed! Are there any other announcements or questions?"

There was a pause, and Wyatt turned to look at Zach. "Really though," he said, smirking. "What happened to your hand?" Zach let out a sigh and looked at Millie.

"He got that defending us from a tiger," Millie stated, stretching slightly.

Kathryn and Roseline gasped as Wyatt's eyebrows shot up. "No way," he said, eyes narrowing.

"It's true," Millie said sincerely. "We were walking through a town, and for whatever reason, there was a tiger that somebody must've let out of the zoo just sitting on the lawn of a gas station."

Zach nodded. "Quite an adventure, that one."

"You can't just leave it like that," Caprie said, sneezing. "Tell us what happened."

The tale of the tiger went back and forth between them as Zach spun the tale quite large right before Millie brought it down to Earth, over and over again. By the time the story was done, it was dark outside.

"Wow," Drake said, awed. "I do believe that's the best story I've heard in a very long time."

After the group split up for the evening, Zach went back to his room. He was just about to kick off his shoes when he suddenly realized that he no longer had his walkie-talkie. He sighed, realizing that he left it in the diner, and headed back to get it. Crossing the parking lot, he spotted Cleo and Millie sitting by the fire pit and looking at a piece of paper intently. Millie talked too quietly for him to hear, but from the serious face that Cleo wore while nodding slightly, he wasn't about to interrupt.

Entering the Diner, Zach was surprised to see a sliver of light coming from the kitchen's partially-open door. He grabbed his walkie-talkie off the table where he left it, and leaned forward out of curiosity to see into the kitchen. There, standing in the corner of the room, were Drake and Roseline. Roseline smiled and blushed as Drake whispered something into her ear. She let out a small giggle as he brushed a strand of hair out of her face, talking seemingly into the crook of her neck. Zach pulled away from the door awkwardly as Drake's hand cupped Roseline's cheek.

Once he was outside, Zach chuckled to himself. *Well, that answers that question.*

The next day was uncharacteristically hot. Millie wiped her forehead on her sleeve and rolled her buggy to the back of the warehouse as Cleo sorted through boxes nearby. The back of the warehouse was stifling, as the breeze that drifted through the open front doors didn't quite reach the back. Millie bent down to stock some shelves on the bottom of the aisle, and realized immediately after straightening up that she'd stood far too quickly. Her head began to reel, and tiny black dots formed in her vision. She leaned on her buggy, a wave of nausea sweeping over her.

"Help," she said, "I could use some help if someone's not busy." She started to sway back and forth as Cleo stuck her head into the aisle.

"What's wrong?"

"Help me get to the front," she said, waving Cleo over. "I'm about to pass out, it's too hot." Cleo wrapped an arm around her back and quickly helped her to the front of the warehouse, passing everyone else on the way. They all followed, asking what was wrong. Zach ran up right as Cleo guided Millie to one of the lawn chairs at the front of the warehouse and helped her sit down. Millie leaned back, praying that her breakfast would stay put. Suddenly, Drake was there at her side as well.

"What's going on?" He asked.

"It's too hot in here," Cleo stated. "She almost passed out from the heat."

"Water," Millie said weakly, her entire body feeling like it was on fire, "I need it." The dots threatened to overtake her vision and she felt like someone was sitting on her chest.

Cleo looked to Caprie. "Go now."

Caprie nodded, and took off at a run to the middle of the warehouse where they kept the water jug for everyone to use. Zach grabbed a newspaper off of the stack by the front door that was normally used for kindling. He fanned Millie gently as everyone stood around, watching.

"I'll be good," Millie said, panting, "I just…sit a minute."

Cleo folded her arms and shook her head at Drake. "It's too hot to be working in here today. Organization can wait, we don't need people dying here."

Drake met Cleo's gaze as something like anger flickered over his face for a moment. Cleo raised her chin, averting her eyes. "Cleo's right," he said finally. "We need to alter our current course of action."

Millie heard herself mumble as ringing exploded in her ears. "Breaks." She stated as the black dots turned into white dots. "Then it…or it…bad when the heat is too hot." Her brain was fuzzy and she couldn't find the right words; the black dots turned into static that gave her tunnel vision.

"Okay," Zach said, jaw clenching as he shook his head, "We can figure this out later, right now she's our priority." Zach knelt beside Millie, who watched the static dance around. "Hey, can you move? I need you to stand up."

"*You* stand up." Millie said defiantly, eyes unfocused.

Zach's eyebrows knitted and he swallowed hard. "Okay, we're going somewhere cooler." He slipped one arm around her back and the other under her knees as Caprie returned with water.

"*You're* somewhere cooler," Millie muttered, continuing to watch the static. Her head lolled backwards and her limbs hung uselessly at her side as Zach carried her out of the warehouse. The prevalent breeze gave him an idea he could only hope would work.

"Somebody get me that chair," he called behind him, adjusting his grip. "And bring water from the insulated closet, a lot of it." Caprie handed her water jug to Cleo. Caprie, Xavier, and Wyatt all ran back for water jugs as the rest of the warehouse crew followed closely behind Zach. Roseline slid the chair outside and followed as he moved into the shadow of the warehouse. Drake watched the scene with interest as Zach lay Millie in the chair and removed her shoes.

"Hey Mil," Zach said, pulling her socks off, "Talk to me, what's going on?"

"My head hurts," she muttered feebly. "And you took my shoes."

Caprie, Kathryn, and Wyatt returned, each carrying two gallons of water.

"Go back and tear open some of those cardboard boxes," he instructed, and Xavier took off. Zach put a hand to Millie's forehead. "Okay, Mil, you still with me?" She nodded, her vision clearing but her mind still foggy. "You're going to hate this, but it's for your own good." He grabbed a water jug and opened it, pouring it onto Millie's head. She sputtered and cried out, but was too weak to move away. "I'm sorry, we've got to get your temperature down and this is the only way I know how." He picked up the next one and proceeded to pour it over her abdomen, soaking her dark purple shirt. She whimpered, face contorting. Xavier came back with a box, torn into pieces. "Here," he took the pieces from Xavier and handed them to Kathryn, Cleo, Caprie, Roseline, and Wyatt. "I need you to fan her and keep a solid breeze going." He put a hand to Millie's forehead, and picked up another jug of lukewarm water. "This would be so much easier if we had ice," he said through gritted teeth. He poured the jug onto Millie's legs and feet and grabbed another, opening and upending it onto her head again.

"She's already soaked, don't waste water," Wyatt said. Zach ignored him, focusing on Millie. He put a hand to her head, and it seemed to be working.

"Okay guys," he said, "Keep going."

Ten minutes later, Millie's temperature was down enough that she began to shiver. Her mind cleared and she looked up at everyone, embarrassed.

"…Thank you," she managed, sitting up straighter.

"Alright, everyone," Drake said, turning the pseudo-crowd's attention to himself. "Let's all get back to work." He looked to Zach. "I trust you've got this under control?"

"Uh, yeah," Zach replied, giving Millie her damp socks back. "I'll make sure she gets back to her room safe, then come back."

Drake led the Fly residents back into the warehouse as Millie squeezed her feet back into the socks. She wrinkled her nose and shivered.

"Ugh, wet socks."

"You feeling okay?"

"Yeah," Millie said, putting her shoes on. "I'm really tired and my head is still a little wonky, but I'll be okay." She swung her feet over the edge of the chair and looked up at Zach. "Thank you. Really."

"Just returning the favor," the corner of his mouth twitched upward as he held up his injured palm. Blood had seeped through the bandage and dried, and Millie looked alarmed.

"Did I do that?"

"What?" Zach looked at his hand and started to peel back the bandage. One edge of the partially-healed wound had broken open again, hence the blood. "Nah, pretty sure that was me getting too overzealous with the boxes in there."

Millie stood shakily, and Zach instinctively wrapped an arm around her back to make sure she wouldn't fall.

"Thanks." She grabbed his shoulder to steady herself. "Borderline heatstroke can do some weird things." She let go and stood straighter. "You can go back to the warehouse, now. I'll be okay."

"You sure 'bout that?" Zach said, pulling back and watching Millie's slow blinking. "You just said you're still feeling weird."

"Yeah, but I'm okay." Millie smiled blearily.

"Humor me, please. Let me make sure you get back okay."

"If you must."

Zach walked behind and to the side of Millie with his arms at the ready in case she fell, eliciting an amused smile from her.

"I'm okay, really," she told him for the thousandth time, "I just need rest."

"Okay – watch your step – I believe you. I just want to make sure you get there safely is all."

Millie stopped suddenly, staring down the road. Zach looked where she was and…nothing.

"Whatcha lookin' at?" He asked, raising an eyebrow.

Millie continued to stare, before shaking her head hard and covering her eyes with one hand. "Now *I'm* the one who's hallucinating," she muttered.

"What?"

"I coulda swore I saw my Nana standing at the end of the road."

Zach squinted. "…where?"

"That's what I'm saying. The heat just got to me." She sighed and frowned, keeping her eyes closed as she dropped her hand. She opened one eye slightly, then the other. She sighed and started forward again.

When they reached her door, Millie pulled the key from her pocket and turned back to face Zach.

"I've got it from here, thanks." She gave him a sleepy smile and unlocked the door. She dropped her key back into her pocket, and realized something was missing from her belt. "Dang, I left my walky-talky back at the warehouse."

"Here," Zach took his walky-talky off his belt and handed it to her. "Take my radio. I'll just pick up yours and we can swap later or something."

"Thanks. Again," she added, opening the door and stepping inside. "I'm going to sleep now."

"If you need anything, just buzz me."

"Okay."

Dinner that evening was rice and beans, a dish that – according to Kathryn – was seen quite a bit around Fly. Millie came in late, her cheeks still pink from that afternoon. As everyone ate, Drake stood at the head of the table as usual.

"Great work today everyone. Cleo and I talked about it earlier, and we want to propose the idea that because of the heat wave, and the incident this afternoon, we need to make a few adjustments to the schedules. Everyone needs to put their safety above work, and to take care of yourselves. If you're not healthy, the town isn't healthy. I'm very impressed with the way that our town has been working like a well-oiled machine, but as we all know, if one cog gets rusty, the whole machine falls apart. We need to make sure that that does not happen here. So, take care of yourselves, take breaks as you need them, and be sure and keep lots and lots of water nearby, and drink it. Does that sound good?" Everyone at the table nodded in agreement with a few mm hmms thrown in for good measure. "Good, good," Drake said with a smile.

Millie glanced around the room, suddenly unnerved.

"Now," Drake continued, "Tomorrow is Thursday, Maintenance Day, so breakfast will be at 10 AM. I want to thank you all again for your cooperation and switching up the schedule this week; I know that we have some who prefer things to be routine, so I especially thank those who don't like change. Take it easy this evening," he looked at Millie, making her uncomfortable, "And we'll reconvene here at 10 AM." Drake stood, taking his bowl into the kitchen. He returned and passed to the table, going out the front door.

"Are you sure you're okay?" Zach asked Millie as they cleaned up after dinner.

"*Yes,*" she replied, "I'm a little boggled, but I'll be okay."

"Okay," he replied, "If you insist."

"I think I'm going to turn in early again," she said. "Try to sleep some of this off."

"Okay," Zach replied. "Do what you need to do. Oh," he stopped her, "Here's your radio back." They switched walky-talkies and Millie left.

On her way back to the motel, Millie passed by an alleyway and movement caught her eye. She glanced down the alley and did a double take, quickly speeding past. She wrinkled her nose at the sight, and tried to shake the image of Drake and Cleo kissing out of her head.

That night, Millie awoke to the sound of her door hitting the chain lock. She lay on her side facing away from the door, but saw a light fall over her bed. She glanced at the mirror in the corner of the room to see what had happened. She froze. It was too dark to make out the face, but it was a clearly masculine figure holding a lamp. Her heart pounded wildly as she quickly tried to think of an escape plan. Before she could make a move, the door shut again.

Chapter Twenty-One

"Can you hear me?" Louis came to, eyes and brain full of static. Gina's face suddenly appeared above him. He stared at her through half-open eyes, confused. The bus must have flipped, because her face was framed by seats overhead. Yeah, *he tried to say,* I can hear *you. His voice didn't sound, lips unmoving. He tried to sit up, but his muscles didn't respond.* Oh God, he thought, I'm paralyzed! *He reeled inside his head, desperately trying to do something, anything.*

Suddenly, Gina moved closer, placing a hand on his face. It was soft, gentle as she tapped his cheek. "Come on...please don't do this." Fear etched itself into her face – her round, freckled, beautiful, face. The world momentarily flickered out of focus. Sirens. Gina shifted, brows knitting together. She looked up suddenly, face stoic again. She stood quickly and disappeared from his field of vision. No, Louis thought, please don't go. Don't leave me!

*

Hank sneezed.

Louis opened his eyes and looked at the dog panting placidly beside him. They lay in the shade of an abandoned armored truck labeled "Gruff Security Inc.," complete with large cartoon goat head painted above it. It crashed into a tree just past a sign bidding them farewell from Kisatchie National Park. Louis sat up and leaned against the truck, using his backpack as a sort of cushion. Beside him sat a thermal water bottle and a bowl. The dog began to lick and nibble at one of his bandaged front paws, prompting Louis to tap him on the nose.

"No," he said, "Don't do that. You'll pull it loose again." Hank yawned, blowing hot dog breath into Louis' face. "Ugh." The boy waved the stench away. "Don't be gross. Here," he scooted the bowl closer to the dog and upended the water bottle into it. "Drink the last of this and we'll be on the road again." Hank quickly lapped up the water, licking the bowl clean of any leftover droplets. Louis stashed the bowl and the bottle in one of his backpack's many zippers. "On the road again …" Louis sang to the dog as they stood, ad-libbing the lyrics he couldn't remember. "Something something, making friends again…" Louis leaned down to pick his bike helmet with the solar panel duct-taped on top up off the ground. "La la la la, do do dee dee deedle…" He swung his backpack onto his shoulders, grabbed the cord leading to his laptop inside, and plugged it into his helmet. Once the helmet was securely fastened on his head, he picked his bike up off the ground, mounted it, and pushed off on the pedals. "I just can't wait to get on the road again!"

*

Darkness. Louis opened his eyes. More darkness. He blinked and raised his hands to rub his eyes. I can move, *he thought. "I'm not para-!" A dry cough cut off his jubilant cry. He hacked and retched to one side, throat feeling like sandpaper. He swallowed hard multiple times to try and generate saliva in his mouth, to little success. He struggled to sit up, joints popping with every movement. As he reached up to stretch his aching arms, something tugged painfully at the back of his hand. He touched the spot on his hand and felt a tube sticking out of it. "Am I in a hospital?" He wondered out loud. He reached out to one side and felt a metal rail running along the bed – no, the gurney. "H-hello? Nurse? Or, er, somebody?" No response. Wherever he was, it was completely silent, standing his hair on end. Louis carefully un-taped the tube from his skin and slid the needle gently out of his hand, gagging at the sensation. He swung his socked feet off of the gurney and shakily stood, grabbing at the rail as his knees buckled. The socks had rubber grips on the bottom, making is a little easier to keep from falling to the tile. The paper gown he wore crinkled as he slowly moved one leg in front of the other, leaning on the gurney for support. When he reached the end, he ran into a curtain. Brushing the curtain back revealed yet more darkness, setting off an alarm in his head. "Am I blind?" He rubbed his eyes hard and tiny lights danced across his closed eyelids. He followed the edge of the curtain on tiptoe, searching for a wall with a light switch. Suddenly, something cold and metal hit his hip. He ran his hands over it, touching cloth and the edge of a pillow. Another gurney. He reached to push it away, and touched something cold and leathery. He ran he hand over it lightly, and grasped a nose. He gagged and recoiled, stumbling backwards into the curtain. He tripped over something on the ground and landed square on his backside. "Oh god oh god oh god oh god oh god," he gasped to himself, shaking the hand that touched the corpse.* Was that a corpse, *his brain asked,* or was that a sleeping axe murderer? *Louis froze, heart pounding loudly in his ears.* Was that some sort of living dead that you just woke up? Did you touch the face of a cannibal mutant zombie? *The thoughts came rapidly as terror began to seep into every corner of his body.* Are they watching you with their night vision goggles? Are they waiting for you to run so they can chase you? Are they slowly closing in right now, ready to tear into your flesh with their razor-sharp claws? *Louis curled into a ball and protected the back of his neck with his hands. He tried not to whimper as images of things that might be lurking in the dark flooded his head. "I gotta get out of here," he whimpered to the ground, "I gotta get out of here."*

*

Suddenly, two gunshots in rapid succession sounded nearby. Louis immediately threw on the brakes and looked toward the woods up ahead. He could just make out movement in the distance. Hank stared, ears twitching. Another shot rang out through the trees, closer than before, followed by two more. Louis quickly wheeled his bike off the road into the tall grass lining the ditch on the other side and crouched low in the grass. Hank stood stoically on the road, still staring toward the source of the gunshot. Louis clicked his tongue and whisper-called for the dog. He didn't budge.

"Hank! Get over here!" Louis hissed, taking off his helmet and backpack and laying out flat on his stomach. The dog glanced back at him, then to the woods. Louis ducked his head down and watched the trees. A boy and girl looking to be a few years younger than Louis emerged from the woods. The boy was toting a rifle almost as big as himself, and the girl swung a dead rabbit in either hand.

"We got 'em, we got 'em," the boy giggled, doing a small victory dance. He had what appeared to be blood smeared on his camouflage pants, as well as his tan ballcap.

"Tolja I was a good shot," the girl smirked, stepping carefully over a branch blocking her path. Her brown hair was in two messy braids, and a large knife hung from her belt. A strap across her chest held something tied to her back, but Louis couldn't tell what it was from his angle. He glanced at Hank, who seemed to be assessing if they were friend or foe.

"Yeah, right," the boy snorted. He kicked something out of his way as he stepped up onto the asphalt. "You barely even wounded that one."

"Only because I wanted to finish it off proper," the girl retorted, waving one of the rabbits in his face. The boy smacked it out of his face, knocking it from her hand. "Hey!" She exclaimed as the rabbit bounced onto the road. Hank suddenly took a couple steps toward the rabbit and snorted, catching the pair's eye.

"Ey!" The boy raised the rifle to his shoulder, pointing it at Hank.

"Don't shoot!" Louis yelled. He stood, hands flying up when the boy turned his gun on him.

"You a zombie?!" The boy took a step forward, gun still pointing at Louis.

"Where?" Louis shrieked, spinning to look behind him.

"Put it down, Gunner!" The girl screamed, pushing the barrel away and toward the ground as Louis spun back to face them. "Zombies. Can't. Talk," she said, over-emphasizing each word.

He glared at her. "I knew that! I was just making sure." The girl quickly leaned down and grabbed the rabbit off the ground, shoving its hind leg into her belt. The boy, Gunner, turned his glare to Louis. "That your dog?"

"No- I mean, yes!" Louis said quickly.

"Is he or ain't he?" The boy asked, moving back as Hank took another step forward.

"Well, technically I'm watching him for a friend but I don't know if that friend is alive or not and if she is I don't know where she is so I guess he's mine for now," Louis sputtered.

"Call him off," the girl said as Hank moved closer.

Louis licked his dry lips and whistled to the dog, clapping his hands. "Come here, Hank. Here, Hankie-Hankie, let's leave these nice people alone." Hank turned and walked back to Louis, who forced a smile. "Well, we'll just be on our way-"

"Wait," Gunner said quietly to the girl. "What if he's got something we want?"

The girl looked at Louis. "Hey! You got any supplies?"

Louis spoke quickly. "No. I haven't had a chance to get any." He swallowed hard, trying to keep from looking at the tall grass where his backpack was stashed.

The girl turned her back to Louis, revealing a sawed-off shotgun strapped to her back. She stuffed the other rabbit's leg into her belt and put her hands on her hips. "He said he don't."

"I know that, Sissa! I got ears," the boy hissed, giving her a pointed look. He glanced back at Louis. "What if he's lying?" They looked at one another for a moment, then simultaneously turned their heads toward Louis. Sissa swung the shotgun from behind her as Gunner raised his rifle back to Louis. Louis stiffened and shot his hands back up, heart pounding in his ears.

Chapter Twenty-Two

"Happy birthday, dear Abigail, happy birthday to you!" Adam leaned his daughter close to the two candles and helped her blow them out. The girl smiled widely, her pearly baby teeth on full display. Her light brown eyes sparkled as she looked around, searching for someone. She wriggled out of her dad's lap and toddled off, almost bumping into her mother; Marianne smiled down at her daughter and went to cut the cake into pieces.

Abby stopped in front of Ira and held her chubby arms up toward him. "Up, Papaw, up!"

Ira smiled down at the girl and scooped her up, careful not to wrinkle her yellow party dress. "Why hello there, Little Lady," he crooned, setting her on his knee. "Look how big you are now! You're almost a grownup."

Marianne looked up from cutting the cake and said with a smile, "She'll be driving before you know it!"

Ira laughed and shook his head. "You'll have to help her with that one, I've never been good at teaching kids how to drive."

"Oh, I remember," Marianne replied, setting a piece of cake on the table next to her father, "That was the one skill Mama taught us better than you, and she never let us forget it." She laughed, throwing her head back along with Ira.

Abby laughed with them, unaware of what she was laughing at, and clapped her hands. She reached up to pat her grandfather's beard with her tiny hands. "Love Papaw."

"And Papaw loves you too," Ira beamed, hugging her to him.

Suddenly, the girl disappeared from his arms and the chair dissolved, dropping him on the ground with a thud. He sat up slowly, surprised to find himself in the middle of a jungle instead of at his family's home as he was moments prior. Ira's confusion turned to horror as he heard Abby scream from nearby; he scrambled to his feet and ran toward the sound, tearing through the thickets and jumping over ditches. He crested a small hill and tripped, sprawling down it and rolling to a stop in a puddle.

"Help me, please," a young man's voice choked out nearby, and Ira rolled over to find himself under a mangrove tree. Adrenaline and the helmet strap around his neck made it difficult to breathe as he searched for the voice. An explosion boomed up ahead, and he ducked down, clutching his medical bag to his chest. Ira crawled forward until he found the man, hidden under some elephant grass. Ira raised up onto his knees to assess the man's injuries, keeping his face blank as his eyes swept over the bloodied spots leaking from his flak jacket.

"They fragged me, Doc," the injured man coughed out, his face contorting in pain. He clawed at the flak jacket. "I thought these was s'pposed to keep that shit out."

Ira shushed the man and ripped the man's vest open. You got fragged alright, *Ira thought as he set to work,* but they shot you, too.

"Am I gonna die?" The man's blue eyes were wrought with fear as a tear leaked out, streaking the dirt caked on his face. This was no man; this was a scared boy who shouldn't be here. He grimaced as Ira pressed on the wound, biting his lip almost in two to keep from crying out. Gunfire rang out, and Ira dropped over the boy as the ftt-ftt *of bullets whizzing past assaulted his ears. When he pulled back, his face contorted in horror as he looked into the now familiar brown eyes.*

"Dad," Marcus begged, "Help me, please." Ira fell backwards, away from his son's bloodied tan DCU fatigues.

"Marcus, no," Ira managed, looking into his terrified face. Suddenly, Marcus was twelve years old again, playing dress-up in his dad's combat boots.

"Daddy, I'm scared," the boy said with a sob, his too-big tan helmet sitting crooked on his matted head.

Ira scooped him up, sitting on the wet jungle floor as indistinguishable voices sounded in the distance. "I know you are, Son, I know." Ira's voice cracked.

"Why won't you help me?"

"I wish I could, Son," Ira's vision blurred as he rocked back and forth, Marcus' small frame going limp in his arms.

Suddenly, the boy disappeared and Ira was on his feet in a different part of the jungle. Abby's screams sounded again, echoing all around him and making him spin frantically to try and discern the source.

"Go, go!" A fellow soldier barreled past Ira, almost knocking him to the ground. Ira pulled his pistol and ran. He jumped over a ravine and tore through the underbrush, ducking and weaving as gunfire exploded from somewhere nearby. Wish the LT had let me keep that rifle, *he thought.* "Non-combatant" my ass.

An explosion knocked him off his feet, throwing him to the side into a tree. He crumpled to the ground as a blinding pain surged through his upper leg, hip, and side. Abigail screamed again, and Ira clawed toward the sound, crying out in agony as the shrapnel shifted in his flesh. The ground suddenly raised and he began to slide backwards. He looked over his shoulder and cried out again, this time in terror as he felt himself being sucked into a swirling black hole that opened up in the jungle floor. He let out one final scream as the hole swallowed him, enveloping him in darkness.

Ira sat up, drenched in sweat. His heart pounded nearly out of his chest as he spun around in the darkness, the bedsheets tangling on his legs. His hip burned, and he reached out to fumble for the flashlight on his bedside table. Switching it on, he yanked open the drawer and pulled out his pain medicine; he dry-swallowed two, not bothering with water. He glared angrily at his bad leg and sat up further in the bed.

"If you're going to keep doing this to me," he said aloud, voice shaking, "Then I'm just not going to sleep."

He threw the covers off himself and swung his legs over the side of the bed, grimacing as fire shot through his hip down his leg. Seizing his cane, he gingerly pushed himself to his feet, whimpering uncontrollably at the pain. "Don't be a child!" He yelled to the darkness, gritting his teeth and slamming his cane into the ground. He grabbed his flashlight and slowly moved for the door.

Chapter Twenty-Three

Eric's hand shook as he sipped the apple juice, spilling some down his chin. He wiped it off and set the glass down on the tiny nurse's desk. The small clinic wasn't much to look at, but it had burn ointment and pamphlets on smoke inhalation, which was good enough. He cleared his throat and took another drink to try and stabilize his blood sugar. As he put the glass down, his flashlight fell over and rolled toward the edge of the counter. He grabbed it and propped it up against a framed picture on the desk of a man and dog. Gina went into another coughing fit, and he shakily stood to hobble over to her. She was doubled over in a chair, grasping an oxygen mask in one hand and clutching the armrest with the other as the hacking wracked her body. She slowly sat back up, singed hair falling over her right eye. She looked up at Eric, dark circles and the ointment-covered burns punctuating her face. Her left eyebrow was virtually gone and the largest burn extended past her swollen eye, almost to her chin. Welts where the branch hit her face stood out in sharp relief.

"Shaky?" She wheezed, putting the mask back on.

"A bit," he replied, clearing his throat. "But I think I'm leveling out now. How are you feeling?"

"Fine," she said, her voice muffled by the mask. She grimaced slightly as she tried to suppress a cough. She reached up and gently moved her hair out of her face. The welts lined up for a moment. Just looking at the raw skin made Eric wince, but she pretended not to notice.

"Your burns are looking better," he offered. "And the swelling has gone down on your eye considerably since yesterday." Gina didn't reply. Eric looked at the small tube of antibiotic ointment resting at her feet. "Are we out of burn cream?" Gina nodded affirmative.

"I'll go see what I can find," Eric said, pivoting slowly. Stiffly, he picked up his flashlight.

"No rush," Gina replied, the last word ending abruptly as another coughing fit overtook her.

Eric left the room and soon found the supply closet. He rummaged through its contents until he found a basket of various antibiotic and burn ointments. He grabbed the basket and headed back, his stomach growling loudly. *Never a break...* Sighing to no one in particular, he headed toward the lobby to raid the vending machine.

As he opened the door to the lobby, he stopped abruptly. Standing in the midst of machine's shattered glass and flanked by candy wrappers, was a small figure with matted hair. The child turned around and stared at Eric with wild yellow eyes, chocolate smeared across its face and down the front of its filthy tan t-shirt. Eric couldn't tell if the child was a boy or a girl, but he cared less about its gender and more about the sharp garden trowel it clutched in one hand. On the floor beside the child's dirty, sandaled feet was a hammer.

"Hello," Eric said softly, trying to be calm and soothing. The child said nothing, bloodshot eyes unblinking. "I'm Eric, what's your name?" No response. "Are you hungry?" Eric took a small step forward as he spoke. The door's stopper suddenly fell down, catching Eric's eye. The child shrieked suddenly and flew at him, wielding the trowel like a weapon. Eric cried out and jumped behind a row of plastic chairs, ducking as the child swung at him. "Stop! Hey!" Eric yelled, picking up a chair and brandishing it like a lion tamer. "Calm down!" The child shrieked again and dove under the chair and stabbed at Eric's legs; Eric jumped back again with a yelp, slamming the chair down onto the child and knocking it onto its stomach. Eric vaulted over the chair as the child screamed and thrashed, and bolted back through the doorway. The screams echoed down the hall as Eric ran; he slipped on the tile as he rounded the corner to where the nurse's station was. He looked over his shoulder just as Gina appeared in the doorway. He collided with her shoulder and fell to the floor, the wind leaving his lungs with a *whoosh*.

"What-" Gina began, stumbling back slightly. The shrieks of the feral child suddenly amplified, and Gina looked up to see it barreling down the hall toward them. Fear washed over her, and she grabbed Eric's wrists and dragged him into an open storage room. She slammed the door behind them, muffling the shrieks. She locked and leaned against the door as the child hit the door over and over with its trowel. Gina began to cough harshly and Eric slapped the ground, trying desperately to force oxygen into his lungs. She leaned over and hooked her fingers into his belt loops, jerking upwards. Eric gasped, huffing and hacking as the air rushed into him.

"What was that?" Gina asked incredulously. "What did you do?"

"I didn't do anything," Eric gasped, sitting up and putting his back against the wall. Outside the slaps and screams of the child continued with ferocity. The door handle rattled, and Gina grabbed it and pulled with all of her might to keep it closed.

"Go away!" Gina wheezed. The banging against the door stopped, and the child let out a long, loud scream, more terrifying than any of the others combined. Everything went silent and Gina and Eric listened intently.

Eric got to his feet and moved closer to the door. "Is it gone?"

Gina didn't respond. She unlocked the door, and slowly, gently eased it open. The trowel suddenly appeared through the doorway almost cutting Gina's face. Gina pulled the door, catching the child's fingers as she tried to shut it. The child screamed and dropped the trowel. Gina locked the door once more, turning to face Eric.

"We need a plan." Gina looked around the room and spotted a box of trash bags. "Grab one of those."

Gina kicked to the trowel out-of-the-way and grabbed the door handle. "Ready?" She whispered, adjusting her grip on the mop and bucket. Eric nodded silently, holding the triple-strength hazmat trash bag open wide. "Okay. Here we go." Gina turn the lock slowly, to minimize sound. When the knob was unlocked, she grasped it firmly and threw the door open wide. The hallway was empty. The hair on the back of Gina's neck stood up as she scanned the darkened room. Eric stepped out as well, brandishing the bag like a shield. Gina gripped the bucket tightly in one hand and pointed the mop out in front of her. Suddenly, a loud shriek sounded from down the hall. The feral child ran at them, barely giving Gina enough time to spin and use the mop to keep her at bay. The child jabbed a hammer at them, and Gina swung the bucket around; the bucket collided with the child's head. "Now!" Gina cried. Eric leapt forward clumsily, throwing the bag over its head and shoulders. He pulled the bag down over its elbows and tied the drawstring tightly around the thrashing child. Gina grabbed the hammer and wrenched it from the child's grip. The child reached up and tried to rip the bag from its face, wildly thrashing on the ground. Gina was kicked twice in the stomach as she tried to seize the child's feet to keep it from getting hurt. The child flipped onto its stomach to try and crawl away. Gina held its feet firm and Eric grabbed the shoulders as well as he could. The pair drug the child into the nearest examination room and slammed the door shut.

Eric grabbed the doorknob and pulled it tightly, giving Gina enough time to wedge the broom up into the door handle and on either side of the door frame to hold it shut. Screams and a lot of bumping around echoed from inside the room as Gina and Eric caught their breath.

"What do we do now?" Eric breathed. "We can't just leave that kid in here." Gina was silent. "I mean… Right?" Eric studied Gina closely as she panted. Gina took a step back from the door, then another. She turned on her heel and headed back for the nurse's station, coughing. She sat down hard and one of the rolling chairs behind the desk. Eric followed, watching intently as she gathered supplies back into her duffel. "That's a human being," Eric stated bluntly. Gina remained silent, putting the oxygen mask back over her face and turning the valve to on. She coughed some more intermittently, trying to get her breath back. "Gina," Eric began. "What are we-"

"Nothing," came the girls muffled reply. "Too dangerous."

"We can't just leave," Eric repeated incredulously. Gina suddenly removed the mask from her face and looked at Eric.

"What do you want me to say? It's crazy. It tried to kill us."

"So you want us to just leave that kid trapped?"

"I don't think there's anything else that we can do."

"They'll starve to death."

Gina remained silent, putting the mask over her nose and mouth again. The feral child's shrieks punctuated the silence.

"If we let it out," Gina said slowly, taking the mask from her face once more. "It could attack someone else. If there is anyone else out there."

"But if we leave them locked up, we will be murderers."

"If we let it out, we can't outrun it. Not in our conditions." Gina turned off the oxygen tank and put it into her duffel bag. "It's just too fast."

"So what do you want to do?"

"I don't know." Gina stood up and picked her duffel bag off the floor. "I don't want to make the decision." Eric rubbed his forehead, and looked back down the hall to where the broom smacked against the wall every time the feral child pulled the handle.

Gina and Eric hiked up the side of a mountain, the air tense and the ground unsteady. Gina fixed her eyes on the trail ahead, but noticed Eric looking nervously at her out of the corner of her eye.

"Gina…"

"I don't want to talk about it." Gina snapped.

"Okay…" Eric wiped his brow and stared at his hands. "Um…"

170

"What?" A hint of annoyance could be heard in her voice. Gina's eyes were weary, and her joints ached painfully. *Just get me out of here...* She thought to herself.

"We should probably find a place to sleep for the night tonight don't you think?"

Gina remained silent.

"It's just it's getting late," Eric continued, "And we don't want to be stranded out here with nowhere to go and-"

Up in the distance Gina spotted an abandoned carnival. "There," she said pointing to carnival grounds. "I want to go there."

"Oh, okay," Eric said, standing up straighter. " They probably have a generator there, and we can salvage it and take it with us back home, wherever that is."

Gina's chest tightened. *Home.* The word made her queasy. "Yeah, okay," she responded unenthusiastically.

"Gina? Are you…are you alright?"

"Yeah, let's just keep moving."

Chapter Twenty-Four

Fly, TN

Millie knocked on Zach's door and leaned against the wall outside. She glanced down the hall and crossed her arms, drumming her fingers before un-crossing her arms again.

Zach opened the door and stepped out, greeting her with a yawn. "Hey." He shut the door behind him, catching the look on her face. "What's wrong?"

"I want to leave." She blurted.

"Huh?" Zach frowned in confusion. "But you were just saying how much you like it here."

"Yeah, well that was before somebody tried to bust into my room last night."

"What?" He followed her second glance down the hallway.

"Something woke me up a little last night, and when I opened my eyes, there was a shadow on the wall. I saw movement in my mirror, there was definitely someone standing there."

"And you're sure it wasn't a nightmare?"

"Oh, come ON." Millie scoffed. "Like I would really dream up something like that!"

"You know that's not what I meant," Zach sighed, "I just...you said it yourself, overheating can mess with your head. Yesterday you saw someone who wasn't there, remember? I was just checking to be sure."

Millie re-crossed her arms tightly. "I know what I saw."

"Okay," Zach nodded slowly, "I believe you."

"I think..." Millie swallowed hard. "I think it was Drake."

"Really." Zach stood up straighter, teeth clenching.

"I think so."

"You think so?" His eyebrows furrowed as his eyes burned into hers.

"I mean...I wasn't fully awake, so I'm not positive it was him, but he's got access to the copies of everyone's room keys. And he's just..." She paused, searching for the words. "He's creepy, okay? He's been really weird this whole time and I get a bad feeling about him."

"That's a pretty serious accusation, Mil," Zach cautioned, folding his arms. "I'm going to need more than 'I think he's creepy' as proof before I start kicking asses."

"I'm not asking you to do that," she said exasperatedly. "I'm just asking you to believe me when I say I don't want to be here anymore. When did you become such a skeptic?"

"Listen," he said, holding his hands up, "I believe that you saw someone. Have you considered that it might have been Cleo or one of the girls just checking in on you?"

"I…" she faltered, stopping. "No."

"I don't think we should jump to conclusions about who it was based on just a shadow. Anyone could have gotten to those keys, they're not exactly in Fort Knox."

"I'm not crazy," Millie said, lifting her chin.

"I'm not saying you are…I just think we should do some more digging before we jump to conclusions and potentially mess this up. We've got a good thing going here."

"How good could it possibly be if I don't feel safe in my own bed?"

Zach's walkie-talkie beeped, and an unmistakably smooth voice came on over the speaker. *"Zach, you around?"* Zach let out a huff of air and unclipped the radio from his belt.

"Are you seriously going to answer that right now?"

"Two seconds." Zach lifted the radio to his mouth and pressed the "talk" button. "I'm here. G'head, Drake."

"Could you grab a toolbox and meet me outside the Warehouse? It looks like maintenance day is getting a jump-start; we've somehow gotten a flat tire."

Zach hesitated a moment, glancing at Millie. "Uh, yeah. I'll be there in a second." Millie's eyes narrowed slightly as he clipped the walkie-talkie back onto his belt. "I know you think you want to leave-"

"I don't think," she snapped, "I *know*."

"Sorry. I know that you want to leave, but maybe we should just see how today goes and pick this up later? See how you feel about it this evening?"

Millie looked away from him. "Sure."

"Thanks." Zach stood awkwardly for a moment before turning and walking away

"'Kay." Millie nodded curtly, dropped her arms, and pivoted, walking quickly back down the hall before Zach could say anything else.

Zach's mind wandered as he unscrewed another lug nut on the rear right tire. Drake and Wyatt talked about something, but Zach was too focused to really hear any of it. He didn't doubt that Millie saw the shadow of someone in her doorway, but he just couldn't see Drake doing something like that. *He's weird, but I don't think he's the sparkly watch-you-while-you-sleep kinda weird*, he thought.

"What do you think, Zach?"

Zach looked up at Drake, who held the toolbox at the ready. "Huh?"

"Is it worth trying to fix?"

Zach looked back at the tire. "Oh. Uh, yeah, I guess. It's still got a fair amount of tread. If there's an automotive shop around we could find a tire patch kit and rig it up. Blow it up with air and listen for the hiss to find the hole."

"Good idea! I'd appreciate if you'd head that up."

"Sure." Zach went back to working on the tire, and soon wrenched the last lug nut off. Wyatt grabbed the tire and pulled it off, with Zach guiding it to the ground. Zach stood and dropped the wrench into the toolbox that Drake held.

"If you wouldn't mind taking Xavier and starting on the doors on the south side of the motel, I'll assist Zach with the tire," Drake told Wyatt. Wyatt looked at him, then Zach, then turned without a word toward the center of town. Zach raised an eyebrow and grabbed the tire, hoisting it off the ground. They walked in silence for a moment, Zach still mulling over what Millie had told him.

"I'm very glad that you both decided to stay," Drake said, the toolbox jostling slightly. "You and Millie are such great assets to the town."

"Thanks," Zach replied, adjusting the tire in his arms.

"Millie's medical knowledge and desire to learn more about it will come in handy, and I believe that you're just the guy to help shape the future of Fly." Drake smiled.

"Yeah?"

"Yes! The way you took charge when Millie had her episode was very impressive." They passed the library, and Drake turned down a road that Zach hadn't been down before. "This is a very exciting time for our generation," Drake continued. "While it's unfortunate that so many were lost to the Great Disaster, those of us who are left have the opportunity to build a better society than we had before."

"True," Zach replied, intrigued. "Everything's a blank slate, now."

"Think about it…we're entering a new age of humanity. We are pioneers, the new Founding Fathers, if you will. We have an opportunity that hasn't been afforded to us in hundreds of years; we get to shape the future, come up with our own system of government, and found our new society on the best principles and practices of history."

"Like what?"

Drake grinned. "Historically, things have always progressed in a certain manner: men and women each have strengths specific to their gender's wiring that should be encouraged, as well as personal strengths. There's a reason that humanity has followed the same general path that has succeeded for thousands of years!" Drake beamed. They rounded another street corner, and reached the auto shop next to the car wash. "Historically, communities have revolved around the idea of family. Yes, it's a well-known cliché that the men provide and protect while the women keep the home and bear children, but it goes beyond that." Drake held the door to the shop open for Zach to walk through. "Take, for example, a wolf pack. The alpha males are the leaders, protectors. They provide for their pack and protect their family from those that would do them harm. They fight to achieve that rank and hold it, and are rewarded thusly. Any male that can't handle those responsibilities or can't hold their own in a battle are beta males, and they essentially will do whatever the alphas tell them to do. Alpha females are the mates of the alpha males, and serve as the leader of the other females who maintains order amongst them."

"Yeah, but people are more sophisticated than wolves." Zach scoured the shelf in front of him, looking for a patch kit. Finding one, he turned and headed back for the front door with Drake in tow.

"True, true," Drake admitted, getting the door for Zach again. "Modern humanity had shaken off most of its animalistic instinct, but the society that supported that model is gone now. We must revert to what has kept the human race going for as long as it has."

Zach knelt beside the air tank, noting that it still had a fair amount of air inside. Drake leaned against the air pump, gazing off into the distance as Zach attached the air hose.

"Consider the hierarchy of the middle ages," Drake continued, "Or of the Vikings. There were three distinct socio-economical classes that were essentially the royalty, the middle class, and the servants. The word 'royalty' carries a negative connotation in America, but it's how humanity was governed for thousands of years across the world." Zach ran his hand over the tire, searching for the hole as Drake talked. "I've always thought that there is a middle ground somewhere between monarchy and democracy that, if found, could be the best move for humanity. As it stands, I lean more toward monarchy simply because in a small society, there is far too much opportunity for a standstill to occur." Zach remained silent, leaning his ear closer to the tire. "Like I said before, history doesn't lie; the best way for us to get the world back to where it needs to be is to embrace our wiring and rebuild using our strengths. The alpha men must lead, the women must bear children and run the home, and those who aren't fit to do either of those things – namely the disabled and mentally or physically weak – must be used elsewhere. I know that sounds harsh, but we must do what's best for humanity going forward."

"Ah," Zach said slowly, finding the hole in the tire. He put his finger on it and reached for the patch kit. "And that's something that everyone here believes?"

"Some find my views to be a bit extreme and are hesitant to switch from the old way, but they can be persuaded," Drake said serenely. "With time, they'll see that my model for the future is a solid one and will guarantee the livelihood of generations to come."

Zach nodded slowly and peeled open the tire patch. He applied it in silence, focusing intently on what he was doing.

"Women only have approximately three decades of fertility," Drake said bluntly, "And that's in the best of times. We also must realize that the rate of infant and mother mortality has just drastically risen with the fall of civilization and disappearance of modern medicine – which again, Millie's medical knowledge and continued research will help with. All that to say: with all factors considered, humanity needs to get a jumpstart on procreating."

Zach didn't respond, choosing to inspect the tire closely instead.

Drake paused a moment. "Are you planning on pursuing Millie?"

Zach stopped and looked up at him. "Why?"

"Why pursue her or why do I ask?"

"Why are you asking?" Zach attached the hose, filling the tire back up with air.

"While I hesitate to possibly endanger the only medically-inclined personnel in our town, she is a female of prime childbearing age."

Zach popped the hose off the tire and attached the cap, raising up to his full height. "What are you getting at, Drake?"

"I was merely probing to see if you had intentions to pursue her," Drake replied, looking slightly up at Zach. "As I've said, your children would be of good stock. But then, with her brains, she might be a good fit for either of the others in town or anyone else who comes to join us."

Zach's jaw tensed slightly. "Nah." He bent down to pick up the tire. "She's a pain in the ass, no other guy would be able to put up with her bad habits."

"So you're considering it, then?" Drake raised his eyebrows. "Or at least, the idea isn't off the table.

Zach shrugged. "Maybe." He turned away to head back toward the warehouse.

Millie dug at her beans and rice, the supper choice of the day. Caprie babbled to Kathryn about planning a day trip to the outlet on the other side of the town, ignoring Millie entirely. The door suddenly opened, and Zach stepped in, uncharacteristically late. Millie looked up and caught his eye. He started forward, but Drake called him from the front of the table. Zach stopped moving and talked with him for a moment before Drake gestured for him to sit down, leaning in intently like the conversation was something serious. Zach glanced at Millie, and sat anyway. She rolled her eyes and went back to digging at her food.

She glanced up as Wyatt returned from the bathroom. He habitually moved to toward his seat next to Drake, stopping short when he saw Zach there. "Hey, man," he said, "That's my seat."

"Oh, sorry-"

Drake held up a hand for Zach to stay put. "I asked him to sit here today, Wyatt," he said placidly. "We need to discuss some things. You wouldn't mind sitting at the end today, would you?"

Wyatt froze a moment. "I guess not." He moved slowly toward the seat next to Xavier.

After a moment, Zach finished his conversation with Drake and stood up again. Kathryn practically leapt from her seat, intercepting him before he could take more than three steps.

"Hey, there," she said, brushing her hair out of her face. "I was wondering, if you're not busy, do you think you could help me rearrange a few things in the kitchen?"

"Actually, I'm-"

"Oh, pretty please?" Kathryn clasped her hands together under her chin, batting her eyes in what could only be assumed was a flirtatious fashion. "It won't take but a minute. You don't even need your bad hand."

Millie stared at her food, stabbing a hunk of stuck-together rice.

Zach sighed. "Yeah, okay. What do you need moved?"

Kathryn grabbed his hand and pulled him into the kitchen, a confused look on his face.

Millie, having had enough, stood abruptly and grabbed her paper bowl, tossing it in the garbage on her way out of the diner.

Halfway across the motel parking lot, Zach caught up with her. "Mil, wait up!"

Millie stopped, and turned on her heel. "What."

Zach stopped short, taken aback by her sharpness. "Uh, how are you?"

"Fine." Millie looked across the lot to her right, purposely avoiding his gaze.

"Is that like an 'I'm okay' kinda 'fine' or an 'I'm pissed' kinda 'fine?'" He asked, half-jokingly.

"What do you want, Zach?" She crossed her arms and looked at the ground.

"…I just wanted to check in and see if your day went okay or not."

"It wasn't good, wasn't bad. It doesn't change the fact that I want to leave, though, if that's what you're wondering."

"That's actually what I wanted to-"

Zach's radio crackled loudly, cutting him off. *"Zach?"* A high-pitched voice sang out, *"It's me, Kathryn. Could you come back to the Diner for a minute? I need help with one last thing, please!"*

Millie smiled bitterly and took a step back. "Go on. Your fan club awaits."

"Mil, don't-"

Zaaaach? I know your radio is on, silly!"

"I don't want to be around these…people anymore." Millie said bluntly, still refusing to look at him. "There's literally nothing here for me."

"Nothing, huh?" Zach uttered, his voice betraying his hurt.

Millie squeezed her eyes shut. "I don't fit in here, and I never will. I'm leaving tomorrow, and you can come with me if you want or…" she paused. "Or you can stay. It's up to you."

Zach nodded slowly, looking to the ground as Millie spun on her heel and marched away from him for the second time that day.

Millie slammed the door to her room and locked it forcefully. She dragged the chair in front of the door and wedged it under the handle, kicking the door for good measure. She pulled the handle, satisfied that it wouldn't open. Kicking off her shoes, she jerked the curtains closed, submerging the room in darkness. She crossed to her bed and threw herself backwards onto it.

You're acting like a child, she heard her dad say. Suddenly she was five years old again and throwing a tantrum because she didn't want to go to sleep. "No," she said aloud, "*He's* acting like a child. *I'm* right about this."

Sometimes it takes a while for truth to sink in. Millie reached over and felt around on her nightstand for her wind-up light/radio. She turned the crank for a while, staring into the darkness. Was he really that obtuse? Could he really not see what was going on out there? She turned the light on dim and set it forcefully on her nightstand, accidentally pressing the "channel scan" button in the process. She sat up and brushed her hair out of her face as the soft hiss-click of the radio gently filled the room.

"Fine," she said, standing. "If he wants to be friends with those people, I'm not going to be a part of it." She stomped into the bathroom and shut the door.

Hissss...click...hissss...click... "...might put you in harm's way. If you're driving a motorcycle and have a wreck, even with the proper safety equipment you may die. Remember...it's a lot riskier to take chances now."

The hair on the back of Millie's neck stood on end as she stuck her head out of the bathroom door. A man. There was a man talking on the radio.

"There are no more ambulance teams and staffed hospitals to come to your aid if you get injured. Whatever you do, take it slow and easy-" Click...

She dove for the radio, snatching it from the table and pressing the "channel back" button.

"Secondly, if you cut or scratch yourself, stop immediately and clean the wound out."

"Oh, my God," Millie breathed, staring wide-eyed at the radio. She hadn't imagined it, there was a living, breathing person, on the radio.

"Carry iodine and a decent first aid kit with you. Stop in a book store, get a good first aid book, and read it."

Millie listened, enraptured. She lost track of time as the man spoke; his voice was soothing, and she felt her anger melt away as the broadcast continued.

"I've said this before, but in case you're just now tuning in or you missed it last time, you're not alone. You are NOT alone. Please hear me when I say that. You mustn't give up; there is always something to strive for, something to achieve. You have a purpose. You are important. As always, this is Ira at Radio Nowhere in Nowhere, Oklahoma. I broadcast from 8 pm Central time to 10 pm Central time every day. I hope that you have a restful night and a safe day tomorrow; I will talk to you tomorrow, friends."

Millie grabbed her shoes from the floor and pulled them on, all resentment and hurt from before dissipating instantly. "Zach has got to hear about this."

The argument he'd had with Millie still burned in Zach's mind by the time lights' out rolled around. The more he thought about what she had said, the more he began to get an uneasy feeling in the pit of his stomach. Drake's views were warped, the conversation they'd had proved that, but…

"No," he muttered, "There is no 'but.'" He sighed and rubbed his face with both hands. Tomorrow he'd talk to Millie about leaving, but for now he needed to sleep. He stood up and crossed to the dresser. As he started to unlatch his belt, there was a knock at the door. He shut the drawer and quickly went to open the door.

"Mil-" he started to say, but stopped. His line of sight dropped down from the empty space directly in front of him. "Oh, Kathryn. Hi."

"Hello, Zach," Kathryn said, looking up at him through her eyelashes. The dramatic eye shadow she wore matched her maroon lipstick almost perfectly. "Mind if I come in for a second?" Without waiting for an answer, she pushed past him into the room and dropped her purse on the floor.

"…I guess not." He said flatly, letting the door shut. "What's up?" When he turned around, Kathryn was only a foot away from him.

"I just wanted to talk about us," she said demurely.

"What?" His eyebrow shot up.

"I know, Zach. I know how you really feel about me." Kathryn moved closer, forcing Zach back against the door. "And it's okay, because I feel the same."

Zach stepped around her so that he was facing the door. "Ok, there's obviously been some miscommunication somewhere."

Kathryn turned and moved closer to him again, starting a dance around the room. "I know," she said, voice taking what could only be an attempt at a seductive tone. "That's why I'm here to clear it up."

Zach suddenly found himself trapped by the chair in the corner. "Ok, I think you'd better-"

Suddenly, she leapt at Zach, wrapping herself around him and kissing him. He tripped over the footstool and landed halfway on the chair, hitting his bad palm in an attempt to stop them both from ending up on the floor. He jerked his head to one side and leaned away as she planted maroon pockmarks all over his face.

"Let go-" he began, but was interrupted as she again latched onto his mouth. "Mmph!" Finally he was able to steady himself enough to grab hold of her arm and forcibly detach her.

"STOP IT," he snapped, pushing her away firmly.

She stumbled back, confused. "What?"

He stood up and wiped his mouth. "Kathryn, I'm sorry if I gave you any reason to think that I'm interested in you, because I'm not. At *all*."

"Oh..." She crossed her arms and bit her lip, eyes glued to the ground. Suddenly, she wasn't the confident teen that had marched into the room earlier; in the span of ten seconds she'd turned into an ashamed little girl. "I'm sorry, I shouldn't have done that." Her voice cracked, cutting off the last word. She turned her back to Zach. "I thought…I mean Drake said…"

Zach stared, unsure what to do. Suddenly, Kathryn uncrossed her arms, wiped her eyes, and adjusted her posturing. She went straight to the door and spun on her heel to face Zach.

"You'll regret this one day when Millie turns into a boring nag," she said with a sniff, grabbing the doorknob behind her. "But until then…have a good life."

Millie rounded the corner of the hallway, clutching the radio to her chest. *Maybe he can figure out how to make this one transmit,* she thought excitedly. *We can find out exactly where this Ira lives, and see if he has a community. Anything would be better than here, and surely Zach would want to go if he knew there was another option.* As she approached Zach's room, she heard muffled voices coming from inside. She stopped short about ten feet from the door, still hidden in the shadow. Suddenly, the door flew open and Kathryn appeared, shutting the door behind her. Millie's chest constricted as she took in the girl's jostled appearance. Kathryn sauntered down the hall, jumping slightly as she suddenly noticed Millie.

"He's all yours," she said flatly, wiping the lipstick from her mouth.

Zach's door opened, bathing them in light. "Kathryn, you forgot your-" he stopped, eyes widening when he saw Millie. He held Kathryn's purse in one hand, and she took a few steps back to grab it. She spun on her heel and clicked down the hall, leaving Millie and Zach frozen in the light.

"Mil, she just-" Zach began.

"You don't owe me an explanation," Millie cut him off, her voice tight. "Goodnight." She turned to leave and Zach moved closer, catching her arm.

"Please don't-"

"Let. Me. Go," Millie said, low and steady.

"Just let me expl-"

"Let me go!" Her voice cracked on the last word as she jerked free of his grip. "Stay the *hell* away from me."

Zach watched helplessly as she stormed off before he could say anything else. "…shit."

Chapter Twenty-Five

Louisiana

Louis's hand slammed into a wall for what seemed to be the thousandth time. He took a step back, making a note on the hazy mental map he'd made of the building. How long had it been? Hours? Days? He'd given up on time when he gave up on finding a flashlight. Louis felt his way along the corridor, hands shakily feeling the walls. His outstretched fingers brushed a doorway. He grasped for a door handle, turning it with ease. Could this be it? Or just another storage closet or bathroom containing a corpse? The door swung inwardly with little resistance. The boy slid his no-slip-socked foot out in front of him and eased forward, feeling for anything that might trip him again. His toes brushed a smooth wall, and he reached out in front of him to run his hands along it. His fingers swiped empty air where the wall should have been. "What?" He carefully raised his foot up, running it along the wall. It leveled off sharply. "Stairs," he whispered giddily to himself, letting go of the door behind him. It swung shut, closing loudly.

Louis clutched the railing as he carefully climbed the steps, only a little afraid that he'd run into a dead body. Or a psychopathic murderer who killed all the people in the hospital and cut the power, *he thought.* "Shut up," *he whispered, moving faster up the stairwell. The stairs stopped suddenly, and Louis felt along the wall to see if there was a –* "Door!" *He yelled. The sudden echo of his voice startled him, and he froze for a moment, listening intently to the silence. He felt for a doorknob, and tried it. Locked.* "No," *he moaned, trying the knob again. He pulled at the door, leaning his full weight into it. It didn't budge. A sudden realization hit, and Louis moved quickly back down the stairs to the other door. He felt for and twisted the doorknob. Nothing.* "No!" *Louis pulled with all his might, twisting his body every which way to try and pry it open.* You're trapped, *his brain hissed,* you're going to die in this stairwell.

*

Sissa jabbed Louis in the back with the end of her rifle, making him lurch forward. "You sure it's up here?"

"Yes, I'm positive," Louis replied, hands level with his ears as they walked down the road. He could still hear Hank barking at them from the tree Gunner made Louis tie him to a while back.

"This is gonna be great," Gunner said, glancing behind them. "An armored truck! Nobody can touch us with that."

"Hell yeah!" Sissa said, smirking. "We got a fortress, ain't no way they're getting in without us knowing."

"Only thing left is to dig that moat."

Sissa jabbed Louis in the back again. "Hey, you any good with a shovel?"

"Um, I think so-" Louis replied, "-I mean, yes! Yes I am."

"You sure do change your mind a lot," Gunner said. He leaned in to whisper in Sissa's ear, unintentionally loud enough for Louis to hear. "He'll be good a distraction when the zombies come."

Louis glanced over his shoulder at them. "Zombies?"

"Was I talking to you?" Gunner jabbed Louis in the back once again.

"No...I mean...no." Louis faced forward again, taking a deep breath. Looking into the distance, he could just make out the shape of the truck a hundred or so yards away. "I just heard you say zombie again, and it made me remember that cemetery I passed a while back."

"What?" Sissa asked.

Louis paused a moment for dramatic effect. "I mean...the ground sure was torn up..." Sissa nudged him again to speed up his walking. "...and that mausoleum looked almost like it had been broken apart from the inside out..."

Gunner grabbed Louis's shoulder, spinning him to face them. "What're you saying?"

"I don't know, it just got me to thinking, maybe *The Hungry Dead* wasn't just a movie after all..."

Gunner and Sissa exchanged a wide-eyed look.

Louis continued, injecting fear into his voice. "...maybe the dead really have risen."

"Go," Gunner shoved Louis forward, "Take us to the truck *now*."

Louis sprinted ahead, smiling to himself as he heard them close on his heels.

*

He sat in the corner of the top of the stairwell, knees drawn up to his chest. "No way out," he whispered to himself, "No way out." He thought of his parents, his dogs, his friends. Never going to see them again, *he thought,* never going to get out of here. *He thought back to the bus. Gina. She'd tried to save him. Louis stood slowly, sliding himself up the wall.* I owe it to myself to try again. I owe it to her to try again. *Resolved, he turned to descend the steps once more.*

*

As they rapidly approached the truck, Louis huffed and puffed to stay ahead of his captors. He slowed, raising an outstretched finger to point at the giant goat's head painted on the side of the truck. "There," he wheezed, slowing to catch his breath as Gunner blew past him.

Sissa grabbed Louis by the arm and drug him with her toward the truck. "Come on, we still need you to dig!"

When they reached the back of the truck, Gunner began to pull frantically at the door handle. "It's locked," he said exasperatedly.

"Well duh, it wouldn't be a good armored truck if it was just open," Sissa retorted.

"Go see if one of the doors is unlocked or something," Gunner snapped, tugging at the door handle some more. A branch snapped in the woods nearby. "And hurry!"

Sissa ran around to the front of the truck and tried the passenger's door. "This one's locked!"

"So try the other one!"

"I *am*, Gunner!"

"Just do it, okay?"

Click. The door swung open, dropping the off-balance body of one Billy-Wayne Gruff onto Sissa. She screamed and fell backwards, firing her gun at point-blank range into Billy-Wayne's shriveled head. Dried innards splattered across her jeans and camouflage shirt, causing her scream to increase in volume.

"Sissa!" Gunner cried, running around to see what the commotion was about.

"IT!" She shrieked, pointing at and stumbling away from the corpse at her feet, "JUMPED ME!"

"Z-zombie?" Gunner frantically stammered, aiming his gun into the truck. No sound came from inside, but Gunner's shotgun shook violently anyway.

Louis seized the opportunity to poke his head around the side of the truck. "Did you hear that?"

"Shh! Shh!" Gunner hissed at Sissa.

"It sounded like a bunch of moaning coming from the woods," Louis said, false terror etched into his face.

"Hurry *up* Gunner!"

Gunner leapt up into the truck and twisted the keys out of the ignition. He jumped back out of the truck and ran around to the back, trying three different keys before finding the correct one. The doors swung open, and both shotguns were trained on the interior to prevent another surprise corpse attack. Inside were three racks of guns of every sort, and Gunner and Sissa leapt eagerly for them, dropping their shotguns outside of the truck.

Louis reacted before he knew what he was doing. He slammed the doors closed and grabbed one of the guns off of the ground, jamming it through the handles and effectively barring the doors.

"Hey!" Came Sissa's muffled protest from inside the truck.

"Let us out!" Gunner yelled.

"I'm sorry, I'm really sorry but I can't," Louis said, grimacing. "You were going to rob and probably shoot me, so I had to do it," he continued over that sounds of the pair yelling and banging against the door. The gun started to slide out of the handles, so Louis bumped it back into place. "...sorry," he said again, before turning and running down the road. *That gun won't keep them contained for long,* he told himself, *better be as far away as possible by then.*

Hank wagged his tail as Louis came wheezing into view and charged over to untie the dog. Louis left Gunner's rope tied to the tree and stumbled quickly across the road to pick up his bike and supplies, strapping on his helmet with gusto.

"Come on, Hank!" He said breathlessly, pushing off from the pedals. "Let's get off this road."

***

Nowhere, OK

Ira slid into his seat in the radio room and studied the Vicodin bottle. Six pills stared up at him, and he hesitated before sighing and popping one. His hip throbbed mercilessly, but he tried to ignore it in the hopes that the opiates would kick in soon. He flipped the notepad he kept by the desk to a new page and jotted down a few thoughts for what to talk about that evening; food and water safety, cleaning wounds, and keeping busy. He set the worn pencil down and leaned against the back of his chair.

Is anyone actually listening to this? He sighed, putting a hand to his forehead. *Or am I just senile and trying to keep myself from going off the edge?* After a moment, he shook the thought out of his head and switched the microphone on.

"Good evening friends, this is Ira at Radio Nowhere coming to you from Nowhere, Oklahoma, once again. I broadcast from eight PM Central time to ten PM Central time every day," he paused, glancing at the clock on the wall, "Though tonight it looks like I'm a little behind schedule. Oh, well. To err is human, as they say. Now…tonight, friends, I'd like to share some tips about food and water safety." He placed his finger on the notebook, running it down the page to review each point. "On the subject of food: I'd primarily like to talk about how you can calculate safe expiration windows, how to check to see if something is spoiled, good ways to get the most out of your meals, thorough cooking techniques, and food storage. When we move on to water safety, I'll be telling you the best and safest ways to boil your water and make it safe for human use. With animals and livestock, you can afford to be a little more lenient with your water source, but you don't want to risk yourself getting sick off of bad water. As I've said in the past, there are no more doctors, so you must be extra careful. Now, on to food expiration…"

Around nine o'clock, Ira began to feel the mental effects of the painkiller, and his mind began to fog. He fought against it, but soon found himself pausing for very long amounts of time in between sentences or even words.

"I'm sorry for the delay, friends," he said, "I seem to be a bit more tired than usual." He blinked rapidly, head feeling very light. "I didn't follow my own advice; I skipped supper, so I'm feeling the results of that decision pretty strongly right now." Ira's vision began to blur slightly, and he felt himself growing very, very tired. "I may have to cut this broadcast short, I'm afraid. But before I do, I want to encourage you all to take my suggestions to heart. I've been in many places where I've had to use these exact methods to keep myself alive, and I would never suggest them to you if I didn't know for a fact that they work."

Ira glanced habitually at his photo of Abigail, and trailed off. *Keep going, Papaw,* he almost heard her say. *Tell them what they need to hear.*

Ira cleared his throat, shaking his head in an attempt to clear the fog. "Friends, I've said this before, but in case you're just now tuning in or you missed it last time, you're not alone. You are NOT alone. Please hear me when I say that. You mustn't give up; there is always something to strive for, something to achieve. You have a purpose. You are important. You can survive." Ira studied Abigail's smiling face, a familiar, painful ache rising in his chest. "If you are lost, or confused, or have no place to call home, know that you are always welcome in Nowhere. My home is open to anyone in need, even if that need is as simple as some company. I can't offer much, but I can certainly try to assist you if you need it." Ira's head began to swim again, and he silently cursed his use of the opiates on an empty stomach. "Anyways. As always, this is Ira at Radio Nowhere in Nowhere, Oklahoma. I broadcast from eight PM Central time to ten PM Central time every day. Or at least," he added, glancing at the time, "I broadcast from eight PM until my old age catches up with me. I hope that you have a restful night and a safe day; I will talk to you tomorrow, friends."

***

Alexandria, LA

In a dark trailer surrounded by flashlights, Louis turned off the radio. Hank lay next to him, his head on the boy's lap, his eyes closed contentedly. Louis scratched the dog's head absentmindedly, staring off into the darkness. "Hank," he said, "I think we have a new plan."

Chapter Twenty-Six

Fly, TN

The full moon gave off more than enough light for Zach to see where he was going without using a flashlight. Oleson always said that the best way to figure things out was to walk and think it over; besides, Zach couldn't have slept if he'd wanted to. He passed the alley between the gas station and Laundromat, shivering as a gust of chilled wind hit him. Walking toward the corner of the building, he suddenly heard voices echoing from across the way. He slowed and looked around the corner toward the carwash.

"…I mean what the hell, man? I was trying to get somewhere with her."

Zach stopped. He could make out two figures moving around in the car wash's first stall. An oil lamp sat on the concrete near the drain, the red maintenance toolbox lying open next to it.

"Patience, Wyatt." The unmistakably calm, second voice could only be Drake. "Kathryn's birthday is in a month, and then she'll be old enough for you." He stood with his back to Wyatt, using a wrench to fiddle with some of the knobs on the wall.

"Kathryn's psycho. I want Rosie." Wyatt shifted on his feet and looked around.

"She's not interested." Drake crossed to the opposite wall and began adjusting some of the bolts on one of the sprayers that hung from it.

Wyatt scoffed and crossed his arms, turning to face Drake. "Yeah? How do you know what she's interested in?"

"I paid her a visit last night," Drake said nonchalantly, moving on to a different sprayer.

"You what?" Wyatt's arms fell to his side.

"We had a nice little...chat. It was very beneficial." Drake replied over his shoulder.

"You son of a-" Wyatt took a step closer, back rigid. "You knew I liked her!"

Drake dropped the wrench into the toolbox and turned around. "You took too long to make a move."

"And what? That somehow gives you the right to go after my girl?" Wyatt fists clenched at his side.

Drake laughed heartily. "She didn't belong to you, not to anyone. Now she does. To me." The last words dripped with malice as Drake's demeanor shifted suddenly. He slowly moved his right hand behind his back. "Granted, she was hesitant at first, but I'm *very* good at persuasion."

Wyatt snarled and swung at Drake, connecting with his jaw. Drake fell, but before Wyatt could jump on him Drake whipped a gun from behind his back. Zach watched in horror as he leapt to his feet and pointed it at Wyatt's nose.

"Hands up," Drake ordered flatly.

Wyatt did as he was told. "What are you doing, man? I didn't mean it like – let's just t-"

"Shh." Drake stepped forward as he talked until the silencer nozzle of the gun was a few inches from Wyatt's brow. "I don't like the way you've been questioning my authority lately." Drake began to circle Wyatt, gun still aimed at his head. "It makes me wonder what your ulterior motives are."

"I don't-"

"Ah-ah, hush. I'm talking now." Drake stopped behind him, swiveling the gun to just above Wyatt's right ear. "See, I don't have much use for subordinates that try to defy me- much less those who threaten and strike me without provocation."

"Drake, please-" Wyatt began to sob.

"Since I really can't afford to be constantly defending myself from you, I hereby sentence you to exile."

A gunshot echoed around the complex. Wyatt fell, the force of the impact sending him face-first into the wall. Zach's jaw dropped as the body hit the bleached concrete, a stream of dark blood running for the drain. Drake put the gun away and nudged the body with the toe of his boot.

"Pity," he sighed, rubbing his jaw, "Such a waste of a perfectly good fighter."

Millie awoke suddenly to a banging on the motel room door. Moonlight leaked into the room through the skylight, casting eerie shadows around the room. She turned the wind-up light on dim, grabbed her pepper spray off of the nightstand, and slid out of bed. She looked out the peephole, and opened the door the three inches that the chain would allow.

"Zach?" There he stood in the sliver of light, wild-eyed and panting like he'd just run a 10k. "What are you-"

"Quick, you gotta let me in." He looked behind him, the horror evident in his face.

"Is this about earlier? Because I don't want to hear-"

"Millie, please!" He was so frantic and obviously terrified that she unlatched the chain and did as he asked. When the door was shut, Zach spoke in a hushed voice.

"Drake killed Wyatt."

"What?" Millie's mouth fell open.

"At the carwash." He leaned against the door, chest heaving as he tried to slow his breathing.

"Oh my God!" Her eyes widened. "Are you serious? What happened?"

"Wyatt hit him, then Drake pulled a gun and 'sentenced him to exile' and just shot him point-blank." Zach peeked out the heavy curtain before drawing it completely closed. "Mil, he's insane. We've got to get out of here."

"I knew he was crazy, but…" Millie shook her head, stunned.

He glanced at his watch. "We can sneak out, get to the bikes, and be halfway out of state by morning if we go now."

"First we need to warn everyone, they have no idea what they're up against."

Zach shook his head. "I don't think we can. They worship him, they're never going to believe us over their beloved leader."

"We can't just leave them with a murderer in charge," Millie said exasperatedly.

"He's probably hiding the body right now. It'd be our word against his, and with the rapport he's built with everyone, there's no way they'd side with us over him. You've seen the way he convinces people – hell, he even convinced *me* – that he's looking out for everyone. If he makes them believe that we're a threat…" Zach trailed off, letting the implied repercussions set in. "I wish we could help them, but right now it's really us or them."

Millie looked around the room for an answer. "Ok…we run. But first we leave a note explaining what you saw and why we left. We hide it somewhere that one of the others would be sure to find it."

Zach nodded. "Fair enough. I'll go pack up and meet you back here."

She looked around the room. "I can have everything together in fifteen."

"Ok. I'll be right back." He grasped the door handle, looking out the peephole. "Be sure to lock up behind me."

"Zach?" Millie's voice cracked slightly.

"Yeah?"

"Be careful."

"I will."

Since most of their collective supplies were in Millie's room, Zach's backpack was only about half full by the time he was done packing up his room. He shut the door carefully behind him, pausing a moment to look both ways and listen for any telltale footsteps. Hearing only silence, he took off at a jog. The contents of his backpack knocked about loudly, forcing him to slow to a walk. The last thing he needed was to wake somebody up.

He went through the gate slowly, stopping in the shadow of the awning for a moment. His heart hadn't stopped pounding since he left the carwash, and the adrenaline made him jittery. He scanned the area around the parking lot before beelining for the door marked 126. He reached the other side of the lot quickly. Suddenly, his foot caught on one of the black wheel stops, sending him sprawling forward onto the concrete. His pressed his lips together hard to keep from yelling when he landed on the not-yet-fully-healed gash on his hand. He quickly got to his feet and started toward the door again. He glanced at his hand to make sure the wound hadn't split open as he stepped onto the sidewalk.

Suddenly, a light exploded on the left side of his face. He threw a hand up and spun to face it, blinking wildly.

"Zach?"

His blood ran cold as the light beam dropped from his face. Illuminated by his oil lamp, a flicker of confusion drifted over Drake's face as he walked up. He looked from Zach to the door and back, a wide grin suddenly spreading across his face.

"Well done, Zach!" He holstered the flashlight in his back pocket.

Be casual, Zach told himself. "Hey, Drake." He gave a stiff head nod.

"Good for you, you finally got the girl." Drake beamed like a proud father at Zach. "I knew it was just a matter of time."

What? Zach glanced at the door. "Oh. Yeah." Zach chuckled twice and cleared his throat. "I, uh, chased long enough for sure."

Drake clapped him on the shoulder. "Marvelous. Simply marvelous." He glanced at the backpack. "Moving in?"

"Uh, yeah. We figured it was selfish to take up more room than was needed." Up close, Zach could see the bruise forming on Drake's jaw. "We thought I'd just move my things in tonight and tell everybody tomorrow." Zach forced a smile. "Well, I guess I'd better-"

"I need to tell you something." Drake's face turned serious, lowering the oil lamp. The shift in lighting made his eyes look sunken and black. "Wyatt... left the group tonight."

"Did he? That's a shame." Zach's mouth ran dry.

Drake sighed. "It was tragic, really. He has been in love with Rosie for some time now, but she doesn't return his feelings. He found me earlier this evening and told me that he couldn't stand to be here any longer, the pain was too much for him. I suggested that he wait until the morning to tell everyone that he was leaving, but he thought it best to slip away quietly." Drake shook his head. "Such a pity. He was so useful to us all."

Zach's jaw tensed. "Yeah, he sure was."

"I'm going to need someone to take over Wyatt's responsibilities. My second-in-command, if you will." Drake gave a placid smile. "I would love for you to take the job."

Zach nodded, a wave of nausea rolling over him. "I'll think about it and let you know in the morning."

"Good!" He clapped him on the shoulder again. "Now," Drake eyed the door, "I'll let you get back to what you were doing." He winked and chuckled, turning to leave. As he walked away, Zach spotted the butt of the revolver sticking out of Drake's waistband.

Millie had everything packed in ten minutes flat. She'd dressed quickly in dark jeans and a navy hoodie so that if anyone should happen to be running around outside, she'd better blend into the shadows. After placing the backpacks next to the door, she unzipped the rolling backpack's middle pocket. She switched on her mini flashlight and turned off the wind-up, sliding it into the compartment.

She sat rigidly on the unmade bed and checked her watch every thirty seconds. Suddenly, she heard voices outside the door. Millie froze, eyes locked on the door. She turned off the flashlight and slipped it into her pocket. As quietly as possible, she slipped off the bed, grabbed her pepper spray, and tiptoed to the door. She bent down a little to look through the peephole. There she saw Zach standing in the light of a lamp being held by…Drake. Millie stopped breathing for a moment. Zach stood rigidly with his back to the door as Drake talked. He was speaking too low for her to make out what he was saying, and she'd never been good at reading lips. Millie stepped away from the door, leaning against the adjoining wall as her heart pounded. Finally, there was a knock. She looked through the peephole again and quickly unlocked the chain. The door swung inward and Zach stepped through and locked it behind him. Millie retrieved the flashlight and switched it on.

"What happened? What was Drake saying to you?" She asked him quietly.

"You saw that, huh?" Zach looked through the peephole for a minute. "He just said that Wyatt left because of Rosie, and he wants me to replace him. I said I'd think about it."

"Did he get suspicious about what you were doing out here after dark with a backpack?"

Zach cleared his throat. "He thinks we're moving in together." Millie raised her eyebrows. "Hey, he guessed, and for the sake of staying alive, I didn't correct him." He looked through the peephole again. A moving light illuminated the edge of what he could see.

Millie sat down on the bed. "So now what?"

"He's still roaming around out there." Zach watched the light disappear for the second time that evening.

"Well, why don't we just wait a while then go. Surely he'll go to his room now," Millie offered.

"Maybe he'll get tired of creeping around soon." Zach turned from the peephole and looked at Millie seriously. "...nothing happened."

"What?"

He cleared his throat again awkwardly. "Kathryn. Nothing happened. She barged in, jumped me, and I kicked her out. That's all."

Millie nodded slowly, looking away from him. "Why'd you kick her out?"

"What?" Zach raised an eyebrow incredulously. "She's ...I mean...she's so...just...no." He stumbled over his words, feeling a heat rise in his cheeks.

Millie continued to nod. "Okay. You didn't owe me an explanation, but thank you."

"Well I didn't want you to think that I was ...y'know, I just..." Zach fumbled again, trying desperately to find the right words. "I'm not into that kinda chick – er, girl, thing."

Millie turned her face away from him entirely to hide an amused smile. "Good to know."

The pair switched off watching the peephole every so often, and after forty minutes Millie was starting to get antsy.

"Hey," she said over her shoulder. Zach, who was lying on the unmade bed studying a map by flashlight, looked up. "There's been no sign of Drake for fifteen minutes. You want to take off now?"

Zach sat up, folding the map. "Yeah, let's go." He stood and stretched, grunting a little as his back popped.

Millie glanced out the peephole one more time and nearly had a heart attack. Walking across the parking lot directly toward the door was Drake. "Abort, abort!" She whispered, backing away from the door. Zach looked at her in alarm. "He's coming!"

"What?" His jaw dropped.

As Zach let loose a string of garbled whispered curses, Millie looked around wildly for a solution. Behind Zach, the bed's covers were rumpled.

"Bed," she said under her breath. "Now!" He stopped cussing and looked at her, then to the bed behind him. There was a soft knock at the door. Millie scrambled for the far side of the mattress, and Zach dove after her. They quickly jerked the covers up over them.

"Cuddle me," she whispered, closing the gap between them. A second tap on the door.

"Is now really the time-" The doorknob squeaked.

"Authenticity!" she hissed, throwing her arm across his chest. She shut her eyes as the lock turned. Zach quickly snaked an arm around her and closed his eyes as the door opened.

The door opened easily, halting just before the chain stopped it. Drake peered inside, blinking to adjust to the darkness. The skylight bathed the room in a soft glow. There in the middle of the room, he saw the two newcomers entangled and fast asleep. He regarded them fondly for a moment before sliding the door shut. A smile danced across his face as he relocked the door and slipped the keychain back into his pocket. The smile broke into a toothy grin as he strode across the parking lot. Everything was working out just the way he'd hoped, and soon the plan would be in full swing. Now if he could just find a way to speed things along. "Patience is key, Mr. Doyle," he reminded himself. He hummed a tune as he started up the steps to the second floor.

Zach and Millie stayed perfectly still for an indeterminate amount of time after the door shut.

"I think he's gone," Millie whispered finally, opening her eyes. She glanced at Zach, whose face was pointed away from her, staring at the door. He didn't seem to hear her. "I said I think he's gone," she said quietly.

"Hmm?" Zach whipped his head toward her, accidentally smashing her nose with his chin.

"Ow!" She pulled her arm from across his chest and grabbed her face.

"Oh, sorry!" He instinctively turned toward her, reaching to touch her nose. "Are you okay?" Millie rubbed the offended nose and frowned at him. "Sorry, I didn't know you were as close as you were." She sneezed twice and he stifled a laugh.

"Real funny," she said, sniffing.

"I'm sorry, I really am." He gave a lopsided apologetic smile.

"Eh, nothing's broken." She gingerly tapped the bridge of her nose and folded her arm against her. "I'll survive."

Zach smiled, which quickly faded. He glanced at the door. "Let's give him a few to get back to his room, and then go." Millie nodded slowly and he continued. "While I'm apologizing," he faltered slightly, looking over at her, "I'm sorry I didn't believe you, Mil. I really should have listened when you first told me something wasn't right about these people."

"It's okay," Millie smiled. "Thanks for apologizing."

"Next time you tell me that our 'leader' is a murderous sociopath who watches people while they sleep, I'll take it," he said dryly.

Millie laughed. "Let's hope there's not a next time for this one."

The room went quiet, and Zach was suddenly aware of the proximity between them. His arm was wrapped around her, hand resting on her hip. One of her arms was wedged behind his back; the other was tucked against her chest, rising and falling with each breath. The room suddenly felt like the inside of a furnace.

"Zach..." Millie trailed off, staring at him.

He swallowed hard. "Yeah?" The space between their faces narrowed. His heart sped up as his grip on her tightened slightly.

"I-" She cleared her throat. "I can't feel my arm."

"...oh." His voice betrayed him as the moment fizzled. The room went quiet again.

"...you're still crushing it."

"Oh!" He sat up quickly. "Sorry."

"It's okay, I don't mind," she said, sitting up and shaking her hand. "I mean, I do, but it's not a bad thing." She wiggled her fingers and looked at him. "I mean, I don't-" she stopped, trying to figure out what she was trying to say. Zach raised an eyebrow. "...never mind. Let's just get out of here."

Chapter Twenty-Seven

Verda, LA

A trail of flyers reading *"Courage Country Carnival!"* snaked their way up the road to the abandoned fairgrounds. The hike had been almost entirely silent, aside from the squeaking of Gina's oxygen tank wheels. Eric glanced at Gina, who kept her gaze straight ahead. The wind blew her hair into her face and caught on her oxygen mask, but she made no move to fix it. Eric looked away quickly, the silence making him uneasy. To his right, a row of canvas tents fluttered slightly in the breeze. To his left sat a vast number of rusting metal structures he could only assume were game booths. He stopped walking as one of them caught his eye. *Penny's Impossible Pins!* A few years ago, Eric spent hours on end practicing how to knock down the dusty old bottles stacked atop one another after Trinity begged him to win her a stuffed animal. He smiled as he remembered how ecstatic she was when he gave her that nauseatingly pink rabbit. He smiled to himself as an idea popped into his head.

"Hey," he blurted, pointing at *Penny's Impossible Pins!* "I bet I could win you that stuffed bear."

Gina stopped walking and glanced at him. "Think so?"

"Oh, I *know* so." He nodded enthusiastically as a small smile crept across her face. "Come on, I'll show you!"

She glanced down the row of tents up ahead. "We really should keep moving if we're going to get to the generator before dark."

"Come on, Gina," Eric grinned. "It'll be fun!" He added in a low, sing-song voice.

Gina's smile vanished. She looked away from him, back rigid.

"I mean," Eric faltered, confused. "I figure we could use a rest from that hike."

Gina glanced at him once more, his puppy-dog eyes blinking up at her. She shifted on her feet and relaxed her shoulders slightly. "…okay."

"Vamos!"

Eric sped walked over to *Penny's Impossible Pins,* slowing down so Gina could keep up. When they reached the booth, Eric picked up one of the dirt-encrusted tennis balls and wiped it on the bottom of his pants leg.

"Alright, are you ready for this mad skill?" Eric wiggled his eyebrows, trying to make Gina smile again.

"Yeah, okay."

Eric wound up his arm like a major-league baseball pitcher and hiked his front leg up. With a mighty "YEEE!" he threw the ball, knocking down the middle tower of pins, and struck a "strong man" pose. He squinted at Gina while puckering his lips and sucking in his cheeks. In spite of herself, Gina cracked a smile.

Eric cracked his knuckles and grabbed another ball. He wound up faster this time, hiked his leg even higher, and let it fly, hitting the left tower in the dead center. The pins fell, sliding off the platform unimpressively. He spun around with his hands forming two finger-guns, pretending to fire them both at Gina with a "pew, pew." Her smile grew as he prepped for the final throw. With a great heave, he lobbed the last ball as hard as he could. The ball smashed through the right tower, ricocheted off the wall, and came flying back toward him.

"Agh!" Eric shrieked as the ball smacked his forehead. He grabbed the stand of plushies as he fell backwards, pulling them on top of him as he landed directly on his backside.

"Are you okay?"

"Ow." Eric's hand stayed firmly attached to his forehead as he pushed the stand off of himself. "I'm fine. Just a small injury. Nothing too bad."

"Are you sure?" She adjusted the mask on her face.

"Yeah, I just need a second. Also," he said holding up a tan bear. "Here."

Gina gave a small smile, running her thumb over the bear's red bow tie and bright, shiny glass eyes. "Thank you," she said quietly.

"Don't mention it." Eric checked his prosthetic before starting to stand. "Anything for a – dog!"

"Excuse me?"

Eric scrambled to his feet and jumped behind Gina, who turned to see what he was looking at. A blue-and-black heeler barreled toward them, tongue lolling.

"Hank?" Gina gasped, pulling the mask from her face. She fell to her knees and threw her arms around the dog as he jumped on her. She squeezed her eyes tight as he licked at her chin and barked happily. "Where on earth-?"

"Haaaank? Haaaaank!" A voice called from nearby, followed by a loud whistle.

Gina's eyes grew wide and her arms dropped to her side. "No way."

"Dog... Dog..." Eric stuttered, backing away as Hank trotted toward him. Gina stood up, her hair falling in front of her face.

"Haaaaaank!" A tall, skinny boy emerged suddenly from behind a tent. He looked at Gina, and his owl-like eyes shot open.

"Louis?" Gina took a step forward, then another.

"Gina, no! Dog!" Eric shouted, pointing at Hank whose tail wagged as he continued toward the boy.

"Gina!" Louis ran over, stopping five feet in front of her. "What are you doing here?"

"Me? What about you? You were dead." Gina wheezed slightly.

"I thought so, too!" Louis exclaimed, throwing his arms up. "But I woke up in a hospital – which *The Ambling Dead* didn't prepare me for because they stuck me in a basement, a *basement*, Gina, it was so dark – and then I found Hank with all his burns that I fixed, don't worry, which made me think that maybe you died too, except that I didn't, but I'm really glad that you didn't either," he sucked in a breath, "Because Hank was really pretty depressed for a while there and now he'll be back to his old self!"

"Thank you for taking care of him," Gina said sincerely, tucking her hair behind her ear.

Louis's face fell as he noticed her burns for the first time. "What happened…?"

"Hey!" Eric cried, "Can someone please get this dog away from me?"

"Hank-"

"-come here, Hank!"

The dog turned away from Eric and trotted back to Gina, who knelt once more to hug him.

Louis, noticing Eric for the first time, waved at him. "I'm Louis."

Eric squared his shoulders. "Eric."

"Hank's Gina's dog," Louis explained, "I was just holding onto him for a while."

"I know."

"He's really quite friendly-"

"-I know."

"…he wouldn't hurt a fly." Louis finished slowly. He glanced back at Gina, still petting Hank, and then looked back at Eric. "So…where are you two headed?"

Eric folded his arms. "What's it to you?"

"Just curious." Louis looked at Gina once more. "I didn't know if you guys were going to Nowhere, like me."

"Nowhere?" Gina looked up at Louis.

"In Oklahoma. An old man named Ira lives there, and he's been broadcasting on a radio to any survivors out there. Well, out here, that is. I heard him the other night on a radio I found and he gives survival tips and encourages people to keep going and says that anyone who needs somewhere to be is welcome to go there, so that's where I'm going. He reminds me of my grandpa, he's got this soothing voice that just makes you feel safe and at home. So I figured why not? I've got nothing else going on and it can get...lonely out here." Louis shrugged, chewing on his lower lip. "Don't get me wrong, Hank is a great companion and I love the open road, but I'd like to find a home, you know? Even just for a little while."

"Yeah," Gina replied, looking back at Hank.

"I don't know, random guy on a radio seems kinda sketchy to me." Eric folded his arms.

"Well, I'm going," Louis shrugged, glancing at Eric, "And if you're willing to risk it, I'd love to have the company."

Gina's brows furrowed a moment. Hank butted her chin with his head, and a small smile worked its way across her face. "That actually sounds-"

"I think we should think about this for a minute." Eric lifted his chin and took a step forward, looking to Gina.

"Why don't you let her finish what she was going to say?" Louis raised an eyebrow at Eric and looked back to Gina. Eric shot the side of Louis's head a dirty look.

"I want to hear him. Ira." Gina said, not looking up from Hank.

210

"I've got a radio," Louis offered.

Gina stood, pausing to breathe a moment. "Let's go find the generator."

***

Mobile, AL

There were far too many family members in the house; that the small boy knew for certain. He fidgeted next to his father, who'd set him on the ground to talk to a distant cousin in a hushed tone. They'd been standing in his grandparents' living room for ages now; he wanted to go play, not be picked up and kissed or pinched on the cheek by anyone who came by on their way to the box. The couch had been moved out of the way to make room for the long wooden box that seemed enormous to the small boy, though he still couldn't figure out what was so interesting about it.

The black dress pants once belonging to his older cousin itched something fierce, and the tie around his neck was too hot. He didn't understand why he had to even wear a tie, it wasn't even Sunday. He huffed loudly and let out a small whine, pulling at the loop around his neck as though it threatened to strangle him.

"Ira," the boy's father said sharply, turning away as the cousin moved on, "Stop that right now."

"It's too hot," Ira whined, pulling again at the tie's steadfast knot.

"If you don't stop that whining," his father warned, "I'll take you out behind the shed and give you something to whine about."

Ira stopped fidgeting, his lower lip jutting out in a pout. He folded his arms across his small chest and stared at the ground. Suddenly, the room went silent. He looked up to see his mother guiding his grandmother, who wore a black veil over her face, over to the box. Ira's father clamped a hand onto the boy's shoulder as Mamaw Honey reached out with a shaking hand to touch the top of the box. Ira's mother looked to his father with tears on her cheeks, and Ira felt strange. He looked around the room again, and noticed that a lot of people were crying. Why?

Mamaw looked slowly toward them, and smiled gently at Ira. She and Ira's mother crossed to them, and she reached down to pick the boy up off the ground. She swept the veil to one side to plant a kiss on his cheek before hugging him tightly to her.

"Mamaw loves you," she whispered, caressing his short hair.

"Where's Papaw?" Ira asked, suddenly aware that he wasn't amongst the people in their church clothes. Mamaw froze, her trembling hand resting gently on Ira's head. She pulled back slowly, looking him in the eye.

"Ira!" Ira's father snapped. He and Ira's mother exchanged a "Didn't you talk to him?" look.

"It's okay, Benjamin," Mamaw said, her kind eyes still resting on Ira. "Papaw...he went to Heaven, baby."

"Why?" Ira didn't understand, Papaw had just taken him fishing.

"Because Jesus called him there."

"When's he coming back?"

One of Ira's aunts let out a sob at his question, turning into her husband's shoulder. Ira's brows furrowed in confusion.

"He's not," Mamaw's voice cracked slightly. "Once someone goes to Heaven, they can't come back."

"I want him back," Ira said, mouth screwing into a pout.

"We all do, baby," Mamaw began to cry and Ira felt himself being taken from her arms. Benjamin turned his son around to hold him better, but Ira wasn't having it.

"I want him back!" Ira yelled, kicking his feet. He looked around the room at the sad people, then fixed his eyes on the cross that hung above the radio on the far wall. He'd learned in Sunday School that the cross was where Jesus was. "Give Papaw back, Jesus!" He yelled, kicking his feet in an attempt to wriggle from his father's arms. "Give him back!"

"Ira you stop that right now," Benjamin said loudly over his son's screams.

"No!" Ira kicked his feet harder, and Benjamin flipped the boy over his shoulder, holding his legs still. "Give Papaw back!" Ira screamed one last time as his father hauled him out of the room.

*

Nowhere, OK

Ira opened his eyes to the dim light of his battery-operated lamp. He lifted his head slowly, groaning at the crick that had formed while he was asleep. The large tan chair in the university library was very good for reading, but rather bad for sleeping. He scooted back in the chair to sit up and the book he'd been reading fell from his lap. He glanced at his watch, and grimaced. 7:54. He had six minutes to get across campus. Ira grabbed his cane and stood, groaning slightly as something somewhere popped. He picked up his lamp and hobbled toward the door.

The clock on the wall read 8:07 when he finally slid into the green wheeled chair at the radio desk. Ira took a deep breath and keyed the mic.

"Good evening, friends, this is Ira once again coming to you from Radio Nowhere in Nowhere, Oklahoma. I broadcast every evening from eight o'clock pm, Central standard time, to ten o'clock Central standard time, barring me being late like today or running out of things to say." He picked up his notes, full of the topics from his previous broadcasts. "Today I'm going to be rehashing some of the things I've already talked about in the past, just in case some of you are just now catching this channel, or maybe you just need to hear it again. Whatever the reason, I feel like I should start by talking about wounds – how to clean them, keep them clean, and what the signs of infection are. As I've said before, there are no more doctors in this world, and if you leave a rampant infection unchecked, it can kill faster than you'd ever expect. Now, suppose you've just gotten cut by a sharp piece of metal…"

***

Verda, LA

Inside the tent of *Madame Marley's Clairvoyant Casuistries*, Eric and Louis sat far opposite one another on worn-out beanbags; Gina sat quietly on a pile of cushions in the corner with Hank's head resting in her lap. They sat in silence at the end of Ira's broadcast, the only sound coming from the generator outside. The string lights hanging from the tent ceiling flickered, giving the room a strange, mystical feel.

"Well? What did you think?" Louis asked finally, his lower lip sucked into his mouth.

Gina shifted slightly on the cushions, careful not to disturb Hank. "I want to go to there."

"Excellent!" Louis grinned, slapping his hands onto his crossed-legged knees. "We can head that way tomorrow if you guys want."

"Okay." Gina cleared her throat and petted the sleeping Hank softly. After a moment she glanced at Eric, who was glaring at the ground. "Eric?"

Eric looked up at her, his face slowly softening. "…yeah. I guess me too."

"Good, good," Louis replied, wriggling his shoulders to slide down into the beanbag. "Let's get some rest now so we can leave at first light."

Gina lifted Hank gently from her lap and adjusted the pile of cushions. As she rolled to face the tent wall, the dog snuggled up against her, and she wrapped an arm loosely around him. She fell asleep almost instantly, the exhaustion caused by the events of the day finally catching up to her.

Chapter Twenty-Eight

Wynne, AR

"This has got to be the single weirdest year of my life," Zach stated, staring out across the park. The can of soup in his good hand was still half full, even though he and Millie had been sitting at the picnic table for well over 20 minutes. "A tiger? A murderous cult leader? I feel like I'm in one of those crappy young adult novels."

"Agreed," Millie replied, eying the soup can. "You should really finish that. We've got a lot of ground to cover today, and you'll need the energy." She cleaned her spoon off with a napkin before putting it in a pocket in her backpack. Taking out a marker, she wrote "Don't give up" and Radio Nowhere's channel number in big letters on the can's exterior. "Just in case," Millie said, standing and placing the can in the middle of the picnic table. She looked at the ground and picked up a rock, dropping it into the can. "You never know what lost people might wander by."

Zach nodded, taking the pen from her. "I sure hope this Ira guy is who he says he is." He wrote on the can's bumpy surface with some difficulty. He handed back the pen, dropped the spoon in his bag, and stood. "I'd hate to get there and him turn out to be a serial killer or something." He swung the bag over his shoulder and gestured toward the other side of the huge park. "Shall we?"

"Just wait until you hear tonight's broadcast before you form an opinion."

"Why, does he say 'I'm not a criminal here to skin you and wear your skin as a suit' or something?"

"Ew." Millie made a face, stepping around a tipped-over trash can. "No, I just mean that his voice is very…trustworthy, for lack of better wording. I wish you could have heard the full broadcast last night or the night before. Or the night before that."

"Me too, but we were a little busy putting as much distance between us and that psycho as possible, remember?" Zach got a bit of a running start and leapt over a ditch.

"Your bike blowing out on us did put a damper on things." She yawned broadly, the exhaustion evident in her face.

"I told you, you didn't have to ditch yours, too," Zach replied, jumping from a small drop-off to the ground. He held out a hand for her to steady herself with as she followed him down.

"Yeah, well. It didn't make sense for me to be riding in circles around you forever, did it?" They reached the middle of the park where a slightly wooded area lay; a stone bridge curved over a gully at the bottom of a hill, and they made their way toward it.

"If we pass a sporting goods store or bike shop ever again, we can get new rigs. We can trick 'em out; you can get one with a basket and streamers on the handlebars," he added with a smirk.

Millie stopped dead in her tracks, eyes wide. Her mouth fell open and she gasped dramatically. "Streamers? A basket? Oh, be still my beating heart!" She tilted her head and clasped her hands together under it. "Oh joy of joys, streamers of my very own!" She twirled around and skipped on ahead, stopping at the top of the bridge. "A tisket, a tasket, a green-and-yellow basket!"

Zach threw his head back and burst out laughing, stumbling back under the weight of his backpack. He lost his breath at one point, he was laughing so hard. After a minute, he had to lean on his knees to compose himself. "Good lord, Mil," he finally managed, "You gotta go without sleep more often."

She gave him a smirk and curtsied. "Glad I could be so entertaining!" Millie laughed as Zach made his way to the top of the bridge. She stopped suddenly, face falling as she held up a hand. "Did you hear that?"

"What?" Zach glanced around.

They stood in silence a moment, listening intently. A faint scream of "help" echoed over the hill. Zach immediately dropped to his knees, rifling through his bag as Millie grabbed her mace and lowered to a crouch. Zach pulled out the emptied revolver.

"You don't have any bullets," she said quietly.

"Yeah, but don't tell them that." He stood, leaving the bag on the ground. Another shriek sounded loudly from over the hill. "Stay behind me." Millie gripped the mace canister as followed as he slunk carefully up the hill. Zach hunkered behind a tree at the top, heart pounding. "Memo to file, get some more bullets." He tensed up as he slowly leaned out to see what was beyond the hill. He turned his head back to Millie, putting one finger to his lips, and beckoned her closer. Still gripping the mace, she tiptoed up to where he was. There, at the bottom of the ridge, surrounded by trees, was a small playground, complete with slide, swings, and rope bridge. Running around on the equipment was a tiny blonde girl, looking to be no more than four.

Millie gasped, whispering to Zach. "She's too little to be all by herself."

"She's not," Zach nodded toward the slide. A matching cotton-top head poked out from behind it before jumping out and clawing at the air.

"Rrrawr! I'm a dinosaur!" The boy roared, stomping around in a circle.

The girl screamed, and ran to the other side of the playground. "Help! Don't eat me! Don't eat me!" She squealed again, prompting a pursuit by the 'dinosaur.'

"We can't leave them here." Millie's brows furrowed in pity.

Zach shook his head. "Wasn't ever an option." He started to stand, but Millie put a hand on his shoulder.

"Let me. They might get scared and bolt otherwise."

"What? Why?"

"You're holding a gun, haven't shaved in a week, and currently look like the definition of stranger danger." He shrugged as she handed him the mace. Stepping carefully down the ridge, she slipped on a branch and landed on her rear with an audible thud. Zach stifled a laugh. The kids stopped playing and looked to the noise, their eyes wide. The girl ran to and stood in front of the boy and he clung to her arm. Millie smiled, carefully easing the rest of the way down the slope. "Hi, there." She waved slowly at the children. "My name's Millie. What's yours?" She crouched down to their level, about 10 feet away. Neither answered, still staring at her like alarmed baby deer. "Are you here by yourselves?" They nodded slowly. Close up, Millie could get a better look at the pair. Both had dirty clothes and faces, unbrushed hair, and the boy wore mismatched shoes. "Is there anyone who's taking care of you right now?" She asked gently. Both shook their heads. "I see..."

"Mama and Daddy went to sleep," the girl said.

"They did?"

"Uh-huh. Daddy was sleepy, so he took a nap. Mama already went to sleep, but before that." The girl scratched her face.

"When did your daddy go to sleep?"

The two looked at each other, and the boy whispered something in the girl's ear before hiding behind her again. "I dunno," the girl shrugged with both hands. "Probably... probably a years ago." Millie smiled at the child's perception of time.

"So nobody takes care of you now?" Millie wanted to make sure before proceeding.

"I take care of him and he takes care of me," the girl pointed to the boy. "But sometimes it's scary." The boy nodded.

"Do you mind telling me your names? I like to know friends' names when I talk to them." Millie smiled at the boy as he peeked shyly from behind the girl's shoulder.

"I'm Ella and he's Joey," The girl pointed again. "We're five, almost."

"Are you twins?"

"Uh-huh. But I'm bigger, a little." The girl pinched her fingers together to show how much older she was.

"It's nice to meet you, Joey and Ella. Do you want to shake hands?" Millie held out her hand. Ella slowly moved forward, took Millie's hand, and shook it heartily. Joey waved, offering a small smile.

Millie stood up. "Are you two hungry?" Both nodded vigorously. "Well, my friend Zach is over that hill, and he's got my backpack which has all our food in it. We can sit and eat and talk about some things if you'd like."

The pair exchanged another look, and Joey whispered something into Ella's ear again. "Ok," she said finally, "That can work." Joey continued to hold onto Ella and she slipped her other hand into Millie's.

As they started up the hill, Millie remembered. "Hey, Zach?"

"Yeah?"

"Go put what you're holding back in your bag so we can talk." The last thing she needed was a gun to scare them off.

After Zach had introduced himself to the twins, Millie opened a can of soup for each.

"What happened to your hand?" Ella asked Zach.

"Well, me and Millie were walking through this town, and there was a tiger that must've gotten loose from the zoo."

The twins gasped. "A TIGER?" Ella's mouth dropped open in awe. Millie handed the twins their soup and spoons.

"Yeah, and it chased us into a store…" Zach spun the story bigger as the twins devoured the soup. "…and right when it jumped at me, fangs bared, ready to kill, I shot it dead."

"Did it bite your hand?" Ella said, mouth full.

"No," Millie interjected, "He cut it on some glass."

"Big glass. Went straight through my hand almost." Zach nodded solemnly, stretching his hands to show how big the glass was.

Millie laughed. "Whatever."

"I think I would be a little more grateful to the one who saved your butt." Zach folded his arms and raised an eyebrow, smirking.

Joey whispered something in his sister's ear. "Butt's a bad word," Ella said matter-of-factly.

"Oh, right… You know, I heard everything that you and Millie were talking about," Zach said as the twins' ravenously ate, "And I got to thinking. Since you don't have anybody here to watch after you, why don't you two come with us?"

Ella paused, speaking with her mouth full. "Where're you going?"

"A town in Oklahoma," Millie replied. "It's far away, but there's people there that we would like to meet. We could be our own little group for now, though."

"Like a family?" Joey spoke for the first time; a wispy, hopeful sound.

Millie shot a glance at Zach. "Yeah, kinda like a family."

"We need our blankets, because they keep us safe, and Joey can't sleep without Roary," Ella told them as she led them down the residential street, pulling on Zach and Millie's hands. The houses were all red brick, with dead grass and built-in garages. They passed a car that had smashed into a mailbox, its mummified driver still leaned into the deflated airbag, but neither twin seemed to notice. "Our house is right over here!" Ella let go of their hands and skipped ahead, prompting Joey to run along behind. "It's this one!" They stopped in front of a small, single-story red brick house with a multitude of toys on the lawn. Zach and Millie followed the twins into the open door. A pungent musty odor washed over them as they hit the entrance, triggering their gag reflexes.

"Gah, what is that?" Zach whispered, bringing a hand to his nose as the twins disappeared down an adjacent hallway.

"Ella said that their parents went to sleep when everyone else did. They're probably still in the house." She glanced around the entry room and saw a cluster of half-empty perfume bottles on the floor by the door. "Looks like they try to mask it as best as they can. Poor things..."

Ella ran back into the room, grabbing the older travelers' hands and pulling them toward an open door. "Come sit down!"

The kitchen floor was littered with food wrappers. Candy, snack cakes, pull-tab cans, and empty chip bags lay on the floor in piles against the walls. Ella pointed to the table against the far wall. "That's where you can sit. We'll go get our stuff."

"Do you need any help?" Millie asked, taking off her backpack and sliding into an open chair.

"Nope!" As the twins set about collecting things they would need for the trip into a pile by the front door, Zach and Millie surveyed the room.

"I'm shocked that they lasted so long on a diet like this," Zach remarked, nudging a ravioli can with his foot. He moseyed into the pantry to check out the cabinets.

"It's a wonder they lasted this long at all." Millie shook her head. "Four years old, coping with all this. I can't even imagine."

"Technically, they're 'five, almost,'" Zach mused, "But I agree. If I were that age, I'd probably have snapped by now." He returned from the pantry carrying three cans of vegetables. "These were all I found. Looks like those two demolished anything that didn't require a can opener." He set the cans on the counter. "Beets and greens, I wouldn't want those, either."

"We can stop by a store on our way out."

Suddenly, a loud rolling thud echoed down the hall. Ella ran in excitedly, pulling a red wagon. "This is our spaceship! It can carry us to the moon," She beamed up at them.

Millie grinned back, taking the handle from her. "Good thinking."

"M-O-O-N, that spells moon! My teacher Mrs. Mabrey taught us how to spell moon and sun, S-U-N."

The pile of things that the twins "had to have" was growing by the minute. For every tiny armful of stuffed animals Ella brought in, Joey would drag up another couple of Tonka trucks.

"How are we going to tell them that we can't bring all this?" Zach raised an eyebrow.

Millie stepped in as a load of coloring books entered the kitchen. "Hey, you two. I forgot to tell you something about the trip," she squatted down to their level, "It's going to be like a camping trip! Have you ever been on a camping trip?" Both nodded. "So you know we can't take ALL these things, right?" Their faces fell a little.

"If we put all those toys and things in the wagon, there wouldn't be any room for you. So how about we only take one toy, blanket, and pillow each? Plus some spare clothes."

The twins deliberated a moment, whispering back and forth in each other's ears, before coming to a decision. "Ok," Ella said, "But one stuffed animal, too, okay?"

Zach grinned. "You should be a lawyer one day." The twins systematically placed their belongings in the red wagon, leaving plenty of room. "We'd better get on. Say goodbye to here and hello to the road." Zach took the wagon handle from Millie and stepped over a trash pile, heading toward the door.

Ella's eyebrows knitted. "Goodbye to here?" She looked over at Joey, cradling a beat-up stuffed dinosaur and wearing a similar expression. Ella turned to Millie. "Will you wait please? We have to do something real quick."

"Sure, take your time."

Zach and Millie waited in the driveway for fifteen minutes for the twins to come out, hand-in-hand. Joey was hugging the dinosaur with his free arm, and Ella wore a somber face.

"Ok, we can go now," she said softly. "We said goodbye."

Chapter Twenty-Nine

Heflin, LA

"Just use the charcoal starter already." Eric stabbed the syringe into his leg, pushing the plunger down. Wind rustled the trees on either side of the narrow blacktop road, and somewhere in the distance a dog barked.

Louis blew gently on the smoldering leaves, willing the sticks to catch flame. "If we use the lighter fluid we can't cook anything over it, it'll release too many toxic fumes."

Eric remove the syringe and wiped the needle off with a disinfecting wipe, putting the cap back on. He dropped it into his bag, leaning on his knees with his forearms.

"It's getting dark," Eric stated, stretching his arms above his head. "If we don't have a fire, we don't have light. Use the charcoal starter and worry about the fumes later."

Gina sat on a log nearby, zoned out of the boys' conversation as she breathed slowly into her oxygen mask. The dial showed that she still had a fair amount left, though she wondered how much exactly she'd need. It had been trial and error up until this point, but she knew enough to take the mask off when she started feeling lightheaded or began to hyperventilate. She turned off the tank and removed the mask, careful to not touch her healing burns. She sighed and reached down to pat Hank on the head. The dog hadn't left her side since the reunion at the carnival, but she wasn't complaining.

"I can do it like this just fine." Louis struck another match and held it to the tinder. "I was in the –"

"In the Scouts," finished Eric as he stood up, "We know." Eric leaned down to rummage in his bag.

"Then you'll know I know how to start a fire," retorted Louis. "It just takes a little time, sometimes, that's all." Louis concentrated carefully on the tiny flame that started to burn through the tinder. His eyes lit up hopefully as it began to spread, then went out with a tiny *fphbt*. His face fell.

"Back up," Eric said, suddenly closer to the fire. He popped the top to the charcoal starter and squirted it all over the tinder and kindling.

"Hey!" Louis protested, jumping back from the makeshift fire pit as the fluid caught the smoldering tinder and went up with a *WHOOMPH!* "You could have burned me!" The boy stood and glared at Eric.

"But I didn't." Eric stretched again, looking over at Gina.

"Yes," Louis said through gritted teeth, "But you could have."

Gina stood suddenly. "I'll be back." She picked up her backpack and stepped carefully over the log, starting off down the road with Hank in tow.

"Where are you going?" Eric asked.

"Girl business," Gina answered briskly without turning around.

"…oh." Eric's cheeks reddened.

Gina continued walking until she could no longer hear the boys' heated "small talk." She glanced over her shoulder and couldn't see them or the smoke from the fire, and relaxed her shoulders, slowing her pace. She turned onto a small gravel road that led into the woods, letting Hank trot ahead of her.

The road turned out to be a driveway, at the end of which was a tiny red brick house. She marched onto the front porch and dropped her bag onto the ground. She reached into the front pocket and pulled out her flashlight, flipping it on. There was a long window next to the front door, so she picked up one of the faded red bricks lining the walkway and heaved it at the glass. It shattered, a loud, satisfying sound that made her smile. After catching her breath, she reached through to unlock the door. Once it was open she covered the glass inside with the welcome mat and ushered Hank inside the entryway. The house reeked of mothballs, and she picked up the brick as she took in the dimness of the house. Lying on the couch in the living room was a man's corpse, raising the hair on her neck. The layout of the room and the way the corpse lay sprawled out reminded her far too much of…she moved away as a chill shot down her spine. In the kitchen, the smell of spoiled food permeated everything. Gina pulled her t-shirt up over her nose as she ventured deeper inside.

Down a hallway lay what looked to be a guest bedroom/home office. Gina set the brick on the desk against the wall and opened one of the wooden drawers, shining her flashlight into it. Inside were countless bills, as well as a stack of photos of, presumably, the old man on the couch and three small children. Gina shut the drawer and went to the closet, opening it to see stacks of board games in one corner and children's toys in the other. The spare bed had a floral bedspread on it, and the pillows had some rogue feathers sticking out of them. Her eyes lit up as the shirt slipped off her nose. Gina tucked two pillows under her arms and grabbed the other two in either hand, heading back to the kitchen; she held her breath and opened drawers until she found a large butcher knife. She went out the back door off of the kitchen, leaving it open behind her.

Outside, she dropped one of the pillows to the ground, taking the case off of the other. She carefully held the pillow in her right hand and slammed the knife into it. She jerked the knife out, and a spray of white feathers flew from the slit. She stabbed the pillow again and again before she suddenly tossed the knife onto a red folding chair by the door and stuck her fingers into one of the slits. She pulled hard, ripping open the hole she'd made and showering the parched lawn with feathers. She re-seized the knife and repeated her actions with the other pillows, flinging the feathers around like snow. Only when the dead grass was coated in a fine layer of white did she stop and survey the feathery carnage.

Something bumped behind her and she wheeled around, chest heaving and knife raised. Hank smiled up at her with that goofy dog grin of his, a tennis ball rolling slightly from where he dropped it. Gina put the knife back in the chair and picked the ball up, smiling as Hank's entire backside began to wag.

As she moved further into the yard, Hank ran circles around Gina's legs. She tossed it as hard as she could toward the trees that surrounded the property, and the dog took off after it. He disappeared into the underbrush and reemerged almost immediately, tearing back toward her to drop the ball at her feet. Gina's smile widened as she picked up and threw the ball again. She wheezed slightly at the exertion, but did it repeatedly anyway, laughing to herself as Hank bounded out of the tree line like a rabbit. Finally, a coughing fit overtook her and she had to stop. She leaned over and patted Hank, scratching his side and making his foot thump. The sun began to disappear into the tree line, signaling to Gina that she should probably go back to the campsite, but she ignored it and turned to walk back through the door. She stopped suddenly as she spotted a small storage cabinet against the house. She crossed to it and pulled it open. Her eyes went immediately to a cardboard box full of old spray paint cans, so she pulled it out. Selecting a dirty can of blue and a newer can of red that matched the chair by the door, she walked around to the side of the house.

Hank lay in the grass a few feet away from Gina as she worked, gnawing on the ball and coating it in drool. Gina breathed hard as she reached up to dot the "i" in her name. She pulled back to inspect her masterpiece, squinting slightly in the rapidly dimming light. *Gina and Hank were here.* She paused for a moment and reached up again to draw a simple flower outline around the dot above the "i." There, finished. She glanced down at Hank, still contentedly slobbering on the ball, and dropped the cans to the ground. She walked around to the front of the house and retrieved her things; she picked up another brick and hurled it through one of the living room windows just for the heck of it, grabbing another and tossing it through the other panes as well. She jumped slightly when Hank bumped the back of her knee with his wet nose, the drooly ball firmly wedged in his mouth.

When she reached the campsite, it was way past dark. Eric and Louis sat on logs opposite one another around the fire, bickering about something. They suddenly stopped when they noticed her approaching.

"Gina?" Louis asked. "What…why do you have feathers on you?"

"No reason." Gina plucked one off her shoulder and tossed it into the fire.

"I was starting to worry," Eric said earnestly.

"No need." Gina replied, dropping her bag to the ground.

"Where did you go?"

"Let's get one thing straight," Gina said firmly, sitting down hard on a log. "I don't answer to you." She stared into the fire, ignoring the stunned expressions on the boys' faces. "I'm in charge of me and Hank. I don't have to tell you where I'm going or where I've been." She paused to breathe for a moment. "I appreciate the concern, but it's none of your business what I do."

"…understood." Louis said softly, sitting quietly on the log and watching Gina with a curious expression. Eric's eyebrows knitted together as he stared at the ground. "Well…anyone hungry?"

Chapter Thirty

Alma, OK

"Do you have any...kings?"

Joey shook his head. The rain pounded mercilessly on the ceiling of the gas station where Zach, Millie, and the twins had taken up refuge.

"Dang," Zach said, drawing a new card. "I was sure I had that one."

Joey smiled and stuck his tongue out of his mouth slightly as he sorted through his cards. He tapped his chin thoughtfully, and held up three fingers.

"Any threes?" Zach glanced at his cards. "Sh-"

Millie looked up from where she and Ella sat on a picnic blanket on the floor making friendship bracelets, catching Zach's eye.

"...Oot." Zach finished. "Shoot." He held out the three of clubs, and Joey took it gleefully.

"Good job, Joey!" Ella called, giving him a thumbs-up. Joey grinned again and set the pair of threes aside. Ella held up the bracelet she was working on for Millie to inspect. "Is it done?"

Millie looked the sloppy blue-and-red braid over, comparing it to her own purple and green one, and smiled. "Yes ma'am, that looks done to me!" She took it from Ella and tied it into a knot. Ella took that one and the green-and-blue bracelet she'd finished previously and hopped up, running over to Zach and Joey's card table.

"Here, Joey!" Ella said, wrapping the green and blue bracelet around his wrist. "This one's yours." She twisted it under, making a loosely folded knot. She then turned to Zach, and grabbed his wrist. "And this one's yours!" She looped the blue and red bracelet around his wrist and tied it off similarly.

"Now we're gonna be friends forever 'cause I got one too." She held up her arm, showing off her red-and-purple bracelet.

Zach grinned and admired her handiwork. "That looks very nice, thank you."

Millie stood and crossed to the counter, reaching into her backpack. She pulled out her map and pencil and laid them out on the countertop.

Zach glanced at Millie, and beckoned to Ella. "Hey kiddo, take my spot for a minute, will ya?" He handed over his cards and stood, going to the counter to look at the map with Millie. "What's the mileage today?"

Millie sighed, charting their progress. "Half of yesterday, which is two-thirds of the day before."

"Damn. We've got to find a better mode of transportation."

"No kidding." Millie crossed to the front door and looked out, glancing down the road at the city in the distance. "We should get bikes again, I'm sure they've got some in town somewhere."

"The twins can't ride, though."

"We can pick up some of those kid seats that fit behind the adult seats." Millie turned around to face him again. "We'll have to figure something out for supplies, but maybe we can find really big baskets to attach to the front."

Zach's face lit up. "I've got an idea." He looked out the window, assessing the rain. It had slowed considerably in the past ten minutes, and the clouds seemed to be breaking finally. "Alright, everybody," he said, wheeling to face the twins, "Who's ready to get smuggled?"

Ella squealed and Joey clapped his hands, dropping the cards to the foldout table. They ran over to the wagon and jumped in, laying as flat as they could in between the other supplies. Millie picked up and folded the picnic blanket, nestling it in beside them. Zach unhooked the tarp he'd attached to the back and pulled it tightly over the twins and supplies.

Millie rolled her eyes, laughing quietly as he tucked the tarp around the bottom and tied it down with a small rope.

"Alright spies, you ready for your secret mission?" Zach called to the twins.

"Yeah!" Ella chirped.

Zach picked his poncho and backpack up off of the floor and slipped them on as Millie did the same. He wheeled the heavy wagon to the front door and charged out into the weather.

Thirty minutes and four stops for fresh air later, they reached a sporting goods store in a strip mall. The front door hung open, allowing Zach to wheel the wagon directly inside. He dropped his backpack to the ground and Millie set hers next to it.

"Alrighty," Zach said, bending to unhook the tarp, "Release the Kraken!"

Joey and Ella popped up from under the tarp with a "ROOOAR!" Zach clutched his chest and stumbled backwards.

"Holy cow," he said, eyes wide, "Those are the scariest Krakens we've ever found!"

"We're hungry," Ella said, baring her teeth, "We're gonna eat you!" The twins hopped out of the wagon and ran at him, prompting a chase around the entrance of the store. Millie laughed and shook her head as Zach skidded around a checkout counter and headed back for the wagon with Ella right on his tail and Joey not far behind her. Zach ducked behind Millie.

"Take her!" He yelled to the 'Krakens,' giving Millie a small push forward.

"Hey!" Millie protested as the twins advanced, 'claws' at the ready and about to pounce. "Hold on," she said, holding her hands out, "Don't Krakens eat Spaghetti-O's?"

The twins stopped and looked at each other.

"Yes," Ella said.

"Do the Krakens want some Spaghetti-O's?"

The twins nodded, and Millie told them to get out the picnic blanket and they could have some. The 'Krakens' did as they were told, and Millie dug out two cans of Spaghetti-O's and a protein shake for herself; Zach took a can of alphabet soup and sat on the edge of the picnic blanket. Handing the cans off with two spoons to the twins, Millie noted that they were running low on food and water.

When the hasty meal was done, Millie stood. "Hey," she told Zach, "If you don't need my help here, I think I'll run down the road and see if I can restock our food supplies at the grocery store down the way."

Zach nodded, reaching into his backpack to grab the wind-up lamp. "Sounds good to me. I was going to go to the bike section and see what I could find to fix up a couple of bikes. I may need the wagon, though."

"Cool." Millie pulled her utility belt out of her backpack and snapped it around her waist, glancing at the twins. "Do you want me to take them with me or are you good?"

Ella, overhearing, piped up. "I want to help!"

Zach shrugged. "I guess that answers that question."

Joey set his can down, got to his feet and walked over to Millie, slipping his hand into hers.

"Do you want to come with me?" Millie asked. The boy looked at Ella, who gave him a thumbs-up, and looked back at Millie with a nod. "Well then, let's go!"

By the time Millie and Joey made it to the other side of the parking lot, the sun was out. Joey let go of Millie's hand and ran to the sliding glass doors, which were, refreshingly, intact and tightly shut. Millie took her flathead screwdriver off her tool belt and raised its handle to break the glass; she stopped after noticing the "emergency procedure" sign by the door.

"Why make a mess when we don't have to?" She told Joey. Crossing to the middle of the door, she wedged the dull flat end between the doors, jimmying them apart so she could get her hands in between. She pulled outwards and the door opened toward her like a normal door would. They stepped inside the grocery store and Millie grabbed two buggies, one to carry things and the other to wedge in between the doors to keep them open. Joey grabbed her leg, hiding behind her. "It's okay," she reassured him, "There's no monsters in here." She glanced around and saw a row of small LED flashlights on the checkout counter nearest her, and took two black ones. She handed one to Joey and told him, "This is your own flashlight so you can see in the dark." He whispered a small "thank you" and they were off.

Millie was pleasantly surprised to find that the aisles seemed mostly intact. The looting that they'd seen through the rest of their journey for some reason hadn't happened here. Millie removed her flashlight from her belt and clicked it on. She aimed it at the signs at the ends of each aisle, heading for the aisle that listed "nuts, jerky, and snacks." Sure enough, the aisle was packed with canned and bagged nuts of every kind, and a wide assortment of jerky. She smiled and reached out to take some packages of jerky.

Suddenly, something clattered loudly behind the aisle in front of them. Joey's eyes grew wide and he clung to Millie's leg. She put a finger to her lips and moved quietly down the aisle to see what had made the noise. Leaning slowly out of the aisle, she came face-to-face with a pair of twitching, bloodshot and jaundiced eyes. She screamed and jumped back, pushing Joey behind her. The man who the eyes belonged to followed them around the corner, his jaw open wide but no sound coming out. Millie's hair stood on end as she realized he was wearing only boxers.

"Stay back," Millie uttered, terror constricting her vocal chords. The man took another step forward, clamping his teeth together. Millie suddenly remembered the mace on her belt and grabbed it, flipping the unlock latch with her thumb. She pointed it at him, pressed the button, and...nothing. The man let out a bloodcurdling scream, and Millie threw the defective mace at his head. She grabbed Joey under the armpits and hauled him down the aisle, beelining for the front of the store. She slipped and almost fell on top of Joey before regaining her footing and running for the door. Suddenly, the man skidded out from behind an aisle, blocking their path. Millie swerved to avoid him and bolted for the back of the store, hoisting Joey onto her hip as she ran. The man howled like a dog and tore after them, making all sorts of terrifying sounds as he went. The man was too fast, circling around and cutting Millie and Joey off again. Millie stopped short and backed up as the man walked slowly toward them, drool leaking from the corners of his mouth. Millie looked around wildly for something, anything to stop him with. A row of salsa jars to her left caught her eye, and she seized one, throwing it at the man. It bounced off of him and shattered on the ground. His mouth broke into a wild, crazed grin as he continued forward, stepping over the broken glass. Millie dropped Joey to the ground and pushed him behind her; she shoved an entire row of salsa jars with all her might, shattering them in front of her.

"Joey, run, get help!" Millie cried, grabbing more jars to throw as the man walked right through the glass as if it were playground sand. The boy took off wobbly toward the front door, and the man's head snapped toward him, honing in. Millie's heart pounded as the man stalked across the glass without a wince, his eyes threatening to pop out of his head as he leered after Joey.

"Hey!" Millie yelled, making the man's head snap back toward her. He made a horrid shrieking sound and reared back to pounce on Millie, who grabbed a can of cheese sauce and heaved it at him, striking him square in the forehead. He howled and she spun, tearing down the aisle. She turned the corner, heading for the front door, where she saw Joey clumsily trying to clamber over the cart wedged in the door. The man shrieked again and Millie looked over her shoulder, horrified as the man headed straight for Joey. Joey looked behind him and cried out, freezing in fear. Millie skidded to a stop and grabbed the nearest thing on the aisle end, a can of soda.

"HEY!" She screamed, running at the man. He glanced at her right as the can struck his shoulder. He shrieked, skidding on his bloodied feet. "I'm over here, you bastard!" The man's jaw dropped open again and his head jerked to one side as he charged toward her. Millie's eyes widened and she took off down an aisle marked "Pest Control and Emergency." The aisle dead-ended into a corner, where Millie spotted a can of Raid. She grabbed in and spun to face her attacker – who wasn't there. She whirled around, looking down the aisle next to her, and spinning back again. The man tore around the corner, arms outstretched. Millie squeezed the trigger, unleashing a stream of white foam directly into the man's bloodshot eyes as he leapt toward her. His hand closed into a fist and socked her in the mouth as he fell, taking her down as well. He screamed and flailed around, bloodied feet keeping him from standing properly, as Millie scrambled in a daze to get away from him.

He grabbed her ankle and began to drag himself up her body. She screamed and kicked with her free foot, hitting him square in the face; he barely flinched as his nose began to gush blood. Millie reached behind her for something, anything to hit him with, and found a hammer. Millie sobbed and brought it down on his head as hard as she could.

A sickening crack, a spray of blood, and the man's shrieks garbled. He convulsed for a minute, then finally lay still. Millie drug herself away, the pain in her jaw finally hitting her. She wept bitterly as she got to her feet and stumbled toward the door, tears and pain blurring her vision.

As Millie pushed past the buggy holding the door open, Zach ran up, gun drawn and pointed at the ground. His eyes grew wide as he took in her blood-spattered clothes and bleeding mouth.

"Oh my God."

"I killed him, I-I killed him," Millie choked out, staggering toward him. "I'm sorry, I killed him."

Zach holstered the gun and grabbed her in an embrace, lowering them both to the ground as her legs gave out. "Are you sure he's…"

Millie nodded into his shoulder, clutching him for dear life. "I'm sorry, I'm so sorry."

"Hey, look at me," Zach pulled back, taking her head in his hands. "Don't you ever apologize for defending your own. You hear me?"

Millie nodded, tears cascading down her cheeks. Her eyes suddenly grew wide and she looked past him. "Where are they?"

"Safe. They're hiding in a cabinet," Zach replied, pulling her slowly to her feet. He looked past her, spotting a pool of blood leaking out of one of the store aisles. He slipped an arm around her and led her toward the sporting goods store. "Come on."

Sitting in the sporting good store's camping display, Zach silently dabbed at Millie's busted lip with a dampened cloth. The room was deathly silent, outside of the quiet hum coming from the wind-up light. The twins sat huddled in a tent a few feet away, quietly coloring by flashlight. Millie stared at the ground, the image of the man writhing and the crack of the hammer splitting his skull replaying over and over in her mind. A tear rolled down her cheek, and Zach instinctively wiped it away with his thumb. Their eyes connected for a moment, and his hand lingered on her face.

"Does it hurt?" He asked quietly.

"Less now, but still a bit."

Zach absentmindedly brushed his thumb over the corner of her bruised lip, cupping her jaw. Millie unconsciously started to lean into his hand, heart fluttering as he moved in as well.

Suddenly, the tent unzipped loudly, breaking the moment. They both pulled back and looked at the tent. Joey rubbed his eye with his fist as he crossed to Millie and climbed into her lap. Ella followed closely behind him, stopping beside the plastic campfire.

"Joey's scared that the bad man is going to come back," she said, looking at Zach.

Zach set the cloth on the armrest of his camping chair and looked at Joey. "You don't have to worry about that anymore, Bud," he said gently as Millie cradled the small boy. "The bad guy is gone forever."

"As long as we are around," Millie said, looking at Zach, "Nobody is ever going to hurt you. We'll make sure of that."

"Can we finish the bikes now?" Ella asked, switching gears quickly, as only a child can.

"What bikes?" Millie asked.

"That idea I told you about," Zach replied, straightening up. "The one I stole from Oleson."

"Tricycles!" Ella sang, throwing her hands into the air. "Over there!" She pointed to the back of the store, beaming.

"I found a few boxes of adult tricycles that need to be assembled; it sounds dopey, but they've got big baskets in the back and we could easily attach kid-seats as well," Zach explained.

"I think that's a very good idea." Millie glanced at Ella and at Joey, who slowly nodded off in her arms. "I think it might be naptime for the twins."

"No," Ella whined, "I want to help!"

"Stop it and do as I say," Millie said, more firmly than she'd meant to. Ella pouted and stomped over to the tent, climbing inside with a huff. Millie put a hand to her forehead, her eyebrows knitting together.

"Here," Zach offered, standing and reaching out to take Joey from her. The boy tightened his grip, clinging to Millie's bloodied t-shirt.

She sighed feebly, the withdrawal of adrenaline making her suddenly exhausted.

"Hey," Zach said gently, "Why don't you get some sleep, too? I'll bring the trikes over and start putting together everything that doesn't require a second set of hands." He glanced to the large empty space beside the camping display. "I'll be right here."

Millie didn't even try to argue. "Thank you." She stood, cradling Joey and taking him over to the tent. Once she and both twins were zipped inside, Zach went over to the bike section. He leaned on one of the trike boxes, closing his eyes a moment. He shook the fear from his head and hoisted the box from the ground, carrying it back to the tent. Dropping the box by the tent, he headed for a different aisle.

Most of the ammunition was gone, but Zach found a box of .357 magnum shells at the very back of a display. He took the revolver from his holster and reloaded it, putting the box in his pocket.

Millie awoke to Zach and a man's voice, and her eyes snapped open. Her heart pounded as she gently slipped her arm out from under the pillow where Joey's head lay and unzipped the tent quietly. She visibly relaxed when she saw Zach sitting on the ground next to a partially-assemble trike; he held a tire in his lap and stared at the crackling radio.

"...As I've said before, there are no more doctors in this world, and if you leave a rampant infection unchecked, it can kill faster than you'd ever expect. Now, suppose you've just gotten cut by a sharp piece of metal. The immediate problem is of course, how to stop the bleeding. Our bodies are wonderfully designed, and for the most part bleeding will stop on its own, though applying pressure is the best way to speed that along."

Zach looked up at Millie. "Whaddya know, Doc," he smirked, the corners of his eyes crinkling playfully. "You got that right." Millie returned a small smile and moved to sit next to him. "I just tried again to transmit back to Ira, but I guess he didn't hear me." Zach sighed. "The kiddos still asleep?"

"Mm-hmm," she replied, staring into the lamplight.

"...how're you doing?"

"I'm..." Millie paused, searching for the words. "I'll be okay."

"It's easy for me to tell you what you should do, but really. Don't ever second-guess yourself when it comes to protecting them." Zach glanced at her, her eyes downcast and studying the floor. He cleared his throat, rubbing the back of his neck. "When I was about eight, my mom whooped three older boys who she caught beating up on me. Hit each and every one of them with a stick she just happened to have on hand. That maternal instinct kicked in and well…they didn't bother me ever again. But more importantly, it taught me that even when things looked as bleak as they could be, my mom would readily kick ass to keep me safe." He glanced at her again, noting the smile that graced her lips.

"…thank you," Millie said after a moment.

"For what?" Zach leaned back slightly.

"Just…everything." Millie shrugged, looking at him out of the corner of her eye. "This whole situation would have shaped up a lot differently if I hadn't met you."

"And to think I was originally going to avoid Pennsylvania altogether."

Millie chuckled, bumping his shoulder with hers. "That would've been one heck of a detour."

"True." They sat in silence for a moment, listening to Ira and the gentle hum of the lamp. Zach studied Millie out of the corner of his eye for a moment before inching his hand toward hers. He nudged her pinky, and flipped his hand over to rest palm-up on the floor. A smile drifted across her face, and she linked her fingers with his. She sighed and leaned into him slightly, resting her head on his shoulder.

"We're gonna be okay," she said softly. "Everything is gonna be okay."

Chapter Thirty-One

Sarepta, LA

The sun beat down on the trio mercilessly, seeming to pierce right through Louis's and Eric's ballcap and bandana, respectively, and Gina's white floppy hat. They'd been hiking with extreme dedication for the past couple of days, keeping their heads down and sunglasses on tightly. The road up the large hill was rough, and Gina often had to stop and jerk her oxygen tank up over a rock or out of a pothole. She felt the need to turn it on less and less as the days went by, but kept it with her just in case.

The usual order in their marches meant that Louis took the lead, with Gina following close behind and Eric huffing to bring up the rear; Hank darted around at random. As the group made their way up a particularly twisty incline, Louis looked back to make sure Gina was doing okay. She took off her sunglasses to wipe her forehead, and for the first time he noticed how her eyes glinted almost amber in the sunlight. He felt himself smile as he continued on. He couldn't help staring, she was just so- *bap!* Louis walked into a pole. He took a step back and shook his head. Looking ahead, he saw train tracks leading into a massive, unnaturally dark tunnel with a train's caboose sticking out of it.

"Hey guys…" Louis swallowed hard. "I think we need to turn back." Gina stopped, and Eric wheezed up to the front.

"What? …oh." Eric stood panting for a moment. "Well…let's just go around it." Eric pointed at a narrow, steep path up the hill, and went toward it.

"Eric, wait," Louis called after him. "Let's think about this for a minute. If we go back, we can bunk for the night and think about a plan for the morning. Let's just go back to that little town a ways back and start back tomorrow."

Eric turned back around, shaking his head. "We're losing daylight. If we go over the hill, it will take less time than going back, and we can bunk at the next town."

"But we have no idea where that is." Louis wiped his forehead and adjusted his hat. "I say we go back."

"Guys…" Gina began, taking off her mask to speak better.

"I say we go over the hill." Eric took a step toward Louis.

"Guys-"

"No, we turn back." Louis took a step toward Eric.

Eric locked eyes with Louis. "The. Hill. Louis."

"Turn. Back. Eric."

"If we turn back, we'll be set back a solid day." Eric lifted his chin. "You want to get to Oklahoma so fast, this is the quickest way."

Louis crossed his arms. "Why do you care? You don't want to go to Nowhere anyway."

Eric's eyes narrowed. "Yes, but I'm going now, aren't I?"

"I never said you weren't." Louis returned the aggravated glare, leaning over Eric slightly.

"Good. Because at this point you couldn't pay me to stay behind." Eric puffed out his chest subconsciously.

"What's this *really* about, Eric?" Louis asked after a moment.

Eric scoffed and shook his head. "Forget it. Why don't we ask Gina what *she* thinks we should do?"

They both turned to look at Gina, but all they saw was her oxygen tank and mask lying on the ground. Eric picked them up.

"Gina?" Louis spun to see where she went. "Hank!"

Eric followed Louis's line of sight to the dog, disappearing into the tunnel. "Gina!"

The boys exchanged a look, then both sprinted for the tunnel. Louis entered the narrow left side where Hank had gone, and Eric took the wider right side.

As Louis entered the cave, he stopped. Eric ran past him on the other side, shouldering the oxygen tank.

Okay, breathe. Louis inhaled. *It's just a tunnel. This isn't* The Stand, *no bodies are going to pop up and…don't think about that. Okay ready? One… Two… Three!*

"Ahhhh!" Louis bolted through the tunnel, screaming like a banshee. As he leapt over a log in the way, he mentally (and mildly) swore. *Please don't let there be zombies, please don't let there be zomb* – WHOOMPH! Louis tripped over a branch and fell flat onto his stomach. He groaned and rolled onto his back, letting out another shriek as he looked dead into the face of a corpse leaning against the passenger car's window. He could almost hear it groan. *Go, go, go.* He scrambled to his feet, took a breath, and bolted toward the exit.

When he re-emerged on the other side, he saw Eric quickly approaching Gina, who stared out past a guardrail over a valley.

"Why did you leave your tank behind?" Eric asked her.

"I don't need it anymore." Gina said simply.

"Oh, okay. Cool."

"Glad you're feeling better," Louis interjected.

"*I* was worried about you," Eric added.

"Don't," she snapped. She pursed her lips, face otherwise blank. Eric looked like he'd been slapped.

"...well, we should probably get moving," Louis said gently. "The next town can't be too far from here." Eric's face was red, but Louis was unsure if it was from the heat, exertion, or embarrassment.

Eric looked around, spotting a tree with a low-set branch. "Hey, I'll scout for it!" He darted towards the tree, grasping the branch firmly.

"Don't-" Gina began, but it was too late. He'd already swung his bad leg up into the tree.

"Eric, get down from there," Louis warned, "You could fall and kill yourself!"

"I'm fine," Eric grunted, pulling up farther into the tree. He wedged his prosthetic into a crevice to gain leverage as he clambered higher. "I can do it." He reached the middle of the giant tree and pushed some of the branches aside. "Hey," he called down, "I see a biggish town down in that valley. It's really close, maybe thirty, forty-five minutes to walk or so?"

"Okay great, now get down," Louis replied.

Eric ignored him, instead stretching further up and shaking his bad foot free of the crevice. He planted it firmly on the next branch up, letting one hand go to push more branches aside. *If I can move out a little more, I can...*

Snap! The branch he stood on broke, sending him toppling to the ground.

"Eric!" Gina cried hoarsely, but it was too late. There was a sickening crunch followed by an almost unholy scream as the boy crumpled to the ground.

"Aw, hell," Louis managed as they ran to his side.

Gina covered her mouth at the sight of Eric's foot, turned inward at an unnatural angle. Louis gagged, clenching his jaw to keep from vomiting. Eric writhed on the ground, sobbing in pain as Hank tried to lick his face.

"Get away!" Eric screamed, lurching away from the dog. Gina grabbed Hank's collar to pull him back, horror still written on her face.

"What do we do? What do we do?" Louis asked no one in particular, putting his hands on his head.

"*Help* me," Eric begged, tears leaking down his face.

"How?" Gina asked, exchanging a horrified look with Louis.

Suddenly, Eric went quiet. His eyes rolled back in his head, and he stilled.

"Oh my God," Gina uttered, mouth dropping open. Hank broke free of her grasp and ran up to resume licking the boy's face. She dropped to her knees beside Eric and grabbed his wrist to check his pulse like she'd seen on TV once.

"It's okay," Louis said unreassuringly, "I think he's in shock."

"How is that okay?" Gina screamed, wheeling around.

The sudden outburst made Louis step back, eyes wider than ever. "I don't know!" He cried, running his hands down his sweaty face. "I just…Ira said something about that the other night, something about shock being the body's way of protecting itself from pain. So as long as he's not hurting we can figure out if it's broken or not, right?"

"Of COURSE it's broken, look at it!" Gina gestured at the foot, still limply turned inward.

Louis gagged again. "Okay, okay, but maybe it's just dislocated or something, we don't know because we aren't doctors."

"There aren't any more doctors, remember?" Gina finally found Eric's pulse, rapid but steady. "He's alive still." She unconsciously put a hand to her brow, jerking away painfully when she touched the burn.

"Good, good," Louis mumbled, nodding. "We need to set it before he wakes up, right? And find him some pain meds stronger than the ibuprofen I've got or whatever this is, it's gonna suck."

"Set it how?" Gina struggled to her feet, wheezing. "And even if we can find pain meds, what if they mess with his diabetes? He hasn't checked his blood or whatever in hours."

"Well…" Louis looked at the tunnel and swallowed hard. "He's too heavy to carry all that way, and we can't risk dropping him and making it worse. I can run back to that little town and find a pharmacy or something and get a splint and different kinds of pain meds." Louis dropped his backpack to the ground, kneeling beside it. "Can you stay with him in case he wakes up?"

Gina nodded, glancing down at the boy's prostrate form.

"Okay." Louis fished around in his backpack, pulled out a blanket, and tossed it to her. "Here, put this on him if he gets cold."

"It's a hundred degrees out here," Gina retorted.

"Well I don't know, he might want it anyway!" Louis exclaimed, opening his bag's side pocket. "Okay, here," he held out a bottle of ibuprofen. "Give him this when he wakes up."

"How much?" Gina took it and looked at the label.

"I dunno," he adjusted his cap once more and stood, leaving the backpack on the ground. "Four, maybe? Double the dose, I think. I had a broken tooth once that I had to wait two days to get fixed and my dad double-dosed me to take the edge off and I'm still here, so he should be okay."

She nodded, looking at Eric. "I hope you're right. I hope it's not broken."

"Me too. Otherwise…" Louis trailed off, chewing on his lower lip.

From the ground, Eric whimpered. His eyes were still closed, but his lower lip trembled.

"Go," Gina said, taking the blanket and ibuprofen over to Eric. "Leave the backpack. Run."

Louis nodded and spun on his heel, tearing towards the tunnel.

"It's okay," Gina told Eric. She swallowed hard and glanced at his foot. "It's gonna be okay."

Chapter Thirty-Two

Broken Bow, OK

Ella sang softly to herself in the seat behind Millie, her feet tapping either side of Millie's hips in time with the song. The tricycle's mountain-bike wheels handled the rough terrain surprisingly well. Ahead, Zach slowed at the hilltop to allow Millie to catch up.

"Looks like rain," Millie panted, allowing her trike to coast slowly down the incline. "Maybe we should fine a resting place?" She glanced around, spotting a building down a dirt path in the near distance.

Zach glanced upwards. "Nah it's just a little thunder."

"Zach…"

"Relax, we have probably a solid twenty more minutes before it-" Zach stopped suddenly as the sky opened up and rain poured down.

"Over there!" Millie called, kicking off the ground toward the dirt road.

As they pedaled furiously, Ella squealed in protest at the weather. "Stop it, rain!"

Upon reaching the building – a log cabin – Zach and Millie pulled under the awning overhanging the roof. Millie looked at Zach, who held up a finger.

"Not a word."

"I didn't say anything." Millie smirked, shaking her wet hair out of her face. She looked at the cabin, then to the clouds. "We might be here a while."

"Yeah…" Zach dismounted the bike and unlatched his leg holster. "I'll check it out; wait here." He removed the pistol and pointed it at the ground, walking to the front door. It was unlocked, so he disappeared inside. Millie unbuckled Ella, then Joey, and set them both on the ground.

After a minute, Zach stuck his head out the door, holstering his pistol. "All clear."

Millie lifted the tarp from her trike's back basket and pulled the clothing backpack out, ushering the twins into the cabin. The front door opened into a combo living room/kitchen; lounging on the couch by the open window were three cats. A fourth meowed from her position perched on a shelf. The cabin was very well-lit, thanks to the numerous large windows in each room, and it was overall a very neat and tidy place.

Millie opened the suitcase and pulled out a set of dry clothes for each twin, sending Ella into the bathroom to change first. Zach wandered over to the sink, noticing that one of the bowls on the drying rack still had water on it.

"Mil," he said calmly, "We need to leave, now."

She turned around, confused. "Wh-"

BAM! The back door flew open, and two baying bloodhounds burst inside.

Millie pushed Joey behind her as Zach grabbed for his gun.

"Easy ladies! What's all the…" A man looking to be a few years older than Zach stopped suddenly in the doorway, carrying a bag of cat food on one shoulder and a bundle of logs on the other. His green eyes flitted to Millie, then to Zach, then to the pistol Zach now gripped tightly in both hands.

"Oh. Hello," the man said, cautiously polite.

"Who are you?" Zach asked, eyes locked on the man.

"Jim Walker," he replied, "Can I ask what you folks are doing in my house?"

"Oh," Millie spoke up, turning to keep herself in between Joey and the hounds as they sniffed at her, "We're sorry, we had no idea this place was occupied."

"No problem at all," Jim said, eyeing Zach's gun again. "If you want to put that away, we can talk like civilized folk." Zach lowered the gun slowly. "'Preciate it." One of the bloodhounds brayed again, and Joey whimpered. "Theodora! Elender!" Jim scolded, continuing into the room. He dropped the cat food and logs onto the ground, snapping his fingers at the hounds. "You two oughta be ashamed of yourselves, scaring people like that." The dogs tucked their tails and plodded away to lie down in front of the fireplace. Zach, Millie, and Joey stared at him blankly. "The dogs came with name tags, and I didn't have the heart to change 'em."

The bathroom door opened suddenly and Ella hopped out, landing with both feet together and holding the wet clothes above her head. She slowly turned to look at Jim, eyes growing wide.

"Hi there, Little Lady," Jim said.

"My name is Ella, *not* Little Lady," Ella said matter-of-factly.

"Ella!" Millie chastised, taking the clothes from her.

Jim laughed. "It's okay. It's nice to meet you, Ella."

"I'm Zach," Zach offered, extending his right hand. "And that's Millie and Joey."

Jim took his hand and shook it. "Pleasure to meet ch'y'all. I was actually just heading in to refill the cats' bowls and get lunch going." Jim looked outside. "Y'all are welcome to stay until the rain lets up."

"Thank you," Zach nodded. "We'll be on our way after that."

Jim carried the bundle of logs over to the fireplace and set them next to the two logs already on the hearth. He knelt beside them, pushing Elender (or was it Theodora?) away as she tried to lick him.

"Your house is very tidy," Millie remarked.

"Thank you, ma'am." Jim replied. He pulled some potato chips out of a zip lock bag in the cabinet by the fireplace, and placed them into the fireplace followed by the smaller of the two dry logs. "In the service, you kept your place clean or you paid the price, and I guess I just kept the habit of keeping things neat." He lit a chip, which quickly spread to the surrounding chips. The log slowly started to burn, overpowering the vaguely unpleasant smell of burning potato chip.

Zach's eyebrows went up. "You're in the army?"

Jim nodded. "Joined on my eighteenth and haven't looked back." He fanned the fire slightly. "Had my eye on Special Forces, already went through jump school at Benning. I was on leave when everything got f-" he stopped suddenly, looking at Millie. "Apologies, ma'am. Sailor mouth ain't just for the navy, still trying the break that."

Millie resisted the urge to shoot Zach a look. "It's okay. Thank you for your service."

"Oh, don't thank me," Jim shrugged. "Didn't really get a chance to do anything." He picked up the cat food and carried it into the spare room.

Millie took the moment to hand Joey a dry set of clothes and usher him into the bathroom to change. She took Ella's clothes and laid them out on the hearth to dry. Zach crossed to the couch and stood by Millie.

Jim came out of the spare room balancing five bowls of cat food in his hands, setting four in a row on the ground.

"That's a lot of cats," Ella said as the cats swarmed the bowls.

"They were here when I got here," Jim replied, petting the black-and-white cat's head, "I wasn't about to run them off. They keep the mice away and are good company, plus it was their house first. The dogs, however, showed up one day without warning and tend to disappear for days at a time before coming back reeking of skunk or covered in mud." Jim stood, taking the fifth cat bowl with him.

"What are their names?" Ella asked. Joey opened the bathroom door, handing his wet clothes to Zach.

"The black one and orange one are Bagheera and Shere Khan," Jim crossed the kitchen as he spoke, "Appropriate since they're always scuffling. That's Duchess," he pointed at the mostly white cat with gray tabby patches, "The solid gray is Dinah, and the mama cat is Nala."

"Mama cat?" Ella asked excitedly.

"Yes ma'am," Jim opened a bottom cabinet slightly and slid the bowl in. "She's under here."

"Baby kittens?" Joey asked, his voice barely over a whisper.

Jim nodded and opened the cabinet slightly, waving them over. Joey and Ella crept up to the cabinet slowly, peeking in to see a gray tabby nursing five small wriggly lumps of different colors.

"Can I pet them?" Ella asked.

"Not right now," Jim replied, shutting the door and standing back up. "They're eating too, but maybe in a little while they'll be done and I can pull one out for a minute."

Joey stood off to the side, trying to pet three cats as they circled and rubbed his legs.

"Where you folks headed?" Jim asked.

"We're meeting up with a friend," Zach replied vaguely.

"His name is Ira and he lives in the radio!" Ella piped up before anyone could shush her.

"Ira from Nowhere?" Jim smiled. "I've got five first-aid kits thanks to him." He gestured to his stockroom.

"Are you and the kitties coming to Ira's house, too?" Ella asked, reaching down to pet the cats still circling Joey.

Jim shook his head. "No reason to. I'm content here in my cabin with my animals; I stocked up on food and've been chopping wood for the upcoming winter. I don't really need anything else."

"Do you ever get scared at nighttime?" Ella asked.

"No. I know I'm well protected."

"Don't you get bored?" Ella continued her battery of questions.

"Ella, that's not nice," Millie spoke up.

Jim smiled. "I think I'm going to take up woodworking and gardening, but for now I mostly chop wood and hike and watch movies."

"Movies?" Ella's eyes grew wide. "How many movies do you have?"

Jim opened up a closet near the front door, displaying a shelving unit of easily over two hundred movies. "I collect 'em as I come across 'em. I've got everything from cartoons to foreign language films."

"Cartoons!" Ella squealed, clapping her hands.

"I can put a movie on while I work on lunch for us," Jim said, "You and Joey just need to pick one out." Ella squealed again, and she and Joey dove into the collection of movies.

"How can we help?" Zach asked.

Jim pulled a big black pot out from a cupboard. "If you could fill this with water, I'd appreciate it!"

Zach obliged, and Millie stepped forward. "Is there anything you need food-wise?"

"I was planning on tuna helper for today, so if y'all got anything that would complement it, feel free to pitch it in."

Millie ducked outside to grab a couple of cans of peas, and a tin of tuna. Ella handed Jim 'The Jungle Book' cartoon, and he popped it into the small battery-powered DVD player. A sudden wave of nostalgia swept over Zach as he heard the opening music, reminiscing for a moment.

Millie re-entered the room as Jim showed Zach where to put the pot - on a rack over the fireplace flame - and helped him get it into place.

"Thank you for sharing your food with us," Millie said, setting the peas down on the wooden countertop.

"You're supposed to help those who need help," Jim said simply, "Keeping y'all dry and feeding you is the least I could do."

Zach glanced at the twins who sat enraptured on the floor in front of the DVD player's screen. "We've got to get us one of those."

The water began to boil, and Jim poured the noodles into the pot, adding a touch of salt.

"Salt keeps the noodles from sticking," he mentioned. Jim set his egg timer and sat back to wait.

By the time they ate and cleaned up, the rain had slowed to almost nothing. Zach loaded their things back into his trike basket as Ella and Joey said goodbye to all of Jim's cats.

"Lunch was wonderful, thank you again for letting us stay for as long as we have." Millie said to Jim.

"No problem. Y'all will be okay out there on the road? You know there's plenty of open cabins around if you need somewhere to rest for the night, just look for one with no cars in the driveway. I'd let you stay here, but my house frankly isn't big enough."

"Oh it's fine!" Millie assured. "We've got to be on our way anyhow."

"Millie, you ready?" Zach called.

"Coming!" Millie replied. "Well, is that everything?"

"Yes ma'am! It's been nice getting to know you folks. If y'all are ever back this way, feel free to stop by."

"Thank you, Jim." Millie smiled.

"Goodbye Miss Millie. Zach." Jim extended his hand to Zach.

"Bye, Jim," Zach replied, shaking his hand. "Thanks."

Zach and Millie loaded up the twins, climbed onto their trikes, and rode off down the road.

Down the road lay another cabin, a two-story home made of redwood.

"Let's go there!" Ella cried upon seeing it, "Stairs!"

Once Zach broke in and made sure nobody was currently occupying the cabin, the twins were allowed to run up the indoor stairs and bump down them on their bottoms until they tired themselves out.

"I'm not sleepy," Ella yawned as Millie carried her up to the bedroom that had two twin beds. Joey followed closely behind, thumb firmly planted in his mouth.

"I think you are, Love," Millie replied, pulling back the checkered quilt and crisp sheets.

"Bedtime story?" Joey asked as he climbed up into the second bed.

Millie thought for a moment. "Okay, but only one." She pulled a teal wooden chair out from the corner and sat down in it.

"Once upon a time," she began, conjuring the story as she spoke, "There lived…" she paused.

"A princess bear!" Ella chirped.

"A princess bear," Millie continued, "And a?" She looked at Joey. The boy's thumb was firmly planted in his mouth, and he smiled around it.

"A knight bear, of course! The princess bear was named Ella, and the knight bear was named Joey."

"Like us!" Ella blinked slowly.

"That's right. And one day, the two little bears were outside playing when they met two other, bigger bears. The two bigger bears asked the little bears if they wanted to go on an adventure to a far-away castle, and the two little bears said 'yes.' So, the four bears all set out on an adventure across the world, heading straight for the magical castle. They had little adventures and expeditions along the way-"

"And a monster," whispered Joey. He yawned.

"Yes…and there was a monster, too." Millie reached out to stroke the boy's hair. "But the big bears told the little bears that the big bears would protect them forever, and that no monsters would ever hurt the little bears, even if the monsters ever popped up and were scary."

"Did the bears get to the castle?" Ella asked, her eyelids drooping.

"They did," a voice said from behind Millie. Millie glanced back at Zach, who'd appeared in the doorway at some point when she was telling the story. "They got to the castle and they lived happily ever after."

"Good." Ella said softly, eyes closing. "I like…happy endings."

Chapter Thirty-Three

Ira leaned away from the microphone off for a moment, settling his notebook in front of him. He took a swig of his water canteen, and leaned forward in his seat. "Friends, I know that things are difficult at present. We've all felt the loss, the profound loss of everyone we loved and the world that we knew, and sometimes it can be tempting to lie down and never get up again. It may feel as though the weight of the world is on your shoulders right now, but know that you are not alone. You are never alone..."

*

Gina pushed as Louis tried to lift the dolly out of the asphalt pothole it'd sunk into. Eric winced, gritting his teeth as beads of sweat ran down his face. The dolly suddenly popped loose and Eric cried out as his splinted foot smacked against the metal.

"I'm sorry, I'm sorry!" Louis said, grimacing. Eric fell back against the dolly, eyes closed tightly in pain.

"Be careful!" Eric hissed through gritted teeth.

"Maybe this wasn't a good idea," Gina stated, wheezing as the heat and exertion began to toll on her.

"You think?" Eric retorted.

"Hey!" Louis marched around to look Eric in the eye. "Don't get snappy at us when you're the one who got yourself into this."

"I'm in agony!" Eric raised up, his eyes wild and hair matted with sweat.

"And we're trying to help!" Louis said exasperatedly, leaning closer to Eric's face. "It's not my fault I couldn't find anything stronger than Tylenol in this awful town, and it's not Gina's fault that this was the best we could do for transportation right now."

Eric's chest heaved raggedly as they stared each other down. Finally, his head drooped, shoulders slumping.

"I'm sorry, okay?" He put his head in his hands, pursing his lips to try and keep his chin from wobbling. "Everything hurts and I just want to go home."

Louis' face softened. "...it's okay, I-"

Suddenly, Hank let out a low growl, staring unblinkingly down the road. The trio stopped and followed his gaze. There, in the exact middle of the road, stood a palomino pony with a long white mane. Astride the pony sat an older woman with long, jet black hair braided over her shoulder. They froze as she nudged the pony forward wordlessly, stopping about twenty feet away.

"What are you young'uns doing out here all by yourselves?"

Louis and Gina exchanged a look.

"Uh...he hurt his leg and we're going to fix it," Louis lied.

The woman raised an eyebrow. "Not like that you're not." She turned her pony slightly, aiming him toward the road she'd just come down. "Come on, we haven't got all day." The pony slowly plodded forward. leaving the trio dumbfounded. The woman stopped and glanced over her shoulder at Eric. "You want your leg fixed or not? Let's go! We need to get y'all out of the heat and into some air conditioning."

Gina glanced at Eric and began to follow, letting Louis push the dolly slowly up the road after the woman.

"Should we really be following a stranger to who knows where?" Louis asked under his breath.

"She's got AC," Eric replied quietly, wiping his eyes. "Plus, three of us, one of her. If things go weird we'll have the upper hand."

"*Two* of us," Louis corrected, "You can't exactly fight anyone right now."

"You wanna test that theory?" Eric said through gritted teeth.

Gina cleared her throat, staring the boys down. Eric looked away as Louis gave her an apologetic grimace.

"We'll be fine," Eric said, just barely loud enough for Louis to hear.

"I hope you're right about that," Louis replied uneasily as the woman and horse turned down a narrow paved road.

*

"...this is an entirely new world compared to what we once knew. In any time of upset and uncertainty, there will be those who will try to take advantage of the good-hearted. You must be vigilant. Look out for the snake in the grass; he'll bite your heel and slither off before you even realize he's there. Stay alert, and always watchful..."

*

Drake shook the can to mix the remaining paint. He planted a hand on the billboard's white surface, slowly and carefully finishing the "N"'s final line.

"Looks great, Drake!" He heard Xavier call from far below, his voice barely reaching. "They'll be able to see it from miles around!"

Drake smiled placidly to himself and stepped back, dropping the can off the side of the walkway. He admired his work, the six-foot-tall blue letters standing out like beacons against the white background. Community, HOPE. Fly, TN. He turned around and looked down the highway where Cleo was putting the finishing arrow on her sign: Come to Fly, We Offer Refuge. She would be rewarded well for the readability of her writing. Drake hummed to himself as he swung his leg over the edge and began to descend the ladder. Everything was going perfectly according to plan.

*

"...you mustn't give up; you have to keep going. There is always a reason to continue on, even if it's not obvious to you at this moment. Find something to do, somewhere to go, someone to be with; loneliness is the new murderer in the night, and you cannot let it take you down. You must keep moving, keeping striving for a reason to carry on. Because trust me, it is out there...Stay safe, stay vigilant, and I will talk to you again the same time tomorrow. As always, this is Ira at Radio Nowhere, signing off until we meet again."

The End

Epilogue

"Hello?"

Ira whipped his head toward the open door and fell silent. *Could...it be?*

"Is there anyone in here?"

The old man switched off the microphone and grabbed his cane, struggling to his feet. He limped out the door and made his way to the edge of the stairway. There, at the bottom of the stairs in the lobby, stood a teenaged boy. His clothes were dirty, and his hair shaggy. The boy suddenly looked up at Ira and straightened.

"Are you Ira?"

"I am." Ira's voice betrayed his relief.

The boy's shoulders relaxed and he looked behind him. A girl about his age stepped into the dim light, holding a small sleeping boy in her arms. A young girl held onto her shirttail, a thumb firmly planted in her mouth.

"My name is Zach Carter," the boy began, stepping to the edge of the stairs.

"Zach," Ira mused, trying to contain his joy. "Yes, welcome."

"We're so glad to meet you," the older girl said, shifting the small boy she held.

"And I'm very glad to meet you all as well. Come," Ira said, gesturing up the stairs, "Let me show you around. We have much to talk about."

CPSIA information can be obtained
at www.ICGtesting.com
Printed in the USA
BVHW071249290719
554566BV00004B/370/P